# From START to FINISH

VERNELL EVERETT

authorHOUSE®

*AuthorHouse™*
*1663 Liberty Drive*
*Bloomington, IN 47403*
*www.authorhouse.com*
*Phone: 1 (800) 839-8640*

*Published by AuthorHouse  01/26/2019*

*ISBN: 978-1-5462-7809-2 (sc)*
*ISBN: 978-1-5462-7810-8 (e)*

*Print information available on the last page.*

The choices that man makes is the determining factors of the life he lives. The characters in these short stories are depicting life as was lived from the characters' own makings. The reader will get an opportunity to share the experiences of people who traveled a different trail to their destination.

# CONTENTS

## WHEN ALL IS SAID AND DONE

## THIS IS MY COUNTRY

# THE
# ENDANGERED
# SPECIES

# CHAPTER ONE

The depression was taking its toll during the last half of the depression storm. The men who were once shade-tree happy people had become grouchy and finger-pointing. A number of the upper-class citizens were suddenly down on the bottom levels of the social ladder along with the people whom they once looked down upon. The biggest problems were there were no trees loaded with reasons that the top men could used to justify their suffering. The top dogs needed an outlet for their bottled up frustrations. The targets for venting frustration on could be any opportunity that happened to drop from the sky. The lower levels of the crowds were used to blame for all social ill when there was no act of God to blame.

Floyd decided that it was not a good time to hang around the big house. There was the hint of trouble blowing in on the cool autumn evening winds. He had been avoiding Shirley for the past several years. The two had been playmates and part-time lovers since they were old enough to play.

It had come time for these two to seek their own kinds to make a safe world for themselves. Floyd was a fifteen year-old slender brown skinned colored boy. He had crossed the line from where the innocent mixed-race children had fun together. Shirley was the same age as Floyd.

"Hay, Floyd! Where are you on your way to?"

"I'm on my way to the store. I thought you might want to walk over there with me."

"Sure, I don't mind, but you could have gone the other way and been there and back by now. What's the matter with you these days? Are you scared of the dark?"

"It's not the dark that I'm afraid of. At least, not the dark that comes after the setting sun."

"Is Shirley after you again? You come this way because you don't want to go by her house."

"She never stops. She thinks this is fun. I don't believe she is aware of the spot that her attention puts me on. Even them old poor-ass McCray boys have started hanging around up there."

"I'll get my cap. This weather sure feels good to these old tired bones."

"If you think you are old now, just wait until I remind you of those same words forty years from now. That is if you will be still here."

"Me? You better wonder if you will be here. These women are going to get the best of you. They have started already. You don't see me and Joe having to dodge women."

"Why don't you shut that mouth of yours. The reason why there ain't any girls chasing you is the girls are scared of the kind of girls you two hook up with. All Gert wants to do is to start something. Her whole family likes to fight.'

"Gert has always been hot-headed. Them darn brothers of hers are the same way. They seem to be in some kind of trouble all the time. You see where I be most of the time. I don't even go to the movies with Bob and Jake. They have such bad manners."

"Those two look for opportunities to fight. They are lucky that everybody in the county knows them, otherwise, they might be taken seriously by some knuckleheads who didn't know them."

"That has happen before. "Remember when that bunch of boys down in Shelby nearly killed the big-mouths?"

"Willie, how would you feel if some white girl had a hard time keeping her hands to herself when she is within touching distances of you?"

"I don't know. I have never had that to happen to me. I do feel shaky when I find myself getting too close to these white women who work the cash registers in these here stores. One mistake could cost a man his life if some crazy redneck hates him enough, or just hate Blacks enough."

"We once were afraid to go to the Smith's house because of their frisky daughters. We could see the expressions on their brothers and cousins' faces."

"Floyd, you had the most trouble. I never could see what these gals see in you. You are too puny to be worth much. How much do you weigh now, Floyd?"

"What has weight to do with anything? I still don't see why they want to pick on me. Come to think of it, being runty may be responsible for their doing what they do. They might be thinking that I'm not big enough to force them to do what they don't want to do."

"I sure wish the county would fix these rutty roads."

"What these people don't know is that I'm about the strongest one of us. You boys might have a bigger gut than me, but no muscles. Look at you, walking along here puffing and grunting like you can hardly walk on these rutty roads. You don't know why the county don't put asphalt on these county roads? Do you know we are in a depression?"

"I can't see much difference between what we have now and what we had when times were good. We still eat the same food, wear the same clothes and so on. What is our big fuss about?"

The men fell silent as they passed the cemetery. The folks of the area showed respect for the ancestors of their kind. It was not the same when they had to pass the cemetery where the Whites were buried.

"You never said what you are going to the store to get?"

"Daddy is about out of chewing tobacco and mama is low on snuff. You know how they get when they don't have something to chew on other than our behinds."

"I believe I have a strong taste for some good old hook-cheese. How do that sound to you?"

"You buy and I'll help you eat it. I don't want you to get too constipated."

"Thanks for looking out for your best friend's guts. I don't know anybody else who would take a chance of becoming constipated just to save me from getting my butt all bound up. "Thanks a lot, my best friend."

"Well I'll be a monkey's uncle. There is none of the poor starving bums hanging out at the watering hole."

"Let's get our stuff and clear out before they show up. You know it's just a matter of time before them drunks show up."

"I show hope Jenny ain't working out there alone. She is one of the prettiest white girls in the area. You know she is the main reason these young white bucks find reasons to hang out here."

Coloreds had more than one pocket filled with reasons to run in bunches. One solitary Black was a sitting duck to be picked on by anybody who had a rough day. There was safety in numbers. The rough riders on the country roads looking for some cheap fun would hesitate before jumping two or more strong pulpwood-working black boys. A popular white girl could start a war among her white sex hounds without much input. She could get a black man killed for nothing more that a hungry stare from the man. The colored felt safer by hanging together for mutual protection from white anger.

"Yep! There she is. It won't be easy, but you better keep your eyes on them there moon-pies. If you don't you will have to go a few extra miles to spend your pocket change in the future. That is if you would be lucky enough to have a future."

"I just keep enough of Jenny in sight to make sure I don't bump her by accident. If I did accidentally bump her, you and me better look for the fastest way out of the country."

"Speak for yourself, Floyd. I'll pretend that I'm not with you. These woods ain't any place to be traveling through at night with all them wild things in there. It's even more scary with a bunch of crazy Whites after one of us Blacks for breaking the rules."

"You were right, Willie. Look back and tell me who just pulled into the parking lot. Those are the meanest white brothers this side of hell itself."

"They don't need a reason to kick a black man's behind. They have been known to beat the daylights out of a man just for the pleasure of it. They will pick on their own kind if they can't stumble upon some poor innocent Blacks to scare half to death."

"I've made up my mind to defend myself and my people to the last breath if it comes to that. I won't give them reasons to do me, or mine, harm, but I won't stand by and let them bastards dog me around."

"Let's hope it never comes to that, Willie. These folks don't know any better. If they knew what they were doing to themselves, do you believe they would continue doing what they are doing?"

"I don't know about these fools. My granddaddy warmed us before he died. He told us to be safe and stay in our places.

He used to tell us how lucky we were to have such good white folks for neighbors and friends."

"He was right on both counts. These jokers are pretty fair with us as long as we stay in what they think is our places. Where our place is often depends on what is going on and who is involved. Our place is where the man says it is. That's the part that drives me crazy."

"Are you still planning on going up north and live with your uncle when you finish the eighth grade?"

"I haven't made up my mind yet of which is the most important at this time, my family or me. My family might need me here with them. I don't know what their condition will be by that time. Daddy and Mommy ain't getting any younger or healthier."

"I sometimes worry about my family too. I might have to drop out of school to help the family feed my little brothers and sisters. You know my six little rats will need to be cared for. Daddy ain't getting any younger the same as your daddy. We have to look out for each other."

Family needs were often talked about among the young men of the southern country folks. There were big families requiring the older children to help support. The older children were expected to do much of the duties of their daddies and mammies did of taking care of the young. Education came far down on the list of important duties to plan for. There were always a few promising smart boys and girls who their families could place high hopes on. They were encouraged to be the highway on which other family members could travel to a better life. But, family came first.

"Willie! I bet you can't guess where I've been all morning. Guess and I'll buy you a double burger."

"You must be happy with whatever has happened to you

to make you offer to buy. Now let me see..uh. You must have a job."

"You hit the nail on the head, boy. Come on let me buy you that burger I promised you. I missed you folks because I was taking care of business."

"Alright, give! What is this that's making you so crazy and unlike the Floyd that I know?"

"You won't believe this. Mrs. Rush offered me the job old Moses have. That old man is too old to cut the mustard now. She says that he will still be there until I learn the ropes."

"That is a good deal, that is if she pays you like she pays old man Moses."

"Listen to this, she is starting me off with more than she paid Uncle Moses. Can you believe
that?"

"I bet that didn't set too good with that old cranky Uncle Moses. He never had any other job."

"He don't know the deal. She said that she wanted a steady worker and she knew that she would have to pay the going rate. But, she made me promise to keep the pay-rate under my hat."

"The job had gotten too much for the old man anyway. She often had to hire outside help to get simple jobs done."

"That's kind of what she told me. She said that her conscious would not let her retire the man before he thought he was ready. But, his arthritis made it easier for her to convince the old bugger to think about sitting on his porch and playing with his grandchildren."

"I'd like to see that. Uncle Moses's grandchildren have grown children of their own. He might play with his great-grandchildren. Yeah, I know. These white folks don't think that we ever get grown."

"This is a good chance for me to educate these folk. I'll have a chance to be around nearly everybody living within thirty miles of here. Yes sir, this will be an interesting job for me. You see she wants me to do the driving for her and old man Rush. The family had a hard time convincing the old geezer to give up his car keys."

"Now don't forget me. You will be in a position to help a few of us poor unemployed cousins get jobs. Don't you do like some of your kind do. They tend to forget where they came from once they draw a few big paychecks."

# Chapter Two

"Floyd, I'll bet you'll have all the girls chasing you. How will you manage to fight them off?"

"No Ma'am. I don't have any girls who I have to fight off."

"You are a good looking boy and I know the little colored girls are falling all over you. When was the last time you were with one of them gals?"

Floyd's heart was in his mouth by this time. He began to pray for somebody to come into the garage where he was polishing the car.

"Why don't you look at me Floyd? You know I'm a woman, the same as them little gals that you mess around with. Have you ever touched a white girl, Floyd?"

Floyd heard somebody calling his name, He knew his prayers had been answered. That was God calling him.

"Will you excuse me, Miss. Flo. I hear Mrs. Rush calling me."

Floyd dashed across the space from the garage to the house as if his britches was on fire. This was one of his most disliked duties of the new job. He was expected to sort of be available to serve not only the immediate family members, but also their distant kinfolks too.

Miss. Flo was a niece of Mrs. Rush. She was somewhere in

her mid twenties and had no intentions of getting hitched in the near future. She didn't even have a steady boyfriend. She seemed to be okay with sharing the boyfriends of the other unmarried women in her end of the county.

"Willie, do you believe we would have been better off if we had stayed in school?"

"That's a hard question to answer. It is said that things will change soon, but, how soon, nobody knows. But, as it is right today, we made a good decision when we decided that we had enough education for what we will need to do our jobs. Look at you? You have a good lifetime job. That is, as long as the Rush family remain whole."

"You might be right. I think I might be good at working on the railroad or construction work. Them jobs pay good money too."

"What's wrong with the job that you were lucky enough to walk right in on? Most black men would give a bushel of peas and a fat hog to have what you had handed to you on a silver platter. What has got you all worked up?"

"I don't like having to work around half these old white women. You know how they are."

"They have always been the way they are. You will have to do what you have to do. You know how it is and has always been."

"I want to live a normal life. I want to get married one of these days and have children. Now what's wrong with wanting what most normal white men want?"

"Not a thing is wrong with it. You might have to take a slightly different road to accomplishing it. I'm planning on the same thing. I can see us now, married with little shavers running all over the place."

"I want to have a chance to do just what we are talking about. I don't want to end up in one of them sinkholes that has no bottom. We have heard of this being the case for a bunch of our kind. We hear the stories all the time."

Signs of fall could be seen and heard everywhere. The northern migrating birds were in the air which was not a good sign for the country's working men. They had to winter-proof their homes, stock up winter kindling and a thousand other chores to get done. The golden leaves were floating to the ground like they had practiced it for years. The floating golden leaves created a beautiful dance to watch.

"We don't know the full story of what that boy did to make them white folks so mad. You know how our people like to make big thing out of nothing."

"That's the thing that scares me to death, making a big thing out of nothing. We've heard of little to nothing getting people run out of town or worse."

"Willie, you hear that vehicle coming? Until I know more about what these folks are mad about, I think it will be a good idea for us to step behind these bushes until we see who this is."

The men were up the bank and into the brush like jack rabbits. They saw no reason to risk their safety to a bunch of nuts to prove anything. The truck was loaded with six young men from the Sunlight area. They were from the trouble area but were headed in the opposite direction.

"Them guys didn't look too mean to me. What did you think?"

"Well, Willie, I just don't feel like taking unnecessary chances when it comes to dealing with men who don't mind violating their most sacred rules to do me harm. This is too nice of a day to run through these beautiful woods with a bunch of hounds on your tail."

"It looks like every light in your house is on, Willie. I hope there ain't nothing wrong."

Willie's mamma met him at the door wearing a panic look.

"Have you two gone crazy? Have y'all heard the news?"

"Yes, Ma'am. We heard the news while we were at the store. We didn't pay too much attention to it because it happened way over in the Sunlight area."

"You young men are old enough to know how that works. These people don't need much of an excuse to go on a rampage and do harm to the innocent."

"I'll see you Willie!"

"You go and get home as quick as you can. Floyd! If you see lights coming hit the woods!"

"If you folks hear a loud noise as if there is a tornado coming through your house grab anything that will crack a head. There is no way a bunch of hillbillies could catch me at night in these woods. They won't catch the boy they are after either. He might be dumb enough to come a whining and asking to be left alone. That might be his last request too."

Fall of the year in the south was the time of the year when the Blacks and Whites had reasons to cross paths. They were usually settling up with the summer's business and getting ready for school and winter hibernating. The men would have plenty of time to hang around with their own kind and drink their own making. Fall and spring were when the trouble was most likely to pop up. There was another kind of trouble that was most likely to happen during the hibernating times. This was also the time when the domestic workers were taking care of the housebound.

'Willie, what do your schedule look like for next week?"

"I don't have much planned, except doing a little shopping for Christmas. What have you got going?"

"My people are having company for the holidays and I have told the boss that I could use some help. He agreed with me. So, there you are. You have some more spending money."

"Floyd, do you really need help with your chores or do you

want company with you. You want some protection from them horny white women. I don't blame you either."

"You know the boy over in Sunlight was running because he had been caught fooling around with the woman down the road from them. They had been fooling around for a long time. They just hadn't gotten caught."

"The woman was nearly old enough to be his mama. She made him have a relationship even though he didn't want to. He was to scared to say no."

"I know how that feels. Why do you think I need you during these holidays?"

"I knew what you were up to before you opened your mouth. I've told you before, you should figure out some way to make yourself ugly to these white folks. You don't see me having white-women troubles. I'm having a rough time getting between the legs of my own kind of women."

"Don't go feeling too bad about your problems with getting women. It might be worse when the ball bounces in the other direction. You see how hard it is for the nice looking girls and women to be good daughters and wives? Even if they ain't done anything, they are suspected of doing everything that has an immoral tag on it."

"I guess you might be right. We have unlimited other ways to get our foot in a crack. It's seems like trouble awaits us at every contact we make with anything. We can barely live pass Saturday night without sticking one of our feet where it ain't supposed to be."

"That's what the Coker boy did when his car was parked and the man from cross the state line drove into Coker's car? You know Cooker was given a ticket for illegal parking."

"I remember what J. Coker had to pay for the damage done to the others' vehicle. You remember?"

"You bet I do. The Blacks made a big fuss about that one, but it did more harm than good."

"The Sheriff made it crystal clear that if there was any further grumbling he would attach more violations to the charges."

"The word is that Mr. J. Coker was never the same after that. Take a look at the man that he is today. He speaks only when he is spoken to. Do you think his present attitude is a result of how he was treated for standing tall and being what he though he should be?"

"It could be. He was not that way before then. He even sold his car and never bought another. The Cokers have always been a proud family of men. They are still ready to fight at the drop of a hat."

"Floyd, do you still dream about what it would be like if you could change your color like one of these lizards can?"

"You mean to change from being colored to being white? Not as much as I once did. I don't hear you talking about it much these days. Come on, let's look for the best Christmas tree in these woods. I don't want to hear no grumbling from that bunch of spoiled people."

"Do you believe they are gonna give you a big check for a Christmas present like they gave the old man?"

"Why do you think I want the biggest and Christmas prettiest tree in these here woods? You just watch me, boy, and maybe you will learn how to make these big-shots do your bidding. You and I are gonna make this a holiday season that these folks won't ever forget."

"Let's hold up here a minute. I'm beginning to get a hunch that my name won't be on the check even if there is one. You and I will have to take a refresher course in our high-school math. I want to make sure you haven't forgotten how to divide and multiply."

"The only worries that you have right now is this tree. I'll do the splitting of the money. You were never worth a darn in math anyway. Have you forgotten who did your math when we were in school?"

"Floyd, whatever happened to John Clayton? That was one smart boy. The teachers didn't want him in their classes because he was smarter than they were."

"The last I heard anything about the boy he was living on the streets in Detroit I saw his mama here a few months ago and she didn't know how he was doing."

"He sure didn't fit here in his hometown. There was no place here for a big-mouth know-it-all black boy like he was. John and Pearl were tighter than dick's hatband. She went to hell after he left."

"That was after she got raped by them white boys. She said that she was raped, but the rumor is that she said that after she learned that she was in family way. She has two half-breed children. They are cute little things. A girl and a boy."

"Willie, would you get serious with a girl who gave birth to two little half-breeds? You would be the laughing stock of the whole community."

"The poor child doesn't go to church anymore. They say that the daddy of the children makes sure that she has what she needs to support them babies. The accused daddy helps her folks out by providing work for the whole family."

"She was, and still is, a pretty little thing. I once could bite her all over if I got the chance. She once said that there were not enough colored men to go around. She said that the ones that were still hanging around were being chased by white girls. What do you think of them apples?"

"Floyd, you are an example of that. Look what you are asking me to do. You are afraid to work around these frisky white women without somebody being with you."

The two hardworking men had to Rush home and get ready for the holidays in time to do their own homes before Santa came. The Coloreds usually earned their Christmas money by working for the white folks. This was the time of year when the highest number of runaway Blacks came visiting their kinfolk. That is, the few who were lucky enough to have their bus fare home on the Trail Way or Greyhound buses. The colored girls would dress for the occasion by spending their hard-earned money on clothes ordered out of one of the mail-order catalogs. The girls that were left at home by the vanishing colored men were looking for a way out of a country that was without enough men to go around.

Half the young colored men who did decide to stay at their birth place were mostly those who were not likely to find jobs in the big cities. These boys were not the pick of the litter.

"Did you men noticed the new jailhouse going up?"

"I did. They will have the thing up and operating before spring. You know why they waited until winter time to build the darn thing."

"So they would have plenty of cheap labor. Willie, you had a chance to work on the government project."

"I thought about exactly that, but, I turned down the chance for the same reasons you did. I've heard you say over and over again that you refused to build your own jail"

# Chapter Three

The new jail was ready for occupants before spring. The darn place were being filled by some of the same men who had worked on it. That was understandable because who else were they gonna fill them empty cells with? Everybody knew the answer to that question. There were few men of color who had no criminal records.

"How did you know that the sheriff and his badge totters were going to raid the Hut?"

"I tell you all the time about my hearing ability. I keep my ears to the opened windows and doors. These folks don't think we Blacks have ears to hear what they don't want us to hear. Sometimes I think they don't even know we are there when they be sharing their news."

"Even I can see that. I don't believe they really know that we can hear what they talk about in our presents."

"Willie, their not being able to hear us hollering for fair treatment is a direct results of their not being able to see us as fully human beings with the same minds as they have. These folks who we are working for today pay us no never-mind at all when they discuss their personal business in our presents. Haven't you noticed that?"

The domestic help always knew the business of the people

whom they worked for. The help knew enough of the white folk's business to win any argument that popped up between the races. The maids and yardmen knew more about the habits of their bosses than the bosses knew about themselves.

The news about the middle age man having to be gotten out of the county through the back woods were mentioned at the Sunday's service. The man had been accused of stealing. This was a common accusation for the people who had something to steal. The black citizens were suspects, and it didn't matter what the evidence suggested, if he was seen in the area where the crime took place. The middle-age black man would have to prove his innocence, that is if he could get a white man or woman to stand up and back him up.

"What was old dumb Jeff accused of stealing? That old bastard of a store owner didn't have much to steal."

"Willie, I believe it was some old worn-out truck parts. You know he hung around them folks too much. It is rumored that the man's own son took the parts and sold them to his cousin at the service station down on US 45."

"Where is Jeff holding up at right now?"

"I hear he is over at their old house where they grew up at. Nobody lives on the few acres now. The last daughter went to Detroit to stay with her son several years ago."

"Maybe he will go where his sister is."

"That would be a good thing to do if they can get him up there. These lawmen and rednecks are cruising the roads and checking his kinfolk's homes, you name it and they are doing it. There is no place where one can hide for too long. He will have to be gotten out of here before this weekend."

"I sure would hate to be in his shoes. These woods and swamps get awful scary at night."

"Why do you think I'm so careful around these folks. We know men who left here on the run and haven't been heard from or seen since. We know they all didn't get away, especially in the old days. Maybe they were better off dead than being lost and helpless in a black slum of some big city."

"Floyd, now that you have it made on this big job, when are you and Ella gonna tie the knot?"

"We have talked about it here lately. You know something Willie?"

"Go on. What is it that I'm suppose to know?"

"What gets on our nerves more than anything we run into every day?"

"You know I know what that is. It's not easy staying out of trouble when dealing with our cousins. We have to tread like we are walking through a brier patch barefooted around out kinfolk."

"What we accomplish during any day still depends on how the man feels. We have to make sure we are not in his line of fire when he get upset or we will become his target for venting his frustrations on. We have to be mind-readers to avoid their hateful moments."

"Floyd, you have become good at working with our people, both Black and White.. Now what have you two decided about getting hitched?"

"Why is all this interest in me and Ella? What about you?"

"I don't have the job that you have. You are in with these money-folks. It would be easy for you to raise a bunch of brats in your position. You would be sitting pretty if your first five children were boys."

"Willie, do you hear what you are saying? Do you know what you just said?"

"Yep, I do. You know I'm telling the truth, Floyd. It takes a steady income to fed a wife and a houseful of eating machines. Can you see me trying to buy shoes and toys for a batch of eating rats?"

"Willie, Willie, we have been talking about this for as far back as we can remember. You and I want more than food and a house to get in out of the rain for our wife and young'uns. I don't want my sons to have to do what I have to do just to earn a living and save their hides. We don't live in a time when we can raise a family with healthy minds."

The weather turned for the worse before the Christmas holidays were over. The children had to remain out of school and under the feet of their mamas and daddies for a few more days. This didn't set good with the old folks at all, It even came a heavier snow than it had been for decades that far south. It was the kind of weather when women were most likely to get in family way.

"I see Billie Ray is back from St. Louis Missouri. He said that we have good weather down here compared to what it's like in St. Louis. The harsh winters are my main reasons for not wanting to move north. I'm thinking about going further south."

"He has been after me to come and visit him for years. The big city never appealed to me. Floyd, If I had your education I might have given it a try. But, I'm pretty set right here where you and me were born."

"The boy was riding in a nearly new automobile. That thing was newer than any vehicle you see around here. I think it was a Buick. He works for a Buick dealer, if I remember right."

"Billie Ray is the only cousin of mine who left us and is doing good. I remember how his daddy worried about him after he got him out of the south. The boy was slaughtering other folk's animals to sell for money in these colored neighborhoods. The sheriff and a group of poor rednecks had set a trap to catch the thief but his aunt who worked for a white family caught wind of their plans. You know how these people tend to forget that we have ears to hear and mouths to speak."

"The man was and still is a natural born wheeler dealer. His kind have the nerves, or lack of common sense, to take the advantages of golden opportunities. He never showed any fear of what could happen to him if he was caught by the wrong people. He was lucky."

"We didn't really think that the man would live to be grown. My uncle could sleep in peace after he received a letter from his sister saying that his son was safe and sound there in St. Louis. He had only one piece of advice for him, 'don't come back this way anytime soon.'"

"Is your uncle getting better? He has been sick for a spell now."

"That was the main reason why Billie Ray came home in this miserable weather. The city of St. Louis was shut down until the weather improved. You know Billy Ray. He has never had good sense when it came to doing things that good common sense tells one to avoid at all cost."

Most of the members had to braved the icy weather when somebody got sick or died. Especially when they drove in from the big cities. The locals went to church to get a look at Billie Ray. This was more true for the young than it was for the older members. It was hard enough to get the young in church when the weather was perfect, but nearly impossible to get them there in weather that was shutting down the entire country.

"Hey, Billie! You look like you have found your pot of gold!"

"Not yet, Floyd, but I'm closer than ever. How have you been doing?"

"I got it made by some of our thinking. I'm top man on the biggest plantation in the county. You might say, I'm the head boy. What else can a poor black country boy, like me, ask for?"

"Floyd, who are you jiving. You would trade all what you have for the rights and freedoms that the poorest of the Whites take for granted."

"I'm beginning to question things that I never had time

to think much about until I got this job. I see something every day that these folks enjoy that people like us can forget about. I mean these are simple little rights and privileges that we don't even think about."

"Floyd, Floyd! Why in hell do you think I had to leave all that was important to me and head for them cold and unfriendly slums up north? I haven't found a real friend since I ran away from home."

"I know now what you were trying to do for yourself or stop others from doing to you. I thought you were just a mixed up hot-headed Black. You were not only trouble for yourself, but you meant trouble for anybody who was foolish enough to run with you."

"You folks were right in a way. It was a good thing that I had people with enough common sense to make me hightail it out of the south before the worst happened to us."

"I hear it was close. You were one of the lucky ones. The swamps are full of the bones of those who weren't as fortunate as you were."

Billie Ray was the most popular man at church. The ladies couldn't get enough eyeballing him while the young men were asking about jobs and other benefits available in the big city. If the man wanted to he could load a greyhound bus with the men and women who were ready to go in search for what they thought Billie had. It would have been easy to haul every able-body man and woman out of Billie's hometown with nothing more than a promise of food and housing.

"What are you planning for tonight, Billie?"

"Well! That all depends on what is available right here. I have my eye on little Miss Maggie over yonder. You see her standing there eyeballing us, don't you? I wonder if she is still ready and willing like she was the last time that I was here. Who is she keeping company with these days?"

"I thought Jack, from the Horn Swamp church, was gonna snatch her up, but he hasn't been seen for a while. I think they might have falling out with the way it was and broke up. I haven't seen the man's truck parked at her house since about July."

"That's all I wanted to hear. If this doesn't work, I'll drop by your place later. See you later."

There were more single ladies in the rural south than men to match them up with. The country men who went to the city slums found that they had the same problems. They were marching back to their hometowns in search of respectable women. Time was running out for some of these people if they wanted to get hitched and raise a family.

"Willie, it looks like this weather is letting up. We'll be able to come out and play in the sun in a few days. Get ready to cut a lot of fire wood because these heaters have been red hot since the storm hit. We can make a few extra bucks doing what we always do under these kinds of conditions."

"Floyd, have you asked your master if we could cut firewood off his place? He has a few trees that he will be better off without."

"It's just you and me, Willie. Mack and Tom won't be here to help us. Them two sorry butts went to St. Louse with Billie Ray."

"Yeah, I know. They left day before yesterday. If this keeps up there won't be anybody left but you and me, Floyd."

"Won't that be a shame. We will have all these ladies to ourselves. I can see us fighting now. We would be at war trying to divide up these beauties so that we each would have the same number."

"You have always been greedy. We would have a problem with your greed."

# Chapter Four

The good old southern god-fearing folks were glad to see the winter become history. They were busy getting ready for a productive spring and summer. Most of the poor Christian folks prayed for God to rain down blessings on their spring planting and other farm properties. They were short of everything due to the long winter. It was easy for these good hard-working folks to be Christians when time were hard and money was in short supply.

"Floyd, listen to the good news. I got a regular job. I have a good paying job with which I will be able to plan a better future for me and my little gal. Yep, things are looking up. I have heard this before and that is hard times brings good things to those who step up to the plate and take the advantages of the opportunities that hard times create."

"Holdup there, boy. Let's back up for a minute. What Job do you have, and what kind of money will you be making?"

"Okay, I got a job at the warehouse. They have boxcars of seeds, fertilizers, plowing and hoeing tools in addition to tractor and cultivators parts. Yes sir, I have a job."

"Don't get too carried away, boy. The same conditions that created the job will disappear and the job will disappear right along with them boxcar loads of farming goods."

"I want to look at this from the bright side, not from the ugly end. I will work seven days a week until the boss stops me. I want to save enough money to afford trips to St. Louse, Chicago and Detroit on a hunt for a better way of living. You know what I'm talking about. You would not be here today if you thought you had a better chance of doing better in the city than what you are doing here. Now, would you?"

"You are right, but you want to make sure that me and your folks don't have to send for you after you go broke. You and I know a lot of our good old southern boys and girls went after the goose that lay the golden egg and ended up busted and forgotten in the big city slums. They found the goose, alright. The goose they found lay rocks"

"I'll leave you back here to bail me out in case I need bailing out. I just might be your ticket off that plantation that you manage. What do you think of that, friend?"

'That's the way a lot of our folks are leaving here. You see how empty their cars are when they return to their homes and how loaded they be when they go back. Anyway, I hope you all the luck in the world. Thanks for including me in your plans. I've been ready for a change ever since You and me were knee high to a short duck."

The highway that southern Blacks used to navigate back and fourth between their birth place and their new homes were usually on the backs of visiting relatives and friends. Life for the ambitious, healthy and bright Blacks was littered with stumbling blocks and life-threatening dangers. The relationships between the races appeared to be getting worse rather than better. The returning homeboys had to be extra careful while traveling the highways because of the precarious relationships between the two good god-fearing folks of this great country living side by side in the good old United States.

"Floyd, did you and Tom hear the news about James McDonald?"

"I didn't, maybe Tom did. He has been sitting here all morning without mentioning it. Have you heard the news, Tom? Speak up boy!"

"Hush, Floyd. You know better than that. Let Willie continue with the news about James."

"James got in an accident up the road a ways. His daddy is trying to get the story right so he can do whatever is needed for his son. The highway people ain't cooperating with our black homeboy. Mr. McDonald is trying to get our sheriff to step in and lend a hand. The word is, none of the fault was his. The white woman was one hundred percent at fault. James told his daddy that he was sitting still when the lady's car hit his car. The law charged him with the accident."

"Let's go over and see what we can do to help. We will have to learn to step up and lend a hand without waiting until it's too late. We, as a race, will have to do better by each other."

The boys loaded up and went to see the worried father. They noticed one thing right off the bat and that was the house was totally dark. The family was sitting on the porch in the cool dark of a nearly perfect evening.

"Y'all come on up and have a seat in the swing over there."

"We didn't come to bother you too much. We just wanted to let you know that we are here with you. You know we are here to do what we can if you need us."

"I'm still waiting for word from our sheriff. He is suppose to get back with me the minute he has any kind of news. Thank you boys for offering a hand. I thank God for people like you men."

"We are here now, you remember that!"

This was the usual way it went when there was an accident between the races. The outcome for the people involved rested on the actions taken by the authorities. Everybody knew how that worked. The Black was guilty until proven innocent while the White was innocent until proven guilty.

"Floyd, you do know that the sheriff will get back with the McDonald family when hell freezes over. I have a hunch the man already knows all there is to be known, but!"

"What would you men think of us putting a trip together and ease into that little town to see for ourselves what the colored population knows? That would not be too hard to do. We will be there going about the business of listening to the story and then getting back on the road home. We would be in and out before the rednecks knew we were there. What do you say Willie?"

"When do we leave?"

"We have time. We won't go there until the mess settles down and the authorities settle down to their business-as-usual routines. Plus we don't want to have to run for our lives the same as the victim did."

"I know the backwoods very good. I know them swamps so good until we would stand a better chance if we ran off and left your boss's pickup."

"We won't run off and leave my boss's truck, no matter what. You see, he'll come and get the truck no matter what. We stand a better chance of being saved If we are with the truck. His wanting his truck, and his boy, will make him give us some help."

"Let's take a cruise up there this coming Friday. The smoke should be cleared away by then. You and I know that unless some outsider interferes with the mess, the local Black will still be in their homes with locked doors between then and their angry white folks."

"Sounds like the thing to do. Who are we gonna take with us?"

"I think the two of us will be enough. After all, we sure don't need hotheads such as Pete, and a few others, with us. These men have our best interest at heart, but, they have no idea how to go about addressing these kinds of issues."

The two scouts rode off into the Saturday morning mist before the Sun got too high in the sky. They wanted to have learned what they wanted to know before the main body of citizens got out into the roads.

"Hey, Floyd! What storm blew you this way?"

"I'm just checking on you folks. We have some bad news about what has been going on over here. Before we get into what we came for, how are you and your family doing?"

"Not bad now that the scare is over. These people are relieved that nothing worse happened than it did. It's a blessing that it was one of the McDonald boys who they accused of misbehaving."

"We were waiting for our old sorry butt sheriff to get with your sheriff and let us know what was what. We all know how that usually work. We stopped by our sheriff's office before we headed out for your place. He acted like he hadn't heard a word. He even acted like he had forgotten that we were in his office earlier in the week asking for his help."

"I know you didn't expect his help when it come to telling on one of his kind, even if they be life-long enemies. They might hate each other, but they hate us even more."

"Is there any news about James? The man couldn't have falling off the edge of the earth. We Blacks know better than to believe that the earth is flat. We have read the white man's books."

"Are we supposed to believe that James was not charged with anything? Not even a traffic violation? We are told that he was just held in custody for his safety?"

"That's where we are today. There was no crime that James

was guilty of, except his being black. He was also a southern boy who had migrated north which was his way of telling our southern Whites to kiss him where the sun don't shine."

The two hotheads went straight to the sheriff's office after they could get nothing out of the local batch of cowards.

"Good evening Mr. Sheriff! How are you today?"

"Now, that will depend on why you boys are here. What can I do for you boys?"

"We are wondering if you knew anything about what happened to James McDonald. We know he must be still here."

"Yes, he is and from what I know, he will be in custody for a spell longer. This will teach you Negroes to be careful while driving through our towns. The boy is lucky that he only got his butt kicked. I had to lock the careless rascal up for his own protection. I didn't want what was about to happen to him to be on my conscious."

"Where is he right now?"

"He's being held up in Southfield. He'll be safe until we can have a hearing for him and charge him with some kind of violation. We know he is guilty, but of what? We will, or I will, have to charge him with something before long."

"He is doing a lot of time before he is charged with anything. Sheriff, do you believe that is a fair way to do your fellow citizen?"

"If you boys could learn from your experiences, y'all would know better than to drive like maniacs in them northern-bought fancy automobiles."

"We heard that he was setting still when the nice lady plowed into his automobile. Did you hear the same thing?"

"Like I told you hard-headed boys, the man is guilty of many violations. It is just a matter of which ones we will charge him with. If he was parked illegally, that's also a violation of the law."

"Thanks a lot Mr. Sheriff! We appreciate your cooperation."

The man of the law did not bother to recognize the men's expressions of thanks. He went back to reading his paper.'

"What do you think Floyd?"

"James will be lucky if he is locked up. I show hope there was no serious injuries to the white woman. When there was a white woman involved, a black man could hang up his expecting any kind of justice. The best the sheriff could do to protect the man would be to turn him loose."

"That would put the poor sap in the hands of the white mob. What chance would he have?"

"That would depend on when he turned the poor bugger loose. The sheriff might give him a running chance to make it to the swamps before the chase got on."

"That would be better than nothing. We will have to do a lot of praying for the man to get out of the area through woods and swamps that he is a stranger to."

"That depends on what is better than nothing and in what way. Let's, you and me nose around the hood and see what we can hear."

The men decided to spend some more time getting the inside scoop on how the locals felt about one of theirs being lynched. Their willingness to lend a hand against their local Whites for a strange Black may be near zero. It wasn't hard to find the common meeting place In the small colored section of the highway stop. The little cafe/bar combination was right on the main street through the colored red-light district.

"Howdy men! What can I get y'all?"

"What kind of sandwiches do you have ready to eat. I'm starved."

"We have some of the best pork chops in the state. How many sandwiches do Y'all want?"

"Give us one each and a bold of that bean soup. That's all right with you Willie?"

"Whatever you order is find with me. I can eat anything that grows hair or feathers."

"This resembles our joints back home. Let's just mention this James's thing and see what she knows. I know all the news has to come through this hangout."

"Here you go! What else can I get you?"

"This look fine, for right now. We were wondering if you knew something about this accident that one of our kinfolk got himself in up here?"

"I thought y'all might be wanting something like that. I knew I didn't remember seeing ya in these parts before. What did you want to know?"

"Just about anything that you know about this mess. It is believed that our cousin was not even moving when the accident happened. The sheriff claims that he is being held somewhere other than his jail and it was for our cousin's own good. What can you tell us about this?"

"What you didn't mention was that the woman who ran into his motor vehicle was the mayor's daughter. Anyway, your cousins' vehicle needs some minor repairs done before he can drive it. The white-owned shops won't touch it until the sheriff gives them the okay."

"We kind of thought there might be more to this than just a bent finder. We figured he would be at fault too. Now the picture is coming clear. What do you think, Willie?"

"As long as James don't get the diarrhea at the mouth, which he tends to get at times."

"Where do you think our cousin is right at this moment?"

"I don't know exactly, but I know who might know. Our pastor usually works closely with the sheriff in these kinds of cases. Our white folks around here don't cotton to colored people getting out of hand, unless they work for one of our sawmill owners or some other big-time white man."

"That's about the same kind of relations as we have back home. Who do you recommend that we talked to who might help us?"

"You can start with our pastor. I'll give him a call. He lives just down the road. I'll ask him to come up here to talk to y'all. He don't like to conduct this kind of business at his house. You men know how that is."

"We sure do. We appreciate your help. Maybe we'll have a chance to repay this favor one of these days."

"I sure hope not. Not this kind of favor."

"You never can tell what we'll have to deal with."

The preacher was expected to sort of keep the races from fighting and doing harm to each other. Both the races would check the racial situation with the church before taking life-threatening actions against the other side.

"Afternoon Reverend!"

"Good afternoon, may God bless you."

"Have you got a few minutes to answer a few questions for us? I'll tell you what it is about without wasting your time. We want to know how we can be of some help to the man who is missing. He is our kin."

"I don't know all there is to know about what is with that case, but I will tell you what I do know and what I do suspect."

"We couldn't ask for more than that. We have collected a few dollars and want to pay his finds, get his car fixed, or whatever our few dollars can help him with."

"The first thing is they don't know what to charge him with. The law is waiting to see what the poor little white gal will want him charged with. She might have some wounds that he will have to be charged for. Chargers of reckless driving is one thing and endangering life while driving recklessly is another. It is possible to be charged with both."

"Do you have any idea of where we can go to talk to the young man?"

"All the law will tell me is that he is safe and sound and for us to stay out of the business of the law. Now, it don't take a smart man to know what he meant by that order."

"Where is his vehicle at? Maybe we can start by having the automobile repaired and made road-ready so he will not have to walk home."

"I'll take you to where the car is."

The car was towed to the nearest dealer and left there to be turned to junk and parts if James could not pay to have the thing fixed. The men were pretty sure that he would not be left with a dime after the law finished with his little savings.

"Good evening sir! We would like to see what damage was done to Mr. James McDonald's car and make a deal if we could."

The repairman didn't answer right away. He stood there staring at the two black men like he had never seen a black man before.

"There it is over there"

The repairman pointed over his shoulders without taking his eyes off the two tall black men.

"It don't look like there is too much damage done to the car. What is you estimate to fix the damn thing?"

"I really haven't totaled it up yet. Give me a few minutes and I'll have that information for you."

"Just fix what needs to be fixed well enough for it to be driven. Do you understand?"

"I think I got what you are asking. Wait here for a minute."

The repairman acted like he was caught between a rock

and a hard place. He didn't know what to do because he and the law had not expected this kind of problem from the Blacks.

"I could do the job for around two hundred dollars, give or take a few dollars. I will have to check with the sheriff before I can release the vehicle to you boys."

"When will the work be done?" We will be back here in the morning when you open to pick up the car. The sheriff can't file charges against the car. We don't care what you have to do, or who you have to see, just have the vehicle ready in the early hours of tomorrow morning. If the sheriff has a problem with that, tell him that we will be at Lula Mae's place."

"Willie, we might have to hire a lawyer to get the car."

Floyd spoke loud enough for the repairman to hear every word. The White folks knew the only lawyers to be hired were Jewish. They would have a hard time fighting against a bunch of Jews.

The car was ready as was told to the man. He didn't mention anything about the law. Floyd and Willie took the car to Lula's place to wait and see what was going on with James. They decided to make another visit to the sheriff's office. They wanted to make something clear enough until a fool could understand.

"Morning Mr. Sheriff!" The two trouble-makers spoke as one.

"Morning, boys! What can I tell you that you don't already know?"

"We are not here to ask you for any information, Sheriff. We are here to tell you what you will be smart to do. We are on our way back home to get ready for whatever it will take to make things right. Do you get that much?"

"Or what?"

"That 'or what' will depend on what you do. You will get with our sheriff as soon as you can square this with your people and let us know what the score is. We will take it from there. But, we want you to understand one fact, we will do whatever is required to make things right. We will expect your answer before the sun sets Monday afternoon."

# CHAPTER FIVE

James could not be found and did not make his whereabouts known. The information was that he had skipped town trying to get away from having to face the chargers and jail time. After all, it was the sheriff's kin that was involved in the accident. There was no way that the young lady could have been at fault.

The community got together and made sure that his family had support in getting thing together and adjusting to life without their main supporter.

'Willie, what do you think could have happened to our man?"

"We know that them white folks have a bad reputation when it comes to the way they treat their colored folks. Remember back about twenty years ago when they lynched them two men for no reason other than they happened to be in the wrong place at the wrong time, and being black?"

"The colored people started to migrate from there hometown after the hangings. The young men could not wait until their eighteenth birthday before they grabbed an arm full of freight train. The relationships haven't changed too much since then."

"It didn't help much when that crazy black boy went crazy and wiped out a bunch of ku klux klan boys while they were in the process of having a good old fashion party by teaching a poor half-crazy black man the rules of the road. It was about this fellow not recognizing the unlimited rights of the white race. He seemed to think that he was due the same breaks as everybody else. He learned the hard way that this was not nearly the way it works."

"We were proud of the poor man who paid the ultimate price for the action. They still celebrate on the day it happened. The man just happened to be hunting in the area when he stumbled upon the lynching. Those K.K.K. Boys were never the same after that."

"Willie! Do you realize what life is like here in the backwoods with legs that don't function like they should? They were stiff-legged until they died. I head that they are all gone now. But, what that black boy did to them changed the way the Whites and Blacks did business together. They say that the hate between the races could be smelled for miles outside the city limits."

Black people were very sensitive and stayed on the alert when visiting, or driving through small southern towns that had a bad reputation from the point-of-view of the Blacks. It didn't take long for a 'we-hate-black' reputation to spread like a wildfire on a hot and dry fall day.

"Willie! What do you think that we could do to make the folks in that little jackass Missouri town remember James?"

"I can't forget how we were treated while we were there. I'm ready to do just about anything short of killing women and children. They had nothing to do with this."

"Let's give this some thought. We are far enough away from the nuts until they would never figure who the wild bunch was. We could warn them to not do anything to the locals for what we do, or they will pay a high cost."

A few brave Blacks were beginning to realize that if any

improvements were to be made between the races it might have to come by way of somebody paying a high price. They were learning that the ball was in their court.

"Floyd, have y'all done any more thinking about doing something about James' disappearance?"

"Yeah, we have. Come to think of it, we are meeting this coming Sunday after services at the church. Why don't you plan to take part. We need all the good help that we can get.

"You won't be able to keep me away with a shotgun. I'll see you Sunday afternoon."

"Be glad to have you on board."

The avengers decided to give the hell hole some time to forget what they did and will not be expecting any retaliation for what they did. The Whites didn't often expect any payback from the Coloreds. Most of the colored men felt lucky it was not happening to them. They usually found a safe place to hide and wait until the stormy weather cleared.

"Listen up you nappy-headed citizens of the good old USA! Willie, Peter and I have decided that it's about time we started looking after ourselves. We are tired of being treated like enemies of our own country and doing nothing for ourselves. We think it's like this. These folks will not do for us those things that we can do for ourselves. Any questions thus far?"

"Give us some ideas of what it is that we can do short of wiping out the entire white population. We know how hard it is to change the minds of them kind of people. They would rather die than to give in or play fair with their neighbors."

"We are taking that under consideration. Yes, we know how determined these folks can be to have their way. But, we also thought about what they hold dear. These folks will do most anything to protect their homes and all that is in them. We will hit him where it hurts; in his pockets. We will destroy every cow and mule he owns. We can even burn his barn, and so on."

"I see what you are getting at. Destroying his property hits where it hurts. He would be nothing without the money in his banks and the land he owns, but can't work."

"The local Blacks won't have to do a thing but refuse to work a few days a month. They can claim that they are scared to report for work. We can help them out by throwing dead dogs, etc. into their yards and on their porches. We want to make sure the law do not suspect their Coloreds. How do this sound so far?"

"You got to me. When do we get this project going?"

"Let's don't get in a hurry. Making haste will be a mistake. We will have to be cool with this evil that we plan to rain down on these poor little white folks. We know how helpless they are without their Negroes to carry them."

The plans had to be so that the locals would not become targets for the white's hate. The project was set to start the first extremely cold day when most of the citizens would be huddled around a warm stove.

"Willie, you and I will do our thing at dusk come this Monday. I don't believe that we need more than just you and me. This way the highway boys won't put two and two together. We will do the hardware store first. This will be a starter. We can do one or two hits a week until we think that justice has been done. The house boys and girls will be told to stay at home while we are at work"

"This will take a while, if that's the case. How much property damage has to be done to pay for a human life?"

"We know there isn't enough property in the world to pay for a human life. We know one can replace property, it's just takes time. But, human life? We can never get that back. There will be other loses. Their black help will be missing while we are making our point"

The two warriors headed out in the early morning just to be

on the safe side of the speed limit laws. They had no intentions of getting caught with a load of explosives. Getting pulled over and search would get them a life sentence in the local lockup.

The warehouse was a safe target as far as it being the least likely that a human would get caught in the blast. It sure was a beauty when the firebombs sent sparks and flames high into the early evening cold sky. The whole town heard and saw the fireworks.

"Pete! What do you think would work in the best interest of all concerned?"

"We got the attention of the white and colored citizens with the fire. Let's wait and keep an eye on what the community do about their destroyed warehouse."

"What about the rest of you men?"

"All I want to accomplish is for the rednecks to stay out of colored folks' business and stop treating our young men like they are the enemies of freedom and democracy. We are not responsible for all the problems that exist in this country."

"I think that's about what we all want, Willie. What more can we ask for? We can't repay anybody for what our granddaddies did. Not directly anyway. We might encourage the powerful people to be a little more understanding of what we have to do to catch up with the Whites, We are not begging for something that don't belong to us. We can't blame the entire white race for the actions of the few."

The men of color had a sticky problem with trying to separate the guilty from the innocent. This was true for sorting out the guilty on both sides of the racial divide. There was a number of Blacks who might be even more guilty of standing in the path of racial justice than many of the good old white boys.

"What did that carload of colored men want yesterday? Where were they from?"

"I'm gonna get to that as soon as Willie and Joe gets here. The four men gave me and Willie something to think about when it comes to lending our fellow colored brothers a helping hand."

"I just happened to drive pass your place when the four men were waving goodbye to you. If I had come by earlier I would have stopped to see if you needed some help."

"They reminded us of something that we often forget. It is not all the Whites who are against equality between the races. It might surprise us to know that some Whites think the same way we do. They have sense enough to know that for us to have the kind of freedoms that we claim we have, and etc, all of us will have to open our eyes to the total picture, instead of closing our eyes to the other side of what is."

"What did they think we should do?"

"They wanted us to do absolutely nothing for the time being. They thanked us for being ready to take action on their behalf. The old man said that just the idea that we wanted to join in the fight was enough. He is using our actions to inspire his people to start paying attention to their ways of relating to their people in order to start their own movements against their unequal ways of sharing the social goodies. Ain't that something?"

"I wonder if the same thing happened right here in our own neighborhood would we be so eager to take actions. Some of these white people are blood related to us. We have shared the goodies of our lands and woods since time began. I don't believe that I could burn down J.D.'s barn and endanger his securities. Shucks, I were brought up in that old building."

"Pete, you know we know what we are about. But, I don't think that what happened up in Missouri could take place here. Again, maybe it could under the same set of circumstances."

"I'm saying that this same craziness could visit us. We have had similar behaviors right here in our own front yards. We haven't had it recently, but we once did."

"We sure did until a few of our crazy Blacks went crazy and nearly wiped out everybody. That was a long time ago, but it could be again."

The feeling of insecurities about one's safety in his home state was still driving the young men to seek refuge in the big northern cities. Safety from being lynched was not quite enough to hold the young generation at home. The boys returning from the wars in foreign countries telling stories of a different way for Coloreds to live and listening to city cousins telling their stories didn't help keep the men home either. The returning Blacks all had bad opinions of their home social conditions.

"I got a letter from my uncle today. He said that the automobile plants are hiring every living soul that can hold a wrench of some kind. You know they were once asking that you needed a high school diploma. He is asking us to come while the gitting is good. They are hiring anybody who can hole a tool. It don't matter whether they can read or write or not."

"What do you think, Tommy? You already have half your family up there now."

"I'm thinking about taking a trip up there just to see how it is. I didn't like it the last time I went. But, jobs are getting hard to find down here at home. The farming business is at a standstill."

"What do you have to say, Willie?"

"I don't see where it could hurt. You could always come back home as long as you don't leave here running from a lynch mob."

"That's the way I see it. It ain't like Tommy has to quit a job, or anything. It would be different for me. I have it made right here in the great state of Mississippi. Don't you agree?"

"Yeah, we do. You are what the northerners call an Uncle Tom. You are the head n... I took a close look at some of the men who left the south for the north and they didn't impress me much at all. Most were living from hand to mouth."

"We know Tommy. They sometimes come back showing off their new cars, and so on. But we know who they are. You take the many who we never see again are the ones who can't come home to their mama's funeral without borrowing their bus fare."

"I hadn't thought much about trying my hand because I don't have a high school diploma. You know what kind of jobs are waiting for a poor ignorant southern country boy? He would be washing cars for a living until he decided to die and get it over with."

"It looks like you got a chance to do better now. You have always been about the best worker in these here parts and that's baring none."

"What about you, Willie? You want to go with me?"

"I don't know for sure. Where would we stay?"

"My cousin rents rooms in a rooming house. He says that he has one waiting for me and whoever."

"I don't know if my head man, Floyd, could do his job without me. He is having a hard time hiring help for his plantation. Half the men and some of the women they once could count on will tell you where to go if you ask them to work in the pulp woods."

"I saw him in the quarters looking for help. He was even offering them transportation to and from the fields and woods."

"I knew he was desperate for workers when I saw him driving the truck. Remember, Mack left for Chicago without even telling Floyd."

"I know. I don't think he could face Floyd with that kind

of information. You know the things Floyd did for him when he was having sickness in his family. Floyd even took up the money to bury Mack's wife and mother-in-law. He sure did."

The Coloreds were having to reduce their own farm sizes due to the fact that their sons and daughters were packing up and going in search of their pots of gold. The roads to new lands were never paved and without hazards.

# Chapter Six

The high rollers of the great country of the United States were still in the dark relative to what was causing the migration of their work force. These men and women were searching for what men have always gone in search for. They went hunting for that promised land that their God had told them was theirs for the taking.

There were no smooth and well-lite roads to these destinations. The migrating Blacks were paying the same prices that all people on the march had paid since Abraham led his God chosen people in search of their promised lands. The migration highways were a second graveyard for the casualties of the roads to somewhere else other than the lands of their birth.

"We have another funeral coming up. Miss Wells died up there in Chicago and her last wish was for her son to bring her body back here for burial."

"Wasn't she kin to your family, Floyd? You know, we all might be just a bit kin to each other."

"It is believed that her son might be our kin. I can't say for sure. Her funeral will be the third this year of people who moved away following their children who could not stand to leave their parents behind."

"At least she had a few good years up there with her son and daughter. She would not have lasted this long if she had remained here with nobody to look after her."

"It has become a big problem for the old folks. They have to follow their children and grandchildren or remain at home to die."

Floyd, when do you think this movement of people from one place to another will end?"

"I don't believe it can come to a stop before man learns to obey the ten commandments. That is, he must learn to treat his fellow men as he want them to treat him. We will have to learn to love each other as we love ourselves."

"It will be a long time before the races can forgive each other and love the way the good book demands. There has been too much wrongs done between the races and the special groups."

"That is one of the big problems. There are the greedy, the lazy, the downright crooks and a million other walls separating the races and groups from being in a state of mind to love others like they love themselves."

"Floyd, do we have that kind of love for our own family members? I haven't seen it."

"If we do have unconditional family love, I haven't seen it either, or I don't know it when I see it. There is more killing going on within the family than it is anywhere else. Husbands killing wives, wives killing husbands and you name it, it is happening."

The leading citizens, such as the preachers and local political leaders, blamed theses inter-family killing on the social conditions at large. It was a commonly held opinion that sin on the parts of man was responsible for the troubles of the world. The convictions that sin was the big bad boy causing the social inequality, also caused Blacks to flocked to

"Everybody here knows the story of how that came to be. We have heard the story a thousand times. They've named one of their county roads, Lynch Road."

"Well, anyway, My uncle is trying to sell his few acres of good bottom land so he will have the financing to pay for his trip out. He told me that his time was running out and he had to make his move soon. My cousin has been trying his best to get the old man to thinking about moving in with him. My uncle has always been pigheaded when it came to depending on others. He needs help with my aunt too. He just can't make it here on his own."

"There is one thing he is thinking about and that is, will he be able to find something to do. He is not the kind of man who can lay up and depend on others to feed and shelter him and his life's love."

"He'll have to start thinking in another frame of mind. There will come times when we all will need to accept help, or die."

"That happens more often than you want to believe. You and I know a few old folks who just threw in their hats and kicked the bucket. The extreme unfortunate in our country never had the opportunities to prepare for their sick years and their old age years. You see, most of the men and women we are part of don't live long enough to worry about their old age. They are too busy making ends meet in their present hard and short lives."

Another killer of the poor hardworking was not having enough wealth saved for their old age and their sick days. The one way people could insure their survival in their later non-productive days would be to save money. They very seldom were paid enough cash to buy their work shoes.

The Negro population was beginning to show a big decrease in their numbers. Part of this declining population was due to there being no Blacks immigrating into our great country. Instead of immigrating into this home of the heavens, they were looking for highways out of the country, or at least out of the south.

The black people had no other country where they looked like the home folks. These Negroes were colored, not black. The American black people would have to be chopped into tiny peaces and sent to a dozen different countries and be part of several different races. They were in their home country.

"I read where you ex-slaves are trying to get a country of your own. You folks know what you are asking for?"

"Yeah, Willie, we do. The American Blacks, or Coloreds, whichever you prefer, don't have a country of origin where they can claim ownership through their ancestors roots."

"It's one thing for sure, these folks are getting out of here one way or another. Those who don't get the hell out of here are killing each other like one kills flies. It sure don't seem like it has always been this bad."

"You are right. We have lost nearly all our young men to the dark. If they aren't killing themselves, they are being sent to jail or the arms services."

"How long can this continue before there is nobody black left In the south?"

"We don't have to worry about this country being without people. The whites and the brown people are flocking to this country by the millions. We are being flooded with legal and illegal immigrants at every gate to this country. Those folks are forcing us Blacks into the slum areas of the big cities. There is another way our black folks are leaving their groups; education. What happens to the Blacks that we are breaking out necks to send to school? Yeah, what about that nose-in-the-air bunch?"

"You have a point Bob. They can't wait to move into some all-white neighborhood. The last thing they want to be is Black. Why Floyd?"

"You really can't blame them either. What have the Blacks got to encourage their educated brothers and sisters to remain in their birth community? Even their black brothers and sisters pick on them. This educated gang ends up not being welcome anywhere. Maybe that's the reason so few Black take education seriously."

"You smart men should come up with something that will save us from being kicked off the maps of human existence. Floyd, Willie, have you men thought about ways to bring us together?"

"We are bringing us together. We are filling the jails, the prisons, the city slums, the nut houses and the grave yards. What more togetherness can we ask for?"

"Good god, Willie, You know what I'm getting at. The things you mentioned are the things that are killing us. The Blacks are falling into them holes to never be seen or heard from again. Is that what we need to save us?"

"Yes, yes, you bet I know exactly what you mean, Bobby. Let's see what our heavy thinker thinks about saving his people from becoming nonexistent. The pure black race has already become over fifty percent extent. It won't be too many more years before the black race as it is and once was will become history. We are fast becoming a race of mixed colors. What do you suggest we do to save ourselves from becoming just notes in history books?"

"The Blacks, who you men are trying to be, no longer exist today. Our African ancestors don't stand a chance of surviving another fifty years. Those original people who fathered and mothered us are gone forever."

"Floyd, what you are saying is that we Blacks of today and the future won't have a one-nation history. How do we classify ourselves when we can't tie our histories to one or two histories?"

"Bob! we have to realize that we aren't the first people who have gone through the evolutionary process of change. We are just the latest. Look around you. Find me a family with all the family members being the same color in the black people. Even the pure Africans that were brought over here during slavery were not from the same tribes or parts of Africa."

"Maybe that's why we are the best of the best. They say when you mix breed anything the best and strongest genes are transferred to the mixed off-springs. Is that what's happened to us?"

"Now you men are getting the point. We have all the best tools from all sides to use to become super human beings. Why don't we use these gifts, you might ask. It's because we, as a people, have been convinced that we are too dumb and too under deserving for such gifts."

"What you are saying is, it is our own fault that we are in the shapes that we are in. That's even worse than it would be If we could blame it on the man."

"Yes indeed. The worst prison a man can be in is the ones he build for himself. The shackles are made by the people that are shackled."

"We are running from our own hell holes that we are tending the fires of. What do you think about what Floyd just told us, Pete?"

"I don't want to think that our social position is created by our own craziness. I don't believe Floyd is saying that our ending up on the bottom of the pile is all due to us being weak and stupid. We have plenty of help keeping us semi-slaves."

"We were better off when we were slaves as far as staying alive is concerned. We were valuable property then which gave the masters reasons to protect us. Our numbers were not shrinking then. Our population was on the rise. We were well housed and fed in those days. We were not allowed to kill each other either. The disgrace of self destruction has kept us 'underdogs' ever since. We still look to the white people for our deliverance."

It didn't matter how the few thought about the black people's situation in the United States. The black realities remain the same. The majority of the Blacks continued to occupy the bottom rung of the social ladder. Even the new comers were higher up on the ladder than the native Blacks. There were a few Blacks being allowed to immigrate to this Unite States to work the farms and they were given more respect than the native black citizens. These incoming Blacks were from the islands and were laborers. All they needed was a speech accent to get the jobs and the respect that goes with being productive.

"Floyd, have you thought any more about pulling up roots and heading north to try your hand at doing some real work for a change?"

"Every day, Willie. My position on the plantation is not what it used to be. It's getting harder and harder to get good help these days, as you are aware of. Plus, the old place and the owners ain't what they were back in the day. What about you Willie?"

"I'm gonna try my hand even though I'm past the age when one should be thinking about starting life over."

"Those are my thoughts too. I want to get married and have a family before it's too late, I can't see you and me plowing a mule to feed a bunch of little pure Americans."

"I know the little woman will be glad to hear that you are beginning to grow up. You won't be able to stand tall and be the kind of man these modern women want while kneeling down to some old dumb white folks."

"When are you leaving for them snow shovels?"

"I'm Heading out later today. If you make up your mind soon, I'll drive down and get you. You just say when."

"Let me know when your plant starts to hire again. I can't see a life in Mississippi being worth a do-do for a colored man anyway soon. I see now what has happened to a few old-timers who decided to stay at home and hope for change. They didn't have the opportunities that we have."

The south's young men continued to fill the public transportation vehicles and the automobiles of returning home boys and home girls with the promised lands as their destinations.

# Chapter Seven

Floyd's big boss died on a cold winter night in February. It was the coldest day of the year. The old man's folks came from all the small communities within twenty miles to pay their respects. The white church was packed to the limits on that cold morning of the burial. It looked like it was too cold to put even the dead in the ground"

Floyd had the gut feeling that it was time for a life change. His guts had never lied to him before and he was paying close attention to them this time, too.

"Floyd, what has been eating you these pass few days. You know, I know when there is something on that dumb mind of yours."

"Yeah, I have been doing a bit of trying to figure out what I want to do with the rest of my life. You are aware that my plantation job is fast coming to an end. I wanted us to start thinking about what our future is to be. What do you think, old lady?"

"I thought you were planning to go visit Willie and see what the big fuss was about up there with the automobile factories was all about. I don't see what's so hard about doing that. I know you ain't use to doing hard work, but it might be time to start getting ready for a different line of work."

"You sound like Willie and Pete. They says the same thing about your hard-working old man."

"You might ought to listen to them men sometimes. You have been riding high on that plantation until the bottom fell out of the good old southern labor market. Haven't you been reading the papers? The south that we know is done for. The southern gentlemen don't even need you men to pick cotton anymore."

"You know babe, what I think about a lot?"

"Probably yours and my life together. That is the same thing that be on my mind most of the time. We will have to figure out what is in our best interest. I've read in the magazines about what others have had to do to make a better life for themselves. Even white folks have to plan their lives too. We are gonna have to start thinking for ourselves."

"Willie told me to call him when I made up my mind to make a move. I have been waiting until I was sure of what your thinking was on this. I know your mother still depends on you a lot. What do she think about moving north, or staying here without you?"

"Mama and I have talked about this a lot here lately. She understands a lot more than you would think she do. You know she has not a sick bone in her body and is able to care for herself, at least for the time being."

"This little talk takes a load off my mind. I was worried about your mama's reactions to the possibilities that I might be dragging you off to unknown lands and people."

"If I were you I'd write, or call, Willie soon and see what's going with the job market. The sooner the better. Don't you worry about mama. You would be surprised at what that young lady be thinking about. Would you believe that she thinks that she might find herself a man in the city? She says that there is no men around here to hang a tag on."

"She is right about that. I don't even have a buddy to run around with, much less talk serious business with. These boys are hightailing it for them northern slums. From what I hear, they'd rather be poor and living in the north than be rich and living here in these sticks."

"Don't you forget that we have mentioned this before Willie left here. Let's face it, you were riding high on the hog when the plantation was busting with bent human and animal backs and the pastures were flooded with roaming stock. Those days are gone forever."

"Let's give old Willie a call and see what is going on up there in the snow. It's too bad that the best time to find jobs up there is in the cold months. I guess that is because the southerners don't like to go north in the winter time."

"Well, you can't much blame them for not wanting to face them cold northern winds half-dressed and thin blooded. But, the better chances of getting a job in the automobile business is in the fall and winter months. Those are the months when the folks buy the new model cars."

Willie's respond to Floyd's questions were promising. Mather of fact, he almost guaranteed Floyd a job before Floyd left the good old state of Mississippi. Floyd was left with no worthwhile excuse for not going north. He had to go if for no other reason than to find something wrong with the whole idea of moving.

Floyd was hired before he reported to the factory. Willie had gotten the application, filled it out and sent it to Floyd for his signature. That took all Floyd's reason for hesitating and dumped them in the trash pile.

"How do that suit you, old man? You got a job and didn't ask for it. They must be desperate for you country boys sweat and tears."

"The only thing that might stop them from giving me

the job is they might find something wrong with my eyes, or something. I'll be leaving here tomorrow so I can report Monday morning. But, I want you to know something right now. You better not even look at another man while I'm gone."

"Are you joking? Who is left here in Mississippi to look at? You point one good Man out to me and just maybe, and I said, just maybe I would give him a side glance."

"I don't want to come back and give one of my own home boys a butt kicking."

"I'm glad you brought that up. Your orders to me give me a chance to tell you what's on my mind. I want you to open up them ears of yours and listen good. I don't want to have to come up there and beat the mess out of you and Willie over them nappy-headed city street-walkers. Do you hear me loud and clear? You country dumb knotty heads tend to go crazy when you get a few dollars in your front pockets. I'll tear that place apart if you go crazy on me. I have put up with you too long while you didn't have a dime. I'm not going to lose you to some fancy-butt city hustler now that you have a way of putting two dollars in your pockets."

"Them city gals won't want a dumb country boy like me. They go for them fancy men in three-piece suits"

"Who are you shucking. They want one thing first and that is the control of a big paycheck. Remember there is a shortage of available black men in the city too. I hear that some of them jobs they give to you southern boys can be downright life threatening. I warn you to not only to stay away from them women, but to be careful on the job too. I don't want to have to shut down the automobile industries for killing my man."

"I'll be writing you every week until I can come for you. You just be waiting for the important phone call."

The job that Floyd got was surprisingly easy and simple. Matter of fact the jobs were too simple. The simple operations were so simple until he became so boring until it was nearly impossible to remain awake. Floyd felt that he had been given a new chance to make a decent life for him and his partner.

"Girl you won't believe how easy these jobs are. They are not much harder than the jobs at home that we do for nothing. So, you remember what I told you about eyeballing other men."

"I don't think it is me you have to worry about. I think you are the one who will have to fight off them city gals. You know how you men are with money in your pockets. There is no critter that can be as crazy as a black man with a pocket full of spending change."

"Hush yo mouth, woman. I'm signing up for all the overtime that they will let me work. I will be able to nearly double my paycheck. They pay time and one-half for weekday overtime and double-time for Sundays and holidays. Now add that up. I will be one rich crazy man in a few weeks. I'll be crazy and rich enough to come and marry you. Now, that is what I call being out of my mind."

"Now you are beginning to make sense. All rich men need sensible wives to prevent them from killing themselves chasing street-walkers."

"You just start packing for a long ride. We will wait until I'm finished with probation and become a regular employee. In the meantime, I'm looking for us a one-room apartment. I will need a good used car too. Cars are a dime a dozen here. I already have a co-signer to help me buy a good used vehicle."

"Slow down now. Don't get ahead of yourself. We have waited this long, a few more days won't be hard to wait. This is why you dumb country boys need a woman, and a good woman at that. A strong woman will make sure you do the right thing. I'm that woman, you hear me?"

The two soon-to-be a couple had a pile of plans to think

through. These two were like the most of their kind in that they had very little experience at thinking for themselves. The ways of life for a colored couple in the south were very simple. The rules were stamped in cement and easy to follow. This was true for both races and all levels of the social stratum.

The happy soon-to-be wife was busy buying and making suitable clothing for the change in residence. She bought magazines and any other books that contained information relative to city living. There was not a whole lot printed about the lives of the migrating **Blacks. She had to play it by ear and watch how the visitors came home and listen to them tell lies about how good it was in the city.**

**Floyd decided to drive all night in order to arrive at his home in the early morning. He had picked a weekend with a holiday which gave him enough time off to make the trip and report for work on Tuesday. He didn't have seniority enough to have vacation days or emergency days he could use for going home purposes. This was part of the problem with moving a thousand miles away from the home where your loved ones still reside. The road would always be jammed with home folks going to see their sick relatives, going to funerals, going on vacation. They would be speeding on the road to one of their homes for any of a number of serious reasons.**

**Floyd settled back and drove on toward home on what appeared to be an empty highway. The radio was playing some great hillbilly music. Floyd came around the curve at a speed much higher than would have been safe if you met another vehicle traveling the opposite direction. But, there are other hazards on the road. He failed to see the stick of pulp wood in the middle of his lane.**

**Floyd had to swerve to the right too much to avoid the log and remain on the highway. His vehicle went**

over the edge of the road and down a steep slope into the trees below. The car had flipped over and trapped Floyd underneath in a shallow stream of water. He hadn't been under the car but a few minutes before a truck stopped to see if help was needed.

"Hey buddy! Hold on friend! Let me see what I have to do to get you out."

The good citizen began to slip and slide his way down the bluff of rocks, bushes and grass to where the trapped driver was. He had to crawl down to get a look at the trapped man to see what he could do to save the man.

"Just you hold on buddy. Don't you die on me. I should have you out...."

The poor good shepherd froze in the position he was in when he saw that the man was black. He didn't remember having seen this man before. At the time he realized that the driver was Black, he thought of his appointment with the doctor.

"Ops! I'm gonna be late for my appointment. I better get on into town before somebody takes my appointment. I'll let some of this fellow's own kind find him. Maybe several of his folks will be able to lift the automobile off his head without a problem. I really don't have time to waste today."

The good white citizen made sure the stick of pulp wood was off the highway far enough for it to be safe for other drivers to be safe. He was thankful that it was no worse than it was. The accident could have happened to anybody.

"God is good! That could have been me down there"

The good citizen left the site of the accident mumbling to himself about his being late for his doctor's appointment. Floyd had enough time above the rushing water to get a glance at the white face as the man turned to make his way back to road level. Floyd didn't have to worry about trying to create a worth-living life any longer. Floyd's life's journey came to an end at the bottom of a bluff under less than twelve inches of muddy water.

# IN THE NAME OF GOD

# Chapter One

The mid-south was experiencing a severe weather condition in the late autumn afternoon when five-year-old J.B heard the truck stop in front of his family's home. As cold as it might be, J.B. Would always make an attempt to meet his daddy at the door. But this afternoon, his daddy didn't come to the door. J.B. waited to hear his daddy's big brogans hit the steps and the porch, but the sounds never came. J.B. Opened the door to see which way his daddy had made off to. That's when he saw the body of his daddy piled along side the drain ditch.

J.B. heard the sound of a little boy's screams but had no idea where the screams were coming from until his mama came rushing through the open door. J.B.'s mama didn't try to help her husband into the house without help. She was eight months pregnant at the time. J.B.'s brother was three and a half years old and his baby sister was one and a half. Mama sent J.B to get his uncle who lived about a mile down the road. J.B ran all the way.

J. B. witnessed the total madness involved in getting his daddy into bed. After they got his daddy into bed, his uncle went for Grandma and the midwife and his aunt May. The dreamlike events of this day would color J.B.'s thinking in racist terms for the remainder of his life, even though he had no proof that his daddy had been harmed by Whites. He and his uncle went for the doctor who lived in town which was five miles away. His uncle drove carefully on the wet and slippery roads. The last thing they could afford was to get stuck in a ditch on their way to fetch the doctor.

J.B. thought that the doctor took too much time before he showed up to doctor on his daddy. It seemed like it took hours for the old white doctor to make his appearance. In the meantime the nearly beat-to-death man had spoken not one word. His jaw bone had been broken in several places. He had several broken ribs in addition to a broken shoulder and knots all over his head, and bruises over the rest of his body.

J.B.'s daddy was a strong man which gave him the strength to pull out of what might have been a sure fatal condition for a weaker man. Mack Smith was bed ridden for months before he was back on his feet and ready to take up the duties of being a husband and father. He was lucky to have relatives and a living mother to provide help for his family until his recovery. Mack was never again the man that he once was. He finally was able to tell what happened that cold and wet Autumn evening in nineteen hundred and thirty-six.

Mack had always been a man who stood his grounds when he felt that his integrity was under attack. This was one of them days. He had just been told that his credit had been cut off until he promise to work for the Walkers during the winter months. Mack could not get the man to understand that he had a better paying job working on the docks which was only thirty miles away. The man told him to get his loan from the docks then. After the encounter with the man, Mack was too angry to wait for a ride home, he decided to walk the five miles.

Mack told his folk that the white men who brought him home was not the same men who had tried to end his days on earth. The Whites who did the good deeds of bringing the half-dead man home were considered good white folk. Whoever they were, they saved his life.

The confusion about who did what was causing J.B. a ton of trouble. He had no single targets to direct his hate at. The young man began to see all white folk in the same way. He began to distrust all Whites. This hatred was building up in J.B.'s guts like pressure builds in a pressure cooker. His daddy and mama started to notice that there was something terribly troubling the mind of their oldest child.

J.B. started to avoid spending time in town more and more as the burning hatred fermented in his innards. Instead of going to the movie house like all the other boys his age, he would buy comic books and spend his time reading them over and over.

"J.B.! Aren't you ready for church yet? You better hurry, or you will miss the ride." His mother yelled through the thin wall of his room.

"I'll be ready when Mr. Turner gets here. I can hear that old truck when he leaves his house."

Daddy Mack was nowhere near ready for church. The old man had slowly ceased going to church every Sunday after his nearly fatal meeting with the gang of thugs. Before that the man was a devoted church goer. J.B. was torn between remaining at home to keep his daddy company or attending church.

"Daddy! You going to church today?"

"No son. You do what your mama tells you to. You go on and get yourself ready for Sunday school. I'll be all right."

J.B. believed that there might be one thing in this world that he could trust to be good for him and his daddy, the church and its teaching. He would read the Bible when he ran out of comic books to read. The Bible made the kinds of promises that sounded good to J.B.'s ears.

J.B. was at the head of his fifth grade class with a straight A grade average. The teachers thought he was still a weird child even with his high grade average. They would have to insist that he go out at recess and play with the other children. The matter was taken up with his daddy and mama at every PTA meeting.

"Mrs. Smith, I think you might ought to think about J.B.'s keeping to himself all the time. I don't believe that's good for the young man. The only children he pays much attention to are his little brothers and sister. I can give him credit for keeping his eyes on them. Yes ma'am."

"He started changing right after his daddy ran into that trouble several years back. You remember that time. I don't think J.B. could handle seeing his daddy lying there in a heap and bleeding from every opening in his body and not be affected awfully."

"I'm not complaining about the young man. He is the best behaved child in the school by far. I have never had any trouble out of the child at all. Is he that way at home, Mrs. Smith?"

"His being unlike other boys his age is what troubles me about the young man. He is too good of a child. He never get sassy with me or his daddy, or anybody else that I know of. He is a good babysitter for his brothers and sister. He do all we ask of him without saying a mumbling word."

Mama Smith noticed just the tip of the monster one day when the family was ask to help a white neighbor finish scraping a few acres of cotton. The Turners usually didn't work for anybody but themselves, with the exception of Mr. Smith. He worked on and off on the docks. This time J.B. turned into a child that surprised both his mama and daddy.

"J.B.! Did you hear me? Mr. Walker wants us to give them a hand in scraping the last of their cotton. We are finished with ours and thought this would be a good chance for you children to earn yourselves a dollar or two."

J.B. just stood frozen in his tracks. He had an expression on his face that his mama and daddy had never seen before. The boy's eyes appeared to be shut, his mouth had an angry crimp to it.

"J.B.! Are you feeling well? What's the matter with you? You look as if you've seen a ghost, or something."

All the images of that terrible evening came rushing back to J.B.'s mind. His heart almost stopped beating resulting in his being barely able to stand. He saw and smelled the blood that covered his daddy that day a few years back. He could not answer his mother's questions that she was asking, or the ones she didn't ask. All he could think to do was to turn and run.

"Mack! You might ought to go see if you can find that boy. You should have seen the look on his face when I mentioned scraping cotton for the Walkers. I have never seen him look like that before."

"Where did he run to?"

"All I could see was his shirt flying in the wind as he went down the hill toward his grandma's. Old King could hardly keep up with the boy, he was running so fast. But, he never said a word."

"Y'all go on to the cotton patch. I'll walk down to mama's and see if he stopped at her place. I'll be on in a while."

J.B. and his dog was not to be found for the next twenty-four hours. The two found shelter in the closed school house. He could not explain what was going on in his mind. All he knew was that he felt like doing some terrible things to any local White he came close to.

J.B.! Your daddy and me would like to ask you a few questions, if you don't mind."

"I'm listening, Mama."

"What went through your mind Monday when I mentioned scraping cotton for the Walkers? Why did you run off and have us worrying ourselves nearly to death?"

"I don't exactly know, Mama. I just went kind of crazy, I guess. I know one thing, I can't work for none of these white folk around here."

"Son, you are gonna have to realize that all these white folk ain't bad. We have some good white folks in this community and if we help them, they will do the same for us. Do you understand?"

"Yes ma'am, I think I do."

"What in the world crossed your mind at the mentioning of scraping cotton for the Walkers? I have never seen you look like you did then. You became a totally different child than what we are accustomed to. I would like to know what was you thinking all them hours out there with just old King."

"I was not thinking anything. I just smelt blood. I could see Daddy like he was the night they brought him home. That's all I remember."

J.B. switched his attention to the Bible and the sermons the preachers preached trying to find the answers to the questions that he did not know how to ask. He was really concerned about the instructions pertaining to love and how one should treat his fellow man. He needed something to take the place of what he felt toward some of his fellow men. He was trying hard to avoid offending his god. "Hey Ann! Get out of the road! You see that bus ain't slowing down none."

"I am out of the road, big brother. Where do you want me to git to?"

"Far enough out of the road so you don't get spattered with mud. That's how far. Now jump to the other side of that ditch."

The white children school bus always seemed to speed up

just to splash mud on the walking colored children. J.B. would repeat the Bible verse of "love thy fellow man as thy brother" or something like that. He did not want to offend God.

J.B. was having a hard time thinking positive thoughts about himself. He was beginning to wish that he was born an Indian, or some other race other than a member of the colored race. He was not as black as some of his race, but he was black enough to be hated by the Whites and some of the Coloreds themselves. They might not have hated him the same as the school bus drivers did, but they did not consider him as an equal.

"Mama! Why do these white folk make fun of the Coloreds?"

"They all don't make fun of us Coloreds. We have some very good white folk. Look how the Walkers treat us. Do you think that little Tommy makes fun of you?"

"Yes ma'am. He sure did last Sunday when his cousins were over here. They made fun of little sister's bow legs. Yes ma'am, he laughed right along with his cousins."

# Chapter Two

J.B. spent his twelfth birthday hunting in the backwoods. He had been given a single barrel shotgun for his birthday. The gun was more for him to supply meat for the table than for anything else. He had been using his uncle's twenty-two for hunting. He had been a crack shot since before he was twelve years old.

"What did you kill on your birthday, J.?"

"You won't believe it if I told you. Come out on the porch and see for yourself, Grandma."

"Praise the Lord. This boy done gone and killed his first turkey, Praise the Lord."

J.B.'s killing his first turkey gave him a means to an end: killing wild game to put food on the table. He used hunting and fishing as excuses to avoid dealing with the white bosses. Old man Smith left the young man to do as he please most of the time.

"J.B.! Don't you stay in them woods until after sundown, you hear?"

"Yes ma'am. I won't let dark catch me across the creek. They say the haunts roam around the old Evan's place as soon as the sun drops below the tree tops. This shotgun won't scare them boys."

"Don't you play with me boy. You just be here at the house when dark comes."

It had never been too safe for a young colored man to be traveling around alone after dark. This was especially true if the young colored man was carrying a twelve gauge shotgun. Nobody trusted what might be an angry black man with a gun. One never knew when a Colored had been wronged.

"J.B.! You can ride into town with us. Your uncle and aunt will pick us up around one. So, don't you go off looking for rabbits."

"I'll be here. I have to buy my school shoes, britches and shirts. I think Uncle Rogers will pay me for cutting his winter wood and a few other jobs he owes me for. He better pay me because I'm the only one who can put up with the old crank."

"Watch what you say about grown folk boy. You better watch your mouth when you speak about old folk. You know what the Bible says about honoring the old folk."

"Yes ma'am. I know he has had a rough time in the last few years. I remember when Auntie was sick. I can't remember a time when she was not sick. I don't ever remember seeing her walk without help."

"That's why you should be careful how you judge others. They might have good reasons for doing the things they do. Do you hear me, son?"

"I sure do, Mama. Then why do people do bad things to others without having a good reason? They haven't had nothing bad happened to them, yet they are horrible to deal with. Why?"

"Only God can answer that, J. We can only obey what the Bible teaches us. We are suppose to love our fellow man in spite of what he do. We can always pray."

J.B. had to shut down his brain for a spell before thinking about the lesson that he had been given. He sometimes wished with all his heart that the good book was right one hundred percent. He felt complete when he was reading the Bible. His only regret was that others whom he had to do business with didn't see it the same way.

Uncle Rogers, that's what everybody called him because he was the oldest member in the church, paid J.B. just like he promised. J.B headed for the one big store that had everything he needed. There were the times when he could be made to feel like he was always in the wrong place.

"Will you stand to the side boy? You are in the customers way."

J.B. moved to the next isle without making a vocal sound. He had to put up with this, or order his school clothes from the catalog which would be just as bad.

"Now, what did you want to buy boy?"

J.B. put his clothing on the counter without speaking. The clerk didn't look at him with any equal consideration for his being a buying customer the same as she did with the white customers..

"That will be seven dollars and ten cents."

J.B. took his time counting the money out on the counter. The only way he could live through these kinds of times was to play stupid. Playing dumb seemed to always work."

"Wait a minute boy until I put that stuff in a bag. Folk will think you might have stolen it. Do you hear me boy?"

J.B. just bowed his head in silence and took the bag and walked out without a backward glance. He could feel that bitter tasting puke boiling up from his guts. He had to get to the colored quarters as fast as he could.

"Hi, Mrs Wells!"

"I see you've been shopping. You buy your own school clothes young man?"

"Yes Ma'am. I worked and made enough to buy my own.

Daddy and mama have enough to buy for without having to buy mine. I'm fourteen years old my next birthday."

"You are a smart young man. You keep that up and you will prosper."

"Can I have a fish sandwich, please?"

"You know I know what you want, son. You are about the only young man who comes down here instead of going to see the movies in town. What don't you like about the movies, J.?"

"I don't like being upstairs over them white folks. I don't know what would happen to all us Coloreds if a fire broke out. I just can't get used to paying the same money to see the movie from such dangerous seats. I read where a lot of Coloreds were burned to death just because the Whites blocked the door when the movie house caught fire. The Whites had to get out first. All the Whites got out, but half the Coloreds got burned. There were some that were burned so badly until they died."

The dangerous balcony seats was not the main reason why J.B. had problems dealing with Whites. This deep felt hatred had to be directed toward something, or it would drive him crazy. He walked back uptown in time to catch his ride home. The other boys and girls never questioned his whereabouts because they knew he was one weird young man.

Daddy Mack was in his favorite chair on the porch when J.B. jumped off the truck. Daddy Mack watched his confused oldest son climb the bank to the house with his bag of clothing and candy and cookies for his little brothers and sister.

"Afternoon son! How did you make out?"

"I made out okay. I bought my school clothes. How do you feel Daddy?"

"I'm doing about as well as the Lord sees fit for me to be doing. I just leave things in the hands of the Lord."

J. went on in the house without commenting. He had a hard time looking in the sad eyes of his father's, especially knowing how much his daddy wanted to help his son. J.B. knew that the help that they both needed was far beyond the powers of his daddy to give. They both would have to look to the Lord for help. J.B. and his daddy didn't believe the problems were within the powers of man to solve.

The farmers had a good season and had to gather their crops while the sun shinned. The cold weather even held off until the sugar cane was cut and turned into syrup, or stump juice. The good farming season the country folks were reaping seemed to be answers to their prayers. They didn't ask for too much. J.B. and his school mates could not totally accept the level of satisfaction that the older folk could. Giving thanks to God was the first thing they voiced in church, at breakfast, before going to bed and just telling others how they were doing. "I'm blessed. We should thank the Lord for what he decided to bless us with."

"J.B.! Did you hear what happened to Big John? The Sheriff gave him a good butt kicking yesterday in town. Big John is now healing up in jail."

"Why did the Sheriff beat the daylight out of the boy?"

"It appears that the Sheriff didn't recognize Big John as being just an overgrown teenager. They thought he was a man, so I hear. Anyway, Big John will have a few scars to help him to remember what side his bread is browned on."

"What I'm concerned about is what in hell did he do? Big John is nothing but a big old baby,"

"He was not charged with doing anything. My daddy thinks that they were just scared of the big old boy. The white lady who yelled for help didn't recognize John. When the Sheriff got there he just started to beat the living daylights out of the boy. The white lady had been in the store alone when the dumb boy went in. Now, you know the average Colored would have known better than that. How crazy could Big John get?"

"Can you remember when his daddy was run out of the county? That's what they say. Some of the old-timers believe the white folks were deadly afraid of the man. There is one thing for sure, he hasn't been seen around here since."

"J., do you think the same thing might happen to Big John?"

Big John never came back to the community. His folk got the boy out of jail and took him straight to the bus station. Nobody made too much fuss about something like this happening once in a while. They understood that all communities had problems once in a while. This was the way the Lord allowed it to be. Most citizens were more than glad to be rid of trouble-makers from their community.

The preacher never mentioned one word, not directly, about the incident involving Big John and his family. The rumor was that Big John got shipped out of the state with the help of some good white people. The colored citizens would not make a big stink when there were the good white folks involved. They would thank the Lord for sending the good white folks to their rescue.

The preacher stuck to the Bible and encourage his congregation to put their trust in God for all their needs. He never got too far away from man's main job which was to love each other and judge ye not.

These kinds of happenings just made J.B. more and more sick in the stomach each time he heard of them. He found a little relief by reading the Bible more. He developed a habit of reading a few verses every night from the parts he loved. This reading about the love that God has for his people helped J.B. to sleep without having them horrible nightmares he sometimes slept with.

"Mama, can I ask you a question and you promise to not preach at me?"

"That depends on what the question is. Go ahead and ask your question, or questions."

"Do you think that God loves the colored folks as much as he loves the Whites?"

"Now what kind of a question is that? Of course he do. What makes you think he don't?"

"It don't always look like he do, not to me. I see a big difference between the way he treats Coloreds and the way he treats the Whites. How can that be if he loves us all the same?"

Neither mama nor daddy attempted to answer J.'s question. They just sat there and gazed at the fifteen year-old son of theirs. J.B. went to the only source he had for the answer. He went into his room and read the Bible until he felt sleepy.

"I pray the Lord that my soul will keep if I should die before I awake……"

# CHAPTER THREE

Daddy Smith woke with one of his severe headaches again. This had started to get worse and worse within the last few years. The only good thing about the headaches was they rendered him unfit for serving in the military. But, these benefits had turned him into an unfit man for just about anything by the year nineteen forty-nine. Daddy Smith could hardly remember his own name at times. The whole family had become babysitters for the man who was getting old before his time.

"Daddy! Hurry up and eat your breakfast so you and me can catch us a way into town. I'm taking you by to see the doctor this morning. Daddy! Did you hear what I said?"

"You just get ready, son. I'll help your daddy get ready. Tell the doctor how often these headaches have started to come. Don't forget to mention that your daddy is losing his mind."

"I have all the information written down. You just don't worry too much about us, Mama."

J.B. registered for the draft while he and his daddy were at the county seat. He was a bit doubtful about ever serving in the arms services of the United States. He thought he would address that problem after he took care of his daddy's problem.

"Mack, I don't know what to tell you except the truth as I see it. You might have a brain tumor. Now I'm not absolutely sure but that's what I see at this point. I'll make an appointment for you to see a specialist next week. He'll be able to tell you more. He is also a surgeon too. Okay? Boy, why don't you stop in before the week is out and see when Mack's appointment is?"

Mack's head problems got worse as time went on. The surgeon made up some kind of medicine to help Mack with the pain. The surgeon thought that the tumor had to be from some head injuries. At the mentioning of head injuries J.B.'s throat started acting up again.

The surgeon didn't talk about performing surgery at all. This was kind of confusing to J.B. and the family. The only thing that made the family feel better was their faith in prayers. They set up prayer night at home in addition to their praying in church.

J.B. got up at his usual time to start the fires going in the heaters and the stove with one major difference; he didn't hear his mama blundering around. He usually could hear bumping and mumbling going on in his parent's bedroom by the time he lit the stove. He felt like something was terribly wrong in his parents' bedroom.

"Mama! Mama! Is everything all right in there?"

No answer came back to his question. J. didn't think asking a second time would matter. He pushed the door open and went in. He would never forget the scene that popped up before his eyes. His daddy was lying on his back with eyes and mouth wide open. J. didn't have to ask his mother the question.

Time kind of stood still after J. B.'s daddy's funeral. J.B. kind of lost interest in everything around him, except Janet. Janet was the one person who took him as he was. She would never ask him the whys of his actions, but would always keep her opinions to herself if they were not complementary to J.B.'s. Janet was the only person in the community who J. could speak his mind to without being thought of as a nut.

"What do you plan to do for your birthday, J?"

"I thought about having a birthday party at home. This will give me a chance to give mama and my brothers and sister something to spruce up their humdrum lives."

"I guess Jed, Moses and Lizzy, in addition to your mama, will be glad to help you celebrate your twenty-first birthday."

"You, mama and Lizzy will have to do all the cooking. I'm sure you special people of mine don't mind."

"I would be glad to do what little bit I can to help you enjoy your becoming a grown man. We can celebrate Uncle Sam refusing to induct you into his army. Can you imagine the old boy thinking that you were as crazy as a loony?"

"It's easy to fool the mess out of these smart folks These folks think all colored people are crazy as a bat anyway. I have learn to let them think what they need to think about me. If they didn't think that I was somewhat nutty I would have a hard time doing business with your white folks."

"You just let me know when and how much. You know how fast these country folks rushes to free food and drinks. I imagine every deadbeat in the neighborhood will be there with bells on."

"I'll bet you there is one bunch who won't be there. They might be dumb, but they ain't that dumb."

J.B. got his mama and uncle to buy up the goodies, using J. B.'s money of course. The party got underway in the early evening after the weather started to cool down. The weather condition was perfect for having an outdoor party.

""J.B! it's 'bout time you started thinking of getting yourself a wife. You'll be an old man on your next birthday!"

"Look at you Junior. How long have you and Mary been married? You are still as broke as a haunt."

"You don't have to be rich to be married, you know."

"You got that right. If one had to be rich to get married,

none of us would be here, not in wedlock anyway. We would all be bastards."

"That's enough of that kind of talk. You boys can find a more pleasant something to talk about"

"Yes mama."

"I'll get the ice cream started. Come on Jed, get some ice busted up."

J.B. had fun for the first time since he was four years old, except when he and Janet were alone. The community came in a partying mood. Everybody was well fed and ready for home before eight o'clock. Most, if not all, had to be in church for Sunday school at eleven the next morning. The few who had a tendency to drown their miseries in stump juice left even earlier. This was because J. B. did not have any alcoholic beverages on his property.

He had never taken a liking to alcoholic nothing. He figured that men were big enough natural fools without making themselves bigger fools. He remembered his daddy, as if the man was sitting on the porch at the party, sipping the only thing that gave him relief from the headaches caused by a hard life. It didn't seem to help the total family much though. J.B. used to watch his daddy, and others, spend food money trying to find solutions to their earthly troubles within a bottle of crazy water.

"Big brother, can I go to the store with you? You promised me I could when I got bigger."

"No little sister. Maybe some times during the week, but not on the weekend."

J.B. didn't take like possibilities for trouble that dragging his little sister around white folks on the weekend could start. It was not that he didn't trust the white men, he didn't trust himself enough to provide security for his little sister. He felt the comfort that his new thirty-eight caliber revolver gave him which was not the same security it provided for his sister. He didn't feel he had the controls necessary to be a security blanket for members of his immediate family.

J. B.'s confusion over how the world treated people of a different race differently because of different colors bothered him. He once thought that he might grow out of this major jungle of depression caused by where he thought his place was in the world. The simple answers from the Bible and it's promises did not quite the roar of the demon in his guts. If anything, the voices he could almost hear continued to call for action.

"Mama, I think I want to try my luck on the river front. I see Mule has found a job down there and is doing good too. I can come home once or twice a week until I get my own vehicle. Until then I'll ride with Mule. How do that sound to you?"

"To tell you the truth, I thought you would have been down there before now. I knew you would not work in this part of the country for long. Anyway, I will worry about you less when you are on the docks than I will if you are hanging around here."

"Thanks Mama. I will be going with Mule come this Monday. If I'm not hired on at the beginning of the week, I'll catch the bus back home and wait until next Monday, or until Mule calls his folks and tell them when they are hiring."

J. B was hired the second Monday that he reported to the union hall. He found the work kind of hard but nothing that he could not handle. The only problem he had was finding some place to sleep. He was hired to help unload one cargo ship and was not yet a union member. Non-union members had to take their chances because they were the last to be hired. They stood a good chance of hiring on when more than one or two ships arrived at the same time. This was okay with J.B.

"I see you like working on them ships, J."

"It's alright. I just wish that you were a little closer to the docks. That is a long thirty-mile distance. Sometimes I feel like walking back here to see you."

"Hush your mouth boy. You wouldn't be worth a dime by the time you walked thirty miles carrying all the presents that you would be bringing."

"I'm a member of the Union now. This gives me first choice at the better jobs, that is first choice over non-union workers."

"Do that mean you will be making more money?"

"No Jed. We all make the same rate of pay. After all we are all doing the same kind of work. Now, I'll make more after I'm promoted to gang leader."

J.B. was overjoyed to have a job where he didn't have to look at white folks all day. There were no Whites hanging around the dirty cargo holes of the iron ore and banana boats. J.B.'s two brothers and his sister did the farm work on the home front. It didn't take all their time to keep the farm in good shape. Mama was slowing down a lot too.

J.B. felt the boiling acid in his guts when he heard about what had happened at the country store.

"Tell me again what happened between you and that boy at the store."

"It wasn't nothing, son. That boy has always been half crazy. All he said was what the others were thinking, that's all."

"Anyway, I want to hear your side of the story before I go up there and tell the skunk off."

"He just wanted to know how I came 'bout having a ten dollar bill this time of the year. His mama told him that I had a son working on the docks. Son, why don't you just leave them kinds of people in the hands of God?"

"Mama, I'm beginning to believe that I am the instrument

of God. It might be time for us to lend God a hand with some of his creations. We have to take care of his other creatures, don't we?"

J.B. shut his mouth after thinking about who he was talking to. He knew his mama would worry herself sick. She had not returned to her old self since his daddy had crossed over. He became the man of the house after they buried his daddy. He was trying to be a good one.

"Will there be anything else, J.B.?"

J.B. didn't bother with an answer, and the boy didn't expect one either. J. fished out a ten-dollar bill and laid it on the counter. J.B. never took his eyes off the young man's face.

"Do you have a question for me, Mr.?"

"About what, J.B.?"

"I thought you might be wondering where and how I came by a ten-dollar bill this time of the year. You sure you don't want to ask me the question?"

"I don't have any idea of what you are driving at."

"I think you know full well what I'm driving at. I know you remember asking a little old colored lady where she had come 'bout having a ten dollar bill this time of the year. I have to believe that you are not that forgetful. Are you?"

"I didn't think she would get mad because I asked a simple question."

"Do you ask all your customers the same question? You see, I don't like people who pick on that old lady. I would appreciate it if this didn't happen again."

J.B. grabbed his bag of goodies and left the young man standing there with mouth open. J.B. never looked back. He knew he had to get out of there as fast as his legs could carry him. Just to be safe he took the short route home. He went across the wet and boggy field. This route offered him a bit more security from being run down by a truck or car. Once he was in the wide open, he checked his revolver and made sure it was loaded and ready for business.

J.B. shuttered every time he thought about what the end would have turned out to be if the boy had gotten nasty. He had to make stronger efforts to control his temper from now on. This was the exact thing that worried his mother nearly to death.

"Son! What have you gone and done? I get a strange feeling when you are around white folks. I pray for you and us all day long. Me and your brothers and sister wants you here with us. I'm begging you to learn to control that hot temper of yours."

"That I have already promised myself and now I'm promising you."

J.B. often thought about his future wife at times like these. He knew that his kind of colored man was not good husband material. He would have to do a lot of changing, or hiding in order to stay out of trouble. He didn't have any ideas of how he could do business with the powers that be and be a full man at the same time. He could not visualize his tucking his tail and hiding from the hard realities of being a responsible man.

Little brother Jed was old enough to begin to worry about his big brother. He was with his mama when the incident at the store took place. He was hoping that his mama would keep it to herself because he knew what his brother might do. He had overheard his brother say to himself after a close brush with the shoe store clerk in town, "I wish I had never been Born."

J.B. and the river front was made for each other. The hard and dirty jobs were just what J.B.'s kind of Negroes needed to survive. The environment of the cargo holes of the ships contributed to the early demise of the workers. J.B. Had to plan for a life after the docks.

"Ike! You and Mark used to be together all the time. What happened to that boy?"

"You don't know about his sickness?"

"If I did, do you think I'd be asking these questions?"

"He has what they call, black lung. Black lungs disease comes from breathing this dust from the iron ore and other dust we breathe while working in the holes. I'm thinking about quitting as soon as I get my daughter through college. Our little piece of property is all paid for."

"How bad off is Mark? He was one of the best workers that worked in the holes. He could be counted on to be here every day too."

"The doctors said that was part of his problem. He didn't give his lungs a chance to clear the dust out. His doctors said that he won't be fit to work the docks any more. The man is in his fifties with a boy still at home. He will have to think of some other way to feed his family."

"I wouldn't want that to happen to my worst enemy. That is one of the reasons I want to be off the docks before I'm thirty. By that time my brothers and sister will be on their own and can help take care of mama. I'll be free to do whatever is available."

"I thank you are forgetting something. What about that little lady that you are holding dear? Huh?"

J.B. was not convinced yet that marriage was for him. He valued something else more than he valued being a husband and father. He thought manhood came first. Being a good husband and father required being a man first. He had few examples of this kind of men within the colored population. He continued down the road to his destiny to a world of the kind that he had never seen.

"Janet, have you ever thought about leaving all that you know and making a new home in a strange city, among strange people and doing strange work? Have you thought much about doing that?"

"No. I haven't, but I know that's all you think about. I know it might be impossible for you to live here in peace. I've always known that."

"Then you know why I have never ask you the big question. I love you too much to be half a man to you and your children. I know what living here under the existing social rules would make me into. I don't believe you want me to become that kind of husband."

"I pray that things will change before it's too late for people like you. The preachers are telling their congregations to have patience with these folks. Our Pastor said that change will come when the good Lord gets ready for it to."

"Yes I know. I heard the same sermons. It has been a many lifetimes and the changes that we are waiting for show no signs of coming galloping over the hill. I'm beginning to be of the mind that the Lord helps those who help themselves. I can't see where the Lord gave the other side what they have. I'm beginning to believe that those folk got where they are today on their own. Did they get help from the good Lord?"

"J.B., you know I'm with you in whatever you decide to do. I'll be right here as long as I can. If I decide to hook up with somebody else, I'll let you know. I really can't see you changing not one bit. Anyway, I don't believe I could love you the way I do if you did change. I respect you the way you are. You better promise me that you will always follow the stars in your own heavenly sky."

J.B. made doubly sure that Janet did not get in family way. He knew that would be bad for both of them and both of their families. He started to come home from the docks less and less. His family was on their own when it came to taking care of the farm. He still made sure that they were well cared for even if he was working full-time as a dock supervisor.

# Chapter Four

J.B. turned in his resignation when he turned thirty years old. He saw no reason to kill himself on the job. His guts were still filled with boiling hot hatred for people with white skin. He begin to believe that he might be the person whom the Lord put here to start the social changes needed to bring about a just social system within which all children would stand a chance of being true to themselves without risking limbs and life. He had his chance to practice what his dreams dictated one cold afternoon.

He was driving from the county seat home when he spotted several young men and women being mistreated by the deputy sheriff. J.B.'s mind went into a mode that took control away from his common sense. It was like the gods had taken over his entire self. His feet automatically slammed on the brake and he was out of the cab of the pickup before he knew what he was planning to do.

The deputy was taken by surprise when he saw who had stopped. It was highly unusual for a black to interfere with the assumed duties of the law.

"What is it that you want boy?"

"I'll ask the questions, if you don't mind. What are you doing to these young folks?"

the church. The preachers became the powerful leaders in the black communities.

"Floyd, you and Willie hold down the fort until I see you again. I'm on my way to Detroit. They tell me that jobs are so plentiful until they are traveling the south in search of men to work the coal mines, the steel mills and the automobile factories."

"We know you will do good if anybody can. Let's have a drink to your trip into the rich world."

"I'll write you and tell you how I'm doing and how the jobs are. Willie, why don't you give this some thought? Floyd don't need you to baby sit him anymore."

"I'm not staying at home on account of Floyd. I have a young lady who wants to tie the knot. You and Floyd better start thinking about what y'all gonna do with the rest of y'all's lives. Time is moving on."

"Once I'm situated I'm coming back for the mother of the children that I will be blessed with. She is the main reason why I want to be in a position to take care of a wife and a batch of young'uns."

"I know exactly how you feel, Roy. Willie and I talk about how we Blacks raise our families. I sure don't want to have to live on my knees in front of some white man in order to feed my children."

"I went to visit my uncle a few days ago and you boys would be surprised to learn what was going on there in Butler county."

"I'll bet you the next pint of ignorant juice that we won't be surprised a bit."

"There is hardly any of the young to middle-aged men left in the county. The farms are turning back to virgin woods. They don't even have cattle on the land to keep the grass and the weeds down just in case a few boys decide to return home. We always knew how much them folks disliked each other."

"I don't think this has anything to do with you, ah ah .What is your name boy?"

"I would not call me boy again, if I was you, boy! Now, are you gonna answer my question, or do I have to beat it out of you?"

The deputy backed off a few steps, turned and crawl into his squad car and eased away. The deputy felt there could have been bigger trouble than he could handle coming his way. He had never been famous for bravery anyway.

"You folks get on my truck and I'll deliver you home."

"Mr. J.B., do you think the deputy will be coming back?"

"Not today he won't. He'll have to take his good old time and think about this day. This is not something that is easy for him to share with his white kin."

"You show got his dandruff up good. Wait till we tell daddy and mama what you did."

"I don't know if they would think that was a smart thing to do. You see when a colored person do something like what I did, he could get himself in a world of trouble."

"You got him told anyway. I have never seen a white man that scared of a colored man before."

The oldest young man didn't seem able to hush his mouth. He never gave the other two teenagers a chance to tell how they thought about the run-in. J.B. delivered the young folks home and drove on home while keeping an eye in his rear view mirror.

The children had the news on the grapevine before their parents could warn them of the possibilities of their getting into trouble talking big about how a black man scared the daylights out of a white man who carried a badge and a gun. The news was discussed at every colored supper table in the community. This was the kind of thing that made the parents fear for their children when they are not using proper and safe manners around Whites.

"J.B.! What in the world is this I'm hearing about you threatening to kick the mess out of our deputy sheriff? Boy, you better get a hold on how you treat these crazy folks. The news is all over the county. Our Pastor was asked to talk to you about this before the high sheriff has to do it for him. You see, the sheriff came out to see the Pastor."

J. B's' two brothers were instant heroes for just being brothers to such a man as J.B. These boys went to church with heads held high. They became heroes of an incomparable kind.

J.B. thought it might be time to take a short vacation. He thought the community needed a few days to forget his standing nose to nose to one of the county's hunky-dory boys.

"I believe I'll drive down to Pensacola for a day or two. I'll let this mess these folks got going cool down a bit."

"I thought about that last night, but I wanted you to figure it out for yourself."

"Janet, you already know this, but I'll tell you again. This is the reason why I would make a bad husband and father here in our home town. I know we have talked about this many times in the last ten years. Nothing has changed except I might be getting worse with each passing day. Let's take what happened out on Red Creek Road for an example. I could never ignore what I saw going on without doing everything in my power to stop it."

"These crazy young boys got you as a sheriff beater. They say you carry two guns around while you drive up and down the roads looking for just such as you were involved in. Now, you know that I know better than that."

"Would you like to ride with me? I promise you that I won't go crazy with you with me. Do you hear me?"

"I'm thinking. I'll have to make sure mama is okay before I go off running all over the country with a crazy black man.

She don't need any extra worry. You do know daddy is not nearly his old self."

"Yeah, I know. These kinds of responsibilities are what keeps me walking alone. It don't matter what you do, it affects somebody you love. If you can ride down there, let me know. I'm thinking of leaving early Monday morning. If you go with me, we will be back before the weekend."

J.B. knew he was walking a tight rope but he felt no regrets. He knew he would not be able to walk away from such a mess no time in his future. He was very proud of the reputation he had throughout the county.

J.B. pulled up to the gas pump at the country store to fill his tank and to buy a few goodies for the family's Saturday night. Earl appeared to be nervous. He kept looking at J.B. as if he didn't recognize him.

"What's the matter, Earl? You are gawking at me like you have seen a ghost, or something. You hear me Earl?"

"I hear you. You don't have to yell, you know. I just thought you would have had sense enough to be a thousand miles away by now. That's all."

"Now what in god's name gave you that idea? What would I be running from? Huh?"

"Oh, I just heard something about you, that's all. How much gas you want?"

"You know darn well I don't stop unless I'm gonna fill it up. You also know what else to do too. Look Earl, do your usual thing. Alright?"

J.B walked into the store without looking directly at the clerk and her company. The reasons he filled up the gas tank and bought a sack of goodies were to reduce the times he would have any business being in the store. There was always that chance of running into a foolish bigot.

"She held $two fifty worth of gas and one quart of oil."

"Thanks Earl. Come on in here and get you something. I'll pay for it."

Earl look as if he had been struck by lightening. His gaze went from one of the ladies to the other. Before he fished a soda from the cooler and grabbed a stage plant from the rack. J.B. wanted the man inside with him for protection against something crazy.

"That comes to six dollars and twenty cents."

J.B. laid a five and a one down on the counter and fished out a two-bit coin. The clerk laid a nickle down for his change. All this transaction were done without J.B. saying one word to the clerk.

"So long Earl. We'll see you the next time."

"Good night J.B. You take good care of yourself, now."

J.B. had noticed that everybody had started treating him like he was a stranger to them. They had always thought he might be a wee bit off his rocker but, these folks has started gazing at him like they were looking at someone who had died and came back to haunt them. The Whites were just as bad. But, the Whites' stares had a different meaning.

"Janet and I should be back sometime Friday night. I like to drive at night when it's hard to see who is behind the wheel. I have never had any trouble out of the police at night. They want to see who they are dealing with."

"Don't you take Janet off and do something crazy. She has her mama and daddy to look after. I'll be praying for the two of you."

"Gosh, do I love this sea breeze. I've never been down here since my uncle died. I had promised myself that one day I would be back, and not to a funeral either. So, here I stand."

"I didn't know you were bent on coming down here that much. We could have been coming here before now."

"That's alright. I'm here now and having a good old time.

My folk won't believe how much sea food I'm eating. At what time will we make it back home?"

"We will be there before ten o'clock tonight. We are only a little over three hours from home. It seems like a far piece but really it ain't that far."

J.B. thought that a few days out of the sights of the neighbors would give them time to get use to what he was becoming and was intending to be. Every time he faced one of the bigots and walked away with his head still on his shoulders, his guts felt less bitterness, his mouth would feel fresher.

"J.B.! Why do you always come this road to get home?"

"I don't rightly know. It's just the way I like to come. I know we could have been home by now if I had gone the Sunlight way. I just like this old Red Creek road."

The night air spoke to the two lovers in ways that they would never forget. Rides like these help these two to tolerate a less than whole life. Life in their parts of the country was not easy for people of their kind.

"Are you and Janet thinking about wedlock anytime soon? You know it's a sin in the eyes of God to lay with each other out of holy matrimony."

"Yes ma'am. We talk about this all the time. We wonder would it be more of a sin to enter a union that you have doubts about it working. Once you enter matrimony it is for life. Neither of us is sure about fighting the heavy winds of inequality that we would have to face in order to live a life that will make life worth the efforts. Mama, believe me we are having a hard time being Christians and trying to deal with this social monster that our people have to deal with. I would not want to bring children into a society like ours. Do you believe that the Lord will forgive us?"

"Sure he will, when you two decide to do the right thing. The Lord will always forgive his children when they ask him in good faith. There might be times when you can't do for your family and yourself the things you think you should do. You might have to ask the Lord for directions and help. That is what we pray for. I pray for you and your brothers and sister. You are your daddy's son. I remember when he had them same kinds of notions in his head. We know what it got him."

"I know that I could never forgive myself if a situation occurred where I was not able to protect my family, or a member there of, just because I'm a black man. I could never live with that experience."

"Son, I can't feel what you feel, but I worry about you all the time. You have to remember you are the role model for your brothers and other black boys here in the community. Remember how these young men became after what you did to that deputy? Remember that? These parents almost had to put their young men under lock and key."

"That's exactly the kind of thing that should not be able to happen here in our country. Our ways of dealing with the other race create opportunities for just such things. Mama you of all people know this first handed."

"Now, let's talk about you and Janet's situation. Which do you think is a bigger sin, man and woman living together out of wedlock, or living the best you can under our Jim Crow system? Look at it through what the Bible says about the wages of sin."

"Mama, I believe the greatest sin pertaining to family life is to bring children into the world and not be in a position to take care of their needs. It tears me apart to stand by and watch how these colored children are taught to put the interest of the Whites ahead of their own. This is not done from love, or by choice, this is a forced thing. I watch this game being played out every day with the children parents standing by without being able to do a thing about it. No ma'am, not a thing. Mama! do you want your boys to be in them kinds of positions every day of their lives?"

"I'm just saying son, I love you children enough to put up with just about anything that will keep you safe from harm. I'm not saying it's right. The only other way to deal with this one-sided justice system is to turn it over to God."

J.B. went off to bed to dream another nightmare about what could happen to those he loved with nothing he could do to prevent it, or to stop it. These nightmares were coming more often the older he got. The only positive feeling that came from the dreams were that he always felt complete after standing his ground.

He would wake in a cold sweat more often than not. But, there was nothing more fulfilling than facing the fears and challenges until he woke up. Somehow he would almost always know it was a dream that he would awake from if he could just hold out long enough. There were times he thought that real life was just about equal to the same kind of philosophy. If one looked at life as a temporary stopover on a journey to somewhere important.

J.B. and his clan had to get ready for the big day at church. The attractive meetings were the days when everybody would dress up to show how good God had been to them during the farming season. The few acres of cotton had done good and J.'s family were eager to get into the county seat and get all dressed up for the big week. J.B. didn't believe in overdressing to go to church, but most of the membership did. He had never been able to make sense out of spending most of your hard earned money getting dressed to impress the Lord. But, this was another of the customs that everybody seemed to be okay with.

"Why don't you pick out yourself an outfit. I don't want you to worry about how much it cost either. Your big handsome man here will dig deep in his pockets just to show you how much you mean to him. Go on and get what I know you already have your eyes on."

"You shouldn't have told me that. You just stay outside here until I come and get you. We don't want you in there flinching and going on."

"You pick it out and come and get me. I'll be over by the hamburger stand pigging out. Just don't lose your mind in there now."

"You just shuffle on over to the hamburger stand. I'll decide how much of your money I want to spend. Go on now!"

There was something mighty humane about a man being able to do for his woman something that brought quality to her life. J, felt like he was worth God's blessings. He often wondered why prayers didn't seem to be answered, even though good people were doing the praying. Was God too smart to waste blessings on the undeserving?

# Chapter Five

"J.B.! Mr. McPherson asked me about you yesterday. He wanted to know where you were and what you were doing now days."

"Why is that old peckerwood suddenly concerned about a crazy black man like me. What did you tell him?"

"I told him that you were in and out. You came and went as you please. That's all I could tell him. I think I know what is on his mind."

"You can never tell what these folk are up to. He has always been a strange bird. He don't have much to do with neither the Whites nor Blacks. The McPhersons have always minded their own business and left other people's alone."

"You haven't heard the last part yet. He told me to tell you to stop by and see him whenever you are out his way."

"He might want to offer me a job, or something. He still runs a logging crew. I haven't seen that boy of his since he got discharged from the Navy. I just might stop by his place when we go into town Saturday."

J.B. could not figure what this old man could have to share with him. All the folks in the community knew that J.B. was half crazy, especially the white folks. J.B. thought if he didn't follow this to the end he would never rest in peace.

Old man Turner had been working for Mr. McPherson for as long as J.B. could recall. He still worked for the family as far as anybody knew. Mr. Turner usually drove the truck and worked as the group leader of the log cutters. That old boy was still around and doing good. He attended church nearly every Sunday.

"Look, there is the old log truck. They must have worked a half day today."

"Yeah, and it's only Friday. Let's go on into town and stop on our way back. I didn't see the pickup nowhere, which means, he is, or his son, is out and about."

Fridays were slow in town. Not many colored folks had time or the money to hang around town during working hours. The white loafing crowd could always be found hanging around the service stations, bus station and shade trees. J.B. would take his mama and whoever else, to town when they would have no trouble getting waited on. They stood less chances of getting in somebody's way.

"Yeah, I see the pickup is there. You guys be patient now. This shouldn't take too long. If you see me coming running at full speed, start the truck."

"Stop that foolishness, boy. Go on and see what the man want with you."

"You guys pray for me. At least I don't see any nigga-eating dogs laying around."

"Good evening. I'm told that Mr. McPherson want to have a word with me. I'm J.B."

"Yes J.B., I'll get him. You may have a seat right there on the porch. I'll be right back."

J.B. got a closeup look at the garage and the garden out back. They had a big vegetable garden that would put the average black's garden to shame. He wonder did some Negro take care of the field. If so, he knew nothing about it. He wondered.

"Glad you could stop by J.B. I hear you are not tied down to a regular job and I thought that you would appreciate working with me and Turner. Turner's eyes are getting too bad for him to be safe on the truck. He could still work with the crew. How would you like to be our driver?"

"This is sort of a surprise to me. What are you offering me, Mr. McPherson?"

"I didn't expect you to decide just like that. I do know something about you. I know you like to know something about the river before you jump in. So, ask your questions and I will supply you the answers."

"I don't have much experience driving a tractor and trailer. It would take a while before I got the hang of it. Plus, what is the condition under which I'll be working?"

"I understand that you and Turner go to the same church. He is the main one who told me to ask you to join us. So, why don't you talk to Turner Sunday and see if you like what he tells you. The deal will be what you two decide it is. Okay Mr. Smith?"

"I surely will talk to the man. I'll give him my decision. Thanks Mr. McPherson."

"I'll be waiting for your answer before I offer the job to somebody else."

J.B. didn't quite know how to deal with the new feelings he was experiencing. That was the first time a White had ever called him Mr. Smith. Maybe he had some learning to do himself, he thought. He climbed into the cab of his pickup without showing any outward signs of queasy emotions at all. He didn't know how to take this new sensation.

"Well, you gonna sit there all day and say nothing? What did the man have to offer you?"

"I don't really know yet. He told me to check with Mr. Turner this Sunday and whatever we two can work out he would honor it. I thought that was strange enough until he addressed me as Mr. Smith. Would you have ever thought something like that would come out of the mouth of one of these hillbillies' mouths?"

"We know they all ain't alike. We have a few who respect people of color. Now these few are far between, but we do have some good Christian white folks. That's exactly what I've been trying to get you to see. They all ain't like what you think they are."

"I'm beginning to see that. But, there is so few who will take the chance of turning their own kind against them by treating Negroes with the respect they give to each other. I realize the good Whites are trapped by the same social rules as we are. They have often been lynched right along with the Blacks who they decided to stand with."

"Let's see what Turner has for you' I hope it's something that will tie you down for a while anyway."

J.B.'s mind had some changes to make. He thought how much he hated all Whites and figured it would be hard for him to work for any white man. He had started planing to start himself something among his people that would earn him a dollar or two. There were many Coloreds who owned large tracks of land. He wanted to start contracting with these folk who would rather do business with their own kind. This was taking a chance and all Blacks knew it.

The Coloreds knew that to do business with the likes of J.B. would be risky. This was true simply because of who and what J.B. was. The Blacks would still have to do business with the white middle and top men.

"Mr. Turner, do you have a few minutes?"

"Absolutely. I know what you want to talk about before you opened your mouth. Let's go over here by the pump."

"Then you know I was out to the McPherson place. He and I had a talk and he sent me to you."

"Well, let me get started here. I have been working for the man nigh all my life. That is ever since I've been on my own. He will do you right and I'm talking about in more ways than you can think about. The white folk don't mess around with the man either. Therefore he can stick his neck out for people like us. You see he don't depend on the Whites, or the Coloreds, liking him too much."

"Now about the job offer."

You do know that I recommended you to him, but not until after he asked about you. Now don't ask me why he would be interesting in you in the first place. He and I split the left-over money, that is after all expense is paid, three ways. He gets one third, I get one third and his equipment gets the other third. Sometimes we do a bill and other times we have to wait. Now he wanted me to offer you a deal similar to what we have already, only this will be a four-way split. How do that sound to you so far?"

"It sounds just about too good to be true. I've never in all my life... Go on with the deal."

"I have done pretty good while working for the old self righteous fanatic. He figures if we all shared the money from the business we would be better business partners. We would give it our best as long as our best benefited us equally. Your job will be getting the logs, or whatever else we are contracted to haul, to the destination. His job will be to sell our work to the highest bidder. You know what my job is, and has been since you were a pup."

"There was one big problem with my driving the rig...."

"I know what that is, You have never driven a tractor and trailer before. That's no problem. I'll show you how. It's nothing to it. Once I get you ready to go without me, I will be in the woods with the men and I'll also be driving the loaders. I don't have to have 20/20 vision to do that. We will be able to get an extra load out most every day. You see what I'm talking about?"

"I understand it was you who recommended me for this partnership. Why did you think of me?"

"Look, I know you better than you think I do. I knew your daddy, remember? This is about the only kind of deal around here that fits you. Now, how do you like them apples?"

"All I have to say is, when do we get this show on the road? The more I here, the more I like what it is that I'm hearing."

"Why don't you meet me out to the McPherson place Monday at about seven o'clock."

"I'll see you there. I got nothing to lose and everything to gain from what I hear."

"See you Monday morning early."

J.B. wanted a snort of good home made ignorant juice for the first time in a while. He had a hard time sitting and paying attention to the services. He did hear the preacher make a profound statement though. He said that God helps those who help themselves. Janet was the first ears J. wanted to hear the news.

"You look as if you found your pot of gold at the end of your rainbow. Tell me if I'm right or not."

"You came close. I'm a genuine business man as of today. I'm partnering up with Mr. Turner and old man McPherson. We will be sharing equally, whatever come as profit. My job will be getting whatever we are contracted to haul to where it suppose to be. Nothing else. Ain't that a deal?"

"I'm glad for us. This won't change the attitudes of these other white folks. It might even make some worse. You know how that works without me telling you."

"Well I'll see you after work tomorrow. I'll tell you how it all turned out."

The man had to get home to inform the rest of the members of his crowd about the good news. He was home earlier than his usual time for a Sunday. He had work to do, come Monday.

"Boy, do you have a glow on your face. I haven't seen that look on your face since you got your first bicycle."

You should have heard the deal Mr. Turner and Mr. McPherson offered me. I won't be working for neither of them. Now, guess who I'll be working for?"

"I have no idea. Why don't you just cut out this guessing game and tell us right out what the deal is.?"

"I am a partner in the business and it won't cost me nothing but work. The profits will be split four ways, evenly. We share the expense by paying it before we split the profit. All my job will be is to drive the rig and make sure the timber gets to where it's suppose to get. I don't have to do business with anybody. Mr. Turner handles the workers and the machines in the woods, Mr. McPherson handles the business on the other end. My job is the middle man's job; drive the hell out of the truck"

"When do I pack your lunch?" Little sister asked.

"I'll be at the McPherson before seven o'clock. It will take me about ten minutes to drive out there. It's only about two miles."

"I'll fix you two of the biggest egg sandwiches that you ever had. Just leave it to me"

The entire family was overjoyed to have a happy J.B. in the house. They might be able to stop worrying about the boy's hot temper when he had to do business with the other side of the mighty wall.

J.B started to feel less hate for his birth in the world as a man of color. He started to believe a little more in the justice of God. He was about to lose his faith in the preacher's translation of what the Bible really said, until this happened.

"What a beautiful day I had. How is all here with you all?"

"Will you cut it out and tell us what happened?"

"Yes mama. I'm still drunk with unbelief. I never thought I would get a deal like what was given to me today. This deal is an answer to my prayers."

"When do you start work? This is what we want to know."

"I started today. Remember I have to learn to handle the big rig before I can do my part of the business. I think I told you all that. I really believe I'm ready to drive the darn thing now. Mr. Turner seems to think it will take me the reminder of the week to get the job down pat."

"Now maybe you will get a good night's sleep tonight. You must have gotten up ten times last night. If you were not going into the icebox, you were walking out onto the porch."

"I'll eat supper after I get back. I want to tell Janet about her big old handsome and smart man. See y'all when I get back."

J.B had never felt the cool evening breeze, and listened to the night sounds like he did this night. It was as if all the sounds, and this included the whispering winds, were speaking his language. He felt like he belonged.

# Chapter Six

It didn't take long for J.B. to realize that he got away with an attitude that would not have been tolerated if he was driving his own rig. Mr. McPherson had his name printed on the doors. This was a warning to the law enforcers to keep hands off. J.B. drove like a maniac at times. His job was to get the timber to the buyers as fast as the crew could get it ready. The three business partners were doing good business.

"J.! How do you feel about your deciding to join our little outfit? I certainly hope you don't regret your decision."

"I'll be frank with you, Mr. Turner. This job is the only thing that helps me to live in the deep south with a little dignity. I was thinking about hitting the road in search of a way of life that allowed me to hate being a Negro less."

"I know exactly what you mean. I would have been out of here a long time ago if I had never run into this job. I once hated to get up in the morning to face what we as Negroes had to face just to survive. Yes, I know how you feel. I sometimes feel the same today, too. You know it is a shame what these people make us Blacks go through just to make a living."

"I have you to thank for this opportunity. I would have gone to jail, or something even worse if this job had not come along. You see how I took to it."

"You had no way of knowing this, but I knew your daddy and what happened to him. I could see you as you became more and more a social outcast. This was the main reason that I suggested to you to take my place behind the wheel of our rig. You and I know, they would torture a Negro to death who owned a rig like the one we got. Man, you would have been written up enough times by now to put us out of business."

"Mr. McPherson don't seem to be a hard man, but yet these white folks stay clear of the old bugger. I would like to know why they think he is so powerful."

"Look at how much property he owns. He has four families sharecropping for him. He is rich now. He is about the richest man in this here whole county."

"I know one thing, he don't even hang around town even. His boy is just about the same way. I hear that the boy plans to live somewhere out of the state after he finishes his education."

"That boy never was into earning his way by tracking through snake infested woods and getting ate up by bugs. No sir, he gave his boy the best. Matter of fact, the boy has been in some kind of school every since he got out of diapers."

J.B. and his business partners were still outside the main stream. Even the log cutters were somewhat spoiled to the point that they had a hard time working for the average Whites. That was one problem with having good humane Whites to work for. This relationship could easily ruin a hardworking Negro for the regular line of work available to the Blacks. These working conditions would sometimes alienate Negroes from their own.

J.B. often witnessed the game played between the average Negroes and the average Whites. These were times when he wished with all his being that he was Indian, or something. It was hard to stand buy and be a part of some of the insulting relationship going on between the races.

"You there! Load them bags of fertilizer into my pickup. You hear me?" Mr. Jack Coon ordered Mo to throw a few bags into his truck.

"Yessuh! I'm a gitting them, I'm a gitting them."

"Don't you bust any of them bags. If you do you'll end up paying for them."

Nossuh, I'll be calful, suh."

J.B. always had a hard time accepting this kind of treatment. He stood stock still and watched his older cousin's manhood be totally disrespected by some poor white trash.

"Hea boy,"

"Thank ya, suh."

Mr. Coon tossed Mo a quarter for loading the truck. Mo. Snatched the two-bit piece out of the air like he was used to doing it all his life. He accepted the insults with a mile-wide grin on his lips.

"Mo! Why did you pay attention to Mr. Coon when he didn't even call you by name. You see what I did. I looked at him like he was talking to the man on the moon."

"Well J.B. Everybody can't be like you. I just play along with these nuts and I get by pretty good. You see I drive a newer truck than you do. I can get just about anything I want from these folks without batting an eye. Would you believe that I have more education than Mr. Coon has?"

"How do that make you feel when you play them dumb roles just to get along with these folks?"

"You see J. I don't care what these Whites think of me. I gave up on them before I reached your age. I just don't give a hoot what they fool themselves into thinking about me and mine. I leave it up to the Lord."

"I'm not too concerned about what they think about me either. But I am really concerned about what I think about myself. I'm also concerned about what my people, and I mean the Coloreds, think about me. It is a matter of respect. I think we will have to earn that level of respect one of these day. You see, these folks might get it in their heads to cross the lines of no return one of these days. Then what?"

"I figure I'll cross that bridge when I get to it. I just pray that the lord knows what he is doing and won't let that happen. I put my trust in the Lord."

J.B had gone this route before and had run into the same dead end. Neither the Coloreds nor the Whites could understand a word he was preaching. He had a long ways to go before he could bring himself to buy into the notion that all of this crummy crap was the will of God. There was something missing from all the socializing bull that the people were led to believe was supposed to be. J. was beginning to believe that there was a very low percentage of the human race who was in search of the truth. The true nature of man, appeared to him, lay in the direction of deception. He was finding the truth to not exist in the hearts of the people of his time.

"Morning Jack! How are you doing this morning?"

"I'm doing pretty good, thanks to God. Now, the old lady had another one of her bad nights. You know she suffers with them migraine headaches. She was up half the night."

"My uncle Oscar suffered with that same kind of headache. There is no cure for it either. Mama said that was what caused him to drank all the time."

"Yea, I bet. I knew that old bugger before he started to have them headaches. Them migraines were not what killed him, like some believed, but his love for drinking rotgut."

"Can I ask you something personal, Mr. Oscar?"

"Show you can. I might not answer it if I feel it won't do neither of us any good to answer it."

"I've wondered about your son, Josh, for a long time. What happened to him?"

"J'B., we don't have enough time in one day for me to tell you about them dark days. Sometimes I think that's where the old lady's migraines are coming from. Josh reminded me of you a little bit. You young men won't take what we older men would. That was Josh's problem."

"Do you know if he is alive or not?"

"Oh, he is alive alright. We know where he is, but the law don't know what we know. He don't write or nothing because of the law. You know he is still wanted for what he did."

"That's another question I've wanted to ask you too. That is if you don't mind. What was he guilty of that made the white folks so mad?"

"You know how good looking he was. His looks made it downright unsafe to be around women, especially white women. This young white gal had the hots for the boy, but he had better sense than to pay her any mind. She came on to him anyway. Finally one day when she was at her worse, she made advances and got caught by her brothers. That's when the mess got started."

"Hold the story until later. It's time for us to get jumping before Mr. McPherson comes out with fire in his eyes. I want to get three loads to the mill today. Do you think we'll be able to get them in?"

"That will be up to you. With Mr. Turner pitching fits all day, we'll get all that you can haul. Now let's get to them woods before that old boy comes looking for us. We don't have to worry about Mr. McPherson as much as we have to worry about your partners in the woods."

"'Tell me more about your son, Josh, as we ride."

"Like I said, Josh was not one who had a deep love for white people. When the brothers decided to teach Josh a lesson that he would never forget, Josh decided to do the same for them. The brothers had picked on the wrong man. They knew what a loose girl their sister was. It took the entire family to keep her out of the arms of every man that came by."

"She is the woman who works at the bus station, ain't she?"

"That's her. You see after all that trouble she couldn't get a man if she wanted to. No white man would even look in her direction after that. You know Negroes avoided her like they avoided the plague."

"What was it they tried to teach Josh?"

"We believe their intentions were to kill him. You know how these folks were back there them days when it came to black men and white women. They made one mistake though. They didn't figure on Josh having a snub nosed thirty-two in his overalls' pocket. He tried to talk some sense into their heads but couldn't. It was three against one which made them overconfident."

"When did y'all get involved?"

"He came home and told us what had happened. You see, he shot all three of the boys, but he killed neither. He wouldn't have been any worse off if he had killed all three. One of the brothers ended up getting infected and finally died in the hospital. Josh was charged with murder after that. It was rumored that he died from bad medical practices in the hospital. But you and I know how that works. Nothing goes wrong around here that the Whites won't try to blame the coloreds for."

"Now what happened to Josh after that?"

"We were too scared to think clearly. We didn't know what to do, so we hid Josh out at my brother-in-law's place. By the next day the news was all over the county that a crazy nigga had gone crazy and was to be shot on sight. Every trigger-happy white man in the county was out hunting for the crazy nigga. They knew who they were looking for. No member of my family could leave home for nothing, not even to go to work. Mr. McPherson got in his truck and came to our house just to see if there was anything he could do for us. He solved our problem before the next day was over."

"What did he do?"

"We knew we could trust the man and we told him the story and where Josh was hiding out at. He wasted no time going and getting Josh and taking him to the McPherson's place until he could be smuggled out of the county on his log truck."

"Thanks for telling me that story. Now I know why you men won't work for anybody else but this old white man."

"You got it down pat. I was working here then and will be working here until my dying day, or until I get too old and sick to work. I can't think of anybody better to work for in the whole world. All of us feel the same way about the old man."

J.B had heard rumors to the effects of what the old boy told him, but he had never gotten the story directly from the horse's mouth. It was good to know that there were a few honest and honorable white men left in the world since Jesus Christ.

J.B. got the nick name "The King of the Road" because of the high speed log hauling he did. Nobody dared to interfere with his style of hauling logs, and whatever else he decided to haul. There were time he used the rig to haul for a few local citizens. Mr. McPherson didn't mind as long as he did not short change him.

J.B. could get some pretty good deal from the middle men if they thought that he was cheating the old white man whom most of the whites had no love for. He didn't dare tell these ignorant buyers that the pulpwood was not stolen from the white man whom they had no liking for.

It was J.B.'s job to make sure his rig was kept in perfect working order. He worked on the thing at every opportunity until he became an expert shade-tree mechanic. The truck was what kept him in the county and maybe in the state as well. It stood between him and the people who he could not tolerate a one on one relationship with. He knew he was the king when he was behind the wheel of his mighty Peterbilt truck.

"J.B.! Have you thought much about anything else lately other than that big old ugly truck? I think you think more of the rig than you do your future here on earth. You know what the Bible says about greed and gluttony."

"Mama, that truck and my business with Mr. McPherson and the boys are what stands between my having good sense and being stone crazy. I know I owe a lot to the Lord, but the Lord don't need me as much as you and the rest of the family do. That ugly old truck makes it possible for me to be true to the Lord and my family all at the same time. I get a chance to help my neighbors out once in a while too. That's what that old Ugly Beauty do for me and ours."

J.B. began to to have bad dreams about the future of his brothers and sister. He had hoped that social change would come with the new federal laws relative to social justice. This was just hopes on the wings of prayers. Nobody in their right mind really thought that these people in power were going to yield without being forced to. He could see nothing in his future that would be incentive enough for the powerful to give anything. The Negros had something to bargain with but, they didn't know it.

"What do you think of making a trip to New York in the near future?"

"First, let me in on what's on that foggy mind of yours. Them trick questions won't work here anymore. Do you know how long I've been putting up with you?"

"Ah come on. I would never ask you to do something that would not be good for you. Now, answer the simple question, pretty please."

"Well! I have never been to New York, as you know. It might be a good experience to see how other more civilized people live. Now tell me what this is all about."

"I was talking with Mr. Jack the other day about his son Josh. You remember his son Josh, don't you?"

"Everybody done heard something about Josh, even the ones who weren't born then. The older folks and the preachers used that story to keep Negroes like you in line."

"That's what they think anyway. Once I got Oscar to talking he told me all he knew except where Josh is now. You know he was not about to give out that information. His story got me to thinking about having ways out of the county, just in case. Do you know what I getting at?"

"I think so. Keep on talking."

"Suppose we had somebody who needed a way out of here quick, what would we have to do? Which way would he have to go? We don't have a plan in place at all."

"That's what this trip is all about. You are looking for a modern underground railroad."

"I hear there is a whole community of Negroes from the south living in New York City. Now if we knew who a few were and how to contact them we would have some place for our trouble makers to run to. We would not have to waste a lot of time trying to figure out where to send the outlaws."

"You want to go up there on an information seeking mission. Who do you know up there now?"

"We have several cousins up there. I talked to Sammy the other day. I told him that I might take a notion to come up to see them. He said they would be glad to have somebody from home coming to visit. You remember his daddy, my uncle Kirt."

"You know I remember him. I thought he was dead, though."

116

"He is. He died about ten years ago. He had two boys and two girls. We'll have plenty kin when we get there. We might not know most of them. You remember Sammy when Uncle Kirt was down for Grand Mama's funeral?"

"Okay, when do you want to crash New York?"

"As soon as the weather warms up a bit. You know I'm not dumb enough to go to New York when old man winter is still hanging around."

"You set it up and let's go. I hope Daddy and mama will be okay then."

"Let's pray that they do. I'll have my folks to keep their eyes on them until we get back."

J.B. was thinking how easy it would be for him to hid a person in his Peterbilt and get them out of the county. But, they would need to have some destination to go to. These folk usually stuck together when it came to fighting a common enemy, which was being true to the Jim Crow rules. He often thought if the Negroes would express that same kind of togetherness when it came to their common enemy they would be a free people. He thought he might share this wild idea with his mama after he got Janet's response.

"Mama! Me and Janet are gonna take a bus ride to New York next week. How do that strike you?"

"What in the world are you wanting in New York? You ain't thinking about running off and leaving the good setup you have here, are you?"

"No way. I could never find anything like this in New York. You are right, I even hear that Negroes ain't doing as well as they want us to believe they are doing up there. From what I hear most of these southern Negroes who run off to the northern ghettos are much worse off than we are here in Jim Crow land. At least we can grow our own food. The food that we can't grow, we can hunt and fish for it. No ma'am, I'm here for the duration. Now what do you think that I would be interesting in, in New York?"

"Son I think I know what this is all about. You have been listening to them men you work with. There were times when we could not run too far simply because we had no place to run to. That was why your uncle made off for New York. If he had remained here he might not have lived as long as he did. I remember that week as plain as if it happened yesterday."

"Then you are in agreement with what I'm trying to do?"

"You know I never stand in your way, except to ask the Lord to guide you and look out for my oldest child."

"I sometimes believe that the good Lord pointed me in the direction that I'm traveling in for a reason. You know I'm in a position where I can help our people if there comes a need. It don't take too much for these nutty southern cousins of ours to go on the warpath against some lone Negro for nearly no reason. I don't think I would be able to stand by and do nothing to help a black brother who was in trouble."

"I've told you before and I'm telling you again; you can't be responsible for what might take place between Negroes and their white citizens. You will be doing a great job if you just look after your own kin."

"Mama, I have a hard time standing by watching my people suffer unnecessarily and don't do the little that I could. No ma'am, I would never be able to do that."

J.B. and Janet had an eye-opening experience in the Big Apple. They learned that their colored folks in New York were in bad shape, socially and financially. These New York Negroes were bunking on top of each other. That was true for those who were lucky enough to have a place to share. There was the group that had no home at all. This was strange to the southern couple. But, these folk had very little physical harm to fear from the average white person. They didn't have anything that the white folks wanted.

"Janet, how would you like living in the big city?"

"I can't imagine us living here under the conditions that I'm seeing. No wonder the first Blacks to settle in the big cities were those who could not come back home. These people don't even speak to each other. I don't believe I could get use to this."

"This is one of the reasons why I wanted you to come with me. I had a hunch that it is far too late for you and me to start living like these folks. We would be show enough miserable cooped up here in one room."

"I noticed that these folks seem to be angry all the time. Who are they mad at?"

"They have to be mad at themselves. I get the feeling at times that we are our worse enemy."

J.B. was more than glad to be back home. He had a renewed appreciation for what he had right there in his own state. He promised himself, and his people, that nothing was gonna run him off from the little that he had that made his life worth the agony.

# Chapter Seven

"I got a letter from your cousin today."

"Which cousin, mama? I have cousins all over the country."

"Floyd wrote and told me that he and his family was having a few problem, but nothing that we have to be concerned about. He also wanted to tell me that they had another baby on the way."

"Good god! How many children do he and Lizzy want? They already have enough to make up an army. I've been promising myself that I would stop to see them the next time I'm within a days drive of them. But you know how that is. My folk want me to keep the wheels rolling on that rig with all the timber that we can get on it."

"His letter sound like he might be having some health problems. He didn't come right out and say so, but you know how we have to read between the lines. I would feel better if you found the time to check on them."

"Yes ma'am. I'll do that the next time I'm over in that part of the county."

J.B. woke up to cloudy skies and the promise of bad weather on Monday just when he and the men had planned to break records all the next five days. It was not possible to haul pulpwood out of the area where they were working when the roads were wet and slippery. He thought he might be lucky enough to get in and out with one load before the storm hit. He and the men wasted no time getting the rig loaded.

"From the way them clouds look, I won't be back for a second load today. I'll be blessed to get to the main highway with this load before the bottom falls out."

"That will be okay. The Lord knows what he is doing. Just let us be thankful to be able to get this one load out. We will continue to cut as long as we can. The four of us can push the pickup up them muddy hills if we have to. See you in the morning if the Lord is willing.

"Mr. Turner had no problems cooperating with the workings of the Lord.

The storm hit just as J.B. entered highway 2. The wind was rocking the rig all over the narrow highway so bad until J. decided to pull into the church yard and wait out the storm. The lightening was speaking loudly and clearly. "Get you behind off the road."

J.B. noticed that the church door was ajar and thought he would go over and close it. The rain came in again just as he made it to the church's door. He thought that he might as well step inside until the big gush passed over. He could think of no safer place to be when God was busy at work than the church. He had no more than sat down when the gush of wind took half the church house with it. J.B. dove under a pew.

"Oh Lord, have mercy." J.B. yield out to nobody or anything in particular. It was a natural thing to do under the circumstances, especially for a believer in the powers of the Lord.

The side of the church where J.B. was glued to, the floor remained intact. He credited the Lord for that. The howling of the wind was enough to make good Christians out of the devil's disciple themselves. The destructive part of the storm lasted no more than five minutes but it seemed like a lifetime to the semi saved man. These were the kinds of times when J.B.'s doubts in his beliefs came to the forefront of his mind.

Old shaking J.D. couldn't make sense out of what had happened to the house of God. Why did the winds take down half of the church? He had no answer for these kinds of events. Once the howling winds died down, J.D. slid from underneath the bench and tip toed to the open end of the building to check on his rig.

The rig was setting there as if there had been no storm at all. J. gave thanks to the Lord for skipping over his truck. He got cold chills just thinking about what his future would have been without that old Peterbilt. He suddenly had his faith back from where ever it took off to there for a moment.

The dirt road were too muddy and boggy to even think about trying to go for another load. Therefore J.B. decided to drive over to see what his cousin was up to. The man had to have reasons above what the letter said for writing to his aunt. At least he would make use of the remainder of the day. He hated to waste the remainder of Monday doing nothing. He drove the twelve miles to his cousin's.

"Ha, ha! I see you folks are in out of the bad weather too."

"Hey J.! How is everything over at the old home site?"

"All is about as good as they will let it be. I see the storm did some damage over here too. Man, this weather is trying to tell us something. I was at Big Rock church when it hit. I hate to say this, but somebody in that church must be sinning. The storm blew half the building all the way over into the graveyard."

"You were in the building when all this took place? You must have dirtied your britches. I know I would have been a bit nervous, especially with that old cemetery almost in the church."

"Where is the family at? Mama is a little worried since she got that letter from y'all. I promised her that I would make a stop over when I got the chance. Today was a good day to visit."

"We are doing pretty good, so far. We were just sitting on the porch talking about y'all when we thought it would be a good idea to write when there was nothing wrong. You know, most of us will write with bad news, but not good news."

"Where did you say Dot and the children were?"

"They are all right. They went to spend a few days with Dot's mother and daddy. You know how they are about the children. Plus, Dot is their only child."

"Well, mama was worried about y'all. She might have been thinking about the children more than anything else. She also remembers how you use to be. God, you were a mess the first few years of your marriage."

"You know I changed after that tree fell on me. I feel it was the will of God that got me through those times. My life flashed before my eyes while I lay there waiting for them to cut that tree off my fat butt. I stopped drinking, gambling and using the name of God in vain. I was a changed man from that time on. Y'all know when I joined Dot's church. Yes sir, those were the days."

"Are you still working with them rednecks down the road here?"

"Yep, I have been with them since right after Dot and me got married. I'm not as lucky as you. Boy you lucked upon a real gold mine. I hear you darn near own the business. How in the world did you get a peckerwood to trust you that much?"

"This man is one of a kind. He hates nobody and he loves nobody. He is neutral when it comes to race. I can't figure him out myself. But, let's leave it to God to judge. Let's hope God sends us more like him. I do know one thing, I would not be here if I didn't have this business."

"Dot and I use to talk about you. You always had a bad taste in your month when it came to white folks. Boy you hated them and that was not what the good book said to do either."

'Getting in the church helped me a lot too. I could always see my broken daddy in the faces of every white face I looked into. I once wished that I could kill them all."

"I think your mama was praying hard that you would get over your hatred and leave revenge up to the powers in Heaven. I know I was warned more than once to not follow you around. Everybody was expecting you to be one bad egg."

"I still do as little business with the Whites as I can get away with. I still get the bitter taste in my mouth when I have to talk to them. I tried to pray that bitterness out of my system, but it's still come on strong when I see certain things that remind me of daddy and that night long ago. Well, I better be getting back cross the county line. I don't like to be out on these highways at night alone. I'm not afraid of what these joyriders will do to me, but what I will do to them. Tell Dot and the children that I said howdy."

"I show will. Take it easy now cousin J."

J.B. could feel that old hate boiling through his innards again as he drove back homeward. He was not sold on the idea that his hatred for Whites was good or bad. He knew for a fact that if he had not this hatred for Whites, he would not be the man that he had become. One of these days he might evolve out of a need to dislike anyone. He often wondered how free he would be walking around this earth loving everybody. That would be heaven on earth. That day hadn't come yet and until it did, he would have to put up with what was.

J.B. was only a mile from the county line when he spotted a truck parked in the road. His heart did a back-over flip. It was common knowledge that these Clark County boys would sometimes hang near the county line just to scare some poor

Negro visitors half to death. J.B. fished his thirty-eight out from underneath the bucket seat and laid it on the seat under his jacket. He might have considered turning around if the road was wide enough.

J.B. drove within a few hundred feet of the parked truck and pulled to a complete stop. He sat there trying to see if there was anybody around. He could see nothing but the truck until he heard a voice coming from behind him.

"What are you doing driving on our roads this time of the week, boy?" The voice said.

"I didn't realize that these roads belonged to you. I thought this was a state road."

"Are you getting big mouthed with me, boy!"

"I'm telling you like it is, or will be."

J.B. felt that white-hot hate boiling up from his soul. This was one more time he would have to play the hand out if he wanted to remain his own best friend. The young white man backed backward a step or two so he could get a good look at J.B.

"Look man, do you want to move your pickup, or do I move it with this Peterbilt?"

"You wouldn't dare! You black folks ain't that crazy."

"Okay, We'll see about that. You see we can be as crazy as you white folks are. Now, you've got one minute to tell your hidden boy, or boys, to start that hunk of junk and move it into the ditch. You hear me boy?"

J.B. revved up the big engine and released the clutch a little while holding the brakes. The big tractor sort of bucked like a wild horse.

"Don't you ram our truck boy. Who are you anyway?"

"Tell your boys to get that damn wreck into the ditch, right now, or I'll push it into the ditch. And another thing, don't one of you let me see a gun, knife or any other kind of weapon, Did you git that boy? Now git moving."

The boy backed all the way to where the truck was without taking his eyes off J.B. J.B. heard him say to his cousins, "That Nigguh is as crazy as a mad dog".

This was another time that J.B. got a chance to see the unlimited fear that Whites had of Coloreds. He drove on by the ditched truck thinking that they would have to go get some help to get their vehicle back on the muddy road. J.D. thought there must be something deficient in a people who have to mistreat their fellow men in order to feel whole. Them boy were looking for reasons to feel special about themselves at the expense of others. Now J.B. was beginning to understand how it worked.

He could recall the few times that he felt like God's chosen and that was when he had to make another human being feel like a loser. He was still high on adrenaline when he got home.

"You are awful spry tonight. You must have had some good luck, judging from the way you are humming and going on."

"Mama, I'll tell y'all all about it at supper time. I've got to clean that mud off my rig before I think about settling in for the night."

"You go right on and do what you have to. We can wait. We always like to hear good news coming from the lips of a black man."

"My news is both good and bad. I learned more of what I already knew today. I'll tell y'all about it. Come on here brothers and help me clean up my beauty."

J. was not about to neglect his one and only money maker. Truck-driving paid about the best income there was for a Negro man in the deep south. That is if you don't count preaching as an income producing job. He had once thought about calling himself to preach, but preaching too would violate his basic personal ideals of himself.

"How long did y'all cut after I left you?"

"Shucks, the wind was much to high to be safe while cutting down trees. Plus the lightening was nothing to play with."

"I had a great day in a way. I drove over cross the county line to check on one of my no good cousins. My mama had been worrying about her favorite nephew. I found him doing about as good as he possibly could. The boy ain't wrapped too tight upstairs."

"Is that what made your day?"

"Oh no! Several white boys were desperate enough for something to do to make their day until they decided to block the road in front of the king here. They hadn't expected to see a Peterbilt eighteen wheeler to show up. Especially one being driven by a crazy nigga."

"You didn't tear them poor boys vehicle up did ya?"

"No, but I don't believe they will block the main road near the county line again. I nearly scared them poor fools to death. Now tell me something, why do men have to make other men miserable just to feel like something special?"

"You must have given them a scare, judging by that grin on your face. They thought that they were dealing with an ordinary nigga. They didn't know who they were messing with."

"I'll bet you they will think twice before pulling that stunt again."

"Was that what gave you a new lease on life?"

"Not quite. I felt fully grown after teaching them boys a lesson. I wonder why it is so necessary for a man to prove his manhood to himself by stomping the mess out of others. Don't that seem strange to you?"

"That's the way it has been since the beginning of time."

"The strange thing about this meeting was they were the one scared to death, not me. That's what made my day. It's very seldom that the Whites put themselves into positions that will reveal their fears. This is especially true when it comes to dealing with Blacks. They showed me the side of their bulling that I wanted most to see. They proved who were the cowards on the road."

"It do you good to find the weakness in these here people of ours."

"Not all. I don't like to see this in my colored folks. I wish that there were ways to past this on to them. I would like nothing better than to see us stand tall in the presents of our white brothers. You see we are all children of the one God. What is it that makes us take the advantage of each other by using the fear route. How do you feel about that, Mr Turner?"

"I've witnessed this so long until I don't think either side would know how to treat each other otherwise."

Old mean white-man hating J.B. would entertain himself with these thought as his rig snaked its way down the highways. The man and his machine were the king of the roads, that is as long as McPherson was written on the doors.

# CHAPTER EIGHT

Good morning Mr. McPherson!"

"Morning Mr. Smith." We better pray that this weather clears up soon. We've got to get back on the road hauling our money producers."

"I don't believe we will be able to do much other than cutting for the next few days. This is that time of the year."

"Did you have something that you wanted to discuss with me today, J.?"

"Nothing in particular. I get a bit frustrated at times with how we treat each other in our home state. I ran into several boys who was looking for trouble the other day. They had the road blocked with their old pickup. I don't think they were after anything but fun. They picked a dangerous thing to do just for fun. How do you think about these kinds of ways to have fun by scaring the daylights out of people?"

"J.B., most of these folks don't see this the same as you do. I don't like these kinds of relations either. You see I came to this county a while back with a pocket full of money. I brought more money with me than all these poor Whites had together. That was one of the things that I had up on them. Being treated as a rich white man was the main reason I got away with what I did."

"This is what bothers me most. Money won't buy equal treatment. It's kind of like colored money is dirty or something. You see what I'm talking about?"

"You take what you ran into the other day had nothing to do with money at all. It was about something else altogether. Thank about that for a minute while I get us a glass of cold water."

"Now J. tell me what you think is the main reason behind the way these idiots treat their people who take care of them? They try to hurt the same people they have to depend on for their lively hood. Now, think about that for a minute."

"I've always had a tough time trying to figure these people out. I'm talking about both races. They could use you as an example. You get along with the Coloreds who work your land, woods and on and on without an argument. Your people are about the hardest working people around here. How do you explain that to one of the idiots? You don't even have to watch your workers at all."

"Me and my people work as partners. You see how we work together. You and the others are partners. When you are in business together what trouble you cause the business, you cause yourself. You can't sink the ship that you and your family are on just to destroy the owner, or the captain."

"It looks like these folk could see that. It's as plain as the nose on your face."

"That's not the whole story J. There is something else at work down here below the conscious mind. I've go to run into town now, but you keep on thinking about this little talk. I'm a lot older than you J.B. which means that I might be able to show you something about the human being that you don't know."

"I'll see you when the weather clears a bit."

J.B. drove back home wondering what the old honest white

man had to teach him that the colored people could make use of. He already knew what white folks could accomplish with a little money and a good heart. Now if the Whites would be better off treating their Coloreds more equally, why don't they do it?" This was the question he asked himself all the way to Janet's house.

"I'm beginning to believe you are liking this bad weather J. I've never seen you loaf around so much. You are all over the place nowadays."

"Yeah, a lot more than at any time in my life. You see I can move about without being messed with as long as these folks think I'm working for you know who. Them boys would have had better sense than to stop me the other day if they had known who I was before they blocked the road."

"How is the folks doing?"

"They are their old selves. You know how old folks are. There is no cure for what ails them. I'm sure you didn't come over here just to ask about my folk's health. Now, what's on that disturbed mind of yours?"

"I just left old man McPherson's. He and I had a long quite talk about race relations here in our state. He had to go into town to take care of some business, otherwise we might have talked all evening. He said we will continue the discussion at a later time."

"Now I guess you want me to give you my opinion, as if you didn't already know it. You see I care less about these thing that I can't change. I just try to live with them without being murdered by them."

"The old man came up with a few good answers to my questions. I think he has the total answer too. He wants me to think about what he is trying to pass on to us. I have a hunch that the boy might be able to show us how to get better treatment from our powerful fellow citizens. You see what New

York was like. I'm not about to take you into a life like I saw my kin living up there. Would you want that?"

"There is no doubt that you and I are doing pretty good here. But this don't apply to the average one of us. I figured that many of your folks are in New York not because they like it up there. They are up there because they had to leave here if they wanted to stay alive. Isn't that what you said when we were up there?"

"What have you got in the kitchen to eat? I'm nearly starved."

"I still have over half that cake you brought the other day. Plus, I have what was left of that backed chicken. You just relax while I go and get a plate to feed my starving old man."

"That's the way you women 'pose to take care of y'all men."

"Keep on talking and you will get bones only from that leftover chicken. I'll strip the meat right off your part and feed it to the dogs. Now be quiet."

The rains finally passed over. The sun and the winds made quick work of the wet and muddy roads. The clay was backed as hard as concrete in less than two days. The big loggers were back in business. J.B. broke every speed law in the book. He was beginning to be angry again. He had to focus this anger onto something. He found himself talking to anybody who would listen about what he thought was bad race relations. Leaving the county was not a solution.

J.B. had all the hauling he could do even though he worked a full six days. This was not what the norm was. These folks figured three or four days per week on the average was too many. Farmer worked parts of the seven-day week on the farm, but working six days per week doing what could wait was out of the question. Old J.B. was not working because he needed the money, he was on some mission that he didn't have a handle on. He was going crazy, he sometimes thought.

"Morning Mr. Jason! Have you got that load of wood all stacked beside the road waiting to jump on my truck?"

"No sir, but I have it close enough to the road until me and my boys can have you loaded in less time than it takes a sinner to tell a long lie."

"That's what I wanted to hear. Let's get it loaded and into town before a lazy hound can wake up. You might be better off doing what we talked about the other day."

"You might be right, Mr. J.B. Let's let the man think that the wood belongs to Mr. McPherson. That is, if your boss will go along with fooling his own folks."

"He will. He is the one who suggested that in the first place. He told me that I could haul for anybody under his name, as long as they were Negroes. Can you imagine that?"

J.B. could haul a lot more than these cutters of his could cut. His Peterbilt had the hauling capacity of two regular trucks and three when j. wanted to drive like a lunatic. That's exactly what he did when he thought he had a need to.

His driving skills came in handy late one afternoon when he just missed killing several white men on Red Creek road. He thought the crazy driver would yield to the loaded truck. The dumb driver thought the eighteen wheeler should do the yielding. It was something about Red Creek Road that whispered troubles.

"Son, don't you think you had ought to slow down a bit. You are out of here before breakfast and come home after supper. I know you ain't doing all this work because you need the money. You don't spend the money that you do make working five regular days a week."

"Mama, I do all that I can to help my people. The Lord knows they need it. How is your day going mama?"

"I thank the Lord things are as good as they are. I have my home and my four children close by. I have pretty good health for an old woman. So, what else could I ask for?"

"Mama, do you ever wished for a different kind of life? I know you and daddy were about as content as it was possible to be under our double standard way of sharing the wealth of this great country. How could you not think about what life would have been like if you were White. Would it have been better, or worse for y'all?"

"I turned the business relating to the justice of what exists between the races over to the Lord. Once I became saved I kind of forgot about them white folk and their thinking."

"Well, good night y'all. I'm out of here before the roaster crows in the morning. I hope to get at least three loads in before the yard closes tomorrow afternoon."

J.B. dreamed about what it was that made folk do what they did. He dreamed that he found something in the Bible addressing an unjust people. He should have been thanking the Lord for being blessed over and beyond what he could see were the blessings of others in the community. He was better off than most of the Whites too. His dreams were about something else. They were not about food, clothes, shelter or a vehicle. There was something else needed before one could be a whole man. It was hard to put his fingers on what that something else was.

J.B. rode hard all day. He got the three loads delivered and loaded up for an early-morning delivery for the next day. It made no difference how his work day went, he was still bothered by what Mr. McPherson almost said, but didn't. J.B. promised himself that he would be talking to Mr. McPherson the next rainy day.

J.B.'s rig was not the only truck on the road early in the morning. He almost didn't see the truck in the pond fifteen to twenty feet off the road. It looked like the pulpwood had completely crushed the cab and the driver. J. stopped in the road, got out to see if there was anything that he could do. He heard the moaning before he got within ten feet of the cab of the old truck. He recognized the truck once he parted the bushes and got a clear look. It was one of the most hated white boys in the county.

"Hey you! Can you hear me?"

"The man answered just above a whisper. "I hear you. Get me out of here>"

"You just lay still and let me see what's pinning you in there."

J.B. freed the man who had a busted leg and a couple of knots on his head. The man was mostly scared to move. He might have been knocked out judging from the lumps on his block. J.B. lifted the skinny bag of bones and loaded him in the Peterbuilt for a trip to the hospital.

The news was all over the county before the day was out. J.B. had started to save white folk instead of wanting to kill them. The poor man's daddy was at J.B.'s house that night asking if there was anything that he could do to pay J. for what he did.

"We want y'all to know how much we appreciate what your boy did for our boy, auntie. If there is anything that we can do, name it."

"There is no cost for what my boy did. The Lord would have it no other way. I'm sure y'all would've done the same for us, Praise the Lord."

"We'll be seeing y'all."

J.B. drove up just as the two white people were leaving. They were going in the directions from the house causing them to not recognize J,D,'s approach.

"Who was that leaving here?"

"Those were the daddy and mama of some boy they said you saved. I didn't have a clue of what they were talking about. I figured it must have been something that you had a hand in.

I didn't ask them any questions because I knew I would know soon enough."

"So! Those were the daddy and mama of the young man. I have seen the days when I might have left the nut there to rot. I'm beginning to see how scared these folks are. I knew the old truck that the man was hauling pulpwood with. I felt sorry for him. Those are just some poor old rednecks trying their best to haul pulpwood off their own place in order to feed themselves. These folks are to be pitted instead of hated."

"Thank God you are learning not to hate these poor children of God. The Lord tells us in the Bible to love our enemies. Not to hate them."

J.B. could not totally understand what was making him change his mind about wishing all white folk dead, with the exception of a very few.

# CHAPTER NINE

It was the fall of the year before the farmers were ready for it. They would have to get down to hard work and get their crops in before the winter snow flakes came. J.B and crew had done a great piece of business across the summer and was ready for a slow down. The wet roads and windy weather gave these big businessmen excuses to take time off without their feeling guilty.

On one rainy day J.B. ended up back over at the McPherson's having a talk with the old man again. He wanted to know more about a man who seemed to be a total success without conforming to the rules that others seemed to be locked in to.

"Morning Mr. McPherson! How is all on this cold and cloudy morning?"

"Morning to you, Mr. Smith."

"I just stopped by to sit a spell and talk. That is if you have the time this morning. I want to start where we left off at the last time we had this serious talk."

"Well1 where did we leave off at? My mind ain't what it once was. You know I'm eighty years old. Now refresh my mind."

"We were talking about there being a level of social consciousness that goes far below what we see and hear all the time. We were looking at the root causes of how we treat each other."

"I'll begin when I was a boy over where I came from. Before I forget, I want to tell you what changes I see in how you behave toward all of us. You are not the young man who I first meet with a chip on his shoulders. You have grown up quit a bit within the last year or two. You proved that by what you did for that boy who was trapped in the cab of his truck."

"All I saw in the man's face was his fears and a need for help. I saw a human being whose needs were no different from anybody's. I would not have been able to live with myself if I had driven off without lending a helping hand."

"Now let me get back to something I've wanted to tell you every since you came to work with us. I took a chance that you would not learn the truth about what happened to your daddy until you were big enough to do the sensible thing. Now I believe you have arrived at that point on your journey down this rocky road called life."

J.B. had become all ears. He got that feeling that always came just before he had to make a big change in the way he did business. Only this time he didn't have a chance to sleep on it.

"The boy's life that you saved the other day was the grandson of one of the men who beat your daddy and left him to die out there on the same road where you saved the grandson of one of them.."

Mr. McPherson and J.B. sat as silent as a grave yard at four o'clock in the morning. Mr. McPherson never took his eyes off J.B.'s face.

"Go on, I'm all ears. That is one time that remain as fresh in my mind as if it had happened yesterday."

"J.B.! Do you have any idea who found your daddy and brought him home? You see, they would have finished your daddy off if these two men had not showed up when they did."

"The only thing I thought was that they were White. I always thought they might have been the same men who did that to my daddy. Daddy could not remember who the men were. He didn't know who did that to him or who brought him home. You see, it was a moonless night. It was so dark until I could barely see the shape of my daddy's body lying side the road in the red clay. All Daddy knew was it was two different sets of Whites."

"I thought about telling you lot's of times but I didn't think it was the right time for you or me. You see, I would have had to tell you the whole story. I knew that neither you, nor your people were ready for this information. I was afraid of what you might have done. You were the oldest child of your daddy's and he needed you more after the incident than he ever needed you. Do you understand what I trying to tell you?"

"Okay, now I know the bastards who did the dirty work. Now, who was the good white folks who brought him home?"

"The two men were not two men. They were a man and his son. It was me and my son who brought your daddy home. You see why we would not be able to let you see us. You see, you would have thought it was us who did that horrible thing to your daddy. The only way we could have vindicated ourselves would have been to tell who did the actual crime. That could have caused great harm to us all. I knew that there was not a thing that you, or anybody else, could have done to make things right. These kinds of things were happening to men like your daddy more times than we would like to admit. You came close to the same thing when you came across the county line a few months back. You see nothing has changed much since your daddy's incident."

J. B. had become as cold as ice once again while listening to the information. This was awaking the devil in his chest once again. He sat motionless and waited for his partner to continue.

"I'm telling you this, not only to relieve my own guilt, but to answer a question that you have carried around in your heart for a long time. I truly believe that you are man enough to do the right thing about what I'm telling you. You will have to be careful who you share this with. This kind of information can cause much harm to all involved and to many who ain't directly involved."

J.B. was still attached to Red Creek Road. He would find himself going out of his way to take Red Creek road to where ever he was on his way to. Now he wondered more than ever about that darn road. What were the connections?

"I think that I'm far beyond the thinking that violence solves social problems. I see by how you conduct business as proof that fighting among people might not be the best way to get where you want to go. Physical harm done to another not only take a person out of the race but makes a criminal out of both. Maybe not a criminal according to the law, but one according to the laws of God."

"I'm show glad to hear you say what you are saying J.B. We all have to sacrifice some sacred beliefs in order to allow others to be whatever they decide to be and to help you to become whatever you decide to become. The two becoming could be in conflict at times. But, the smart man will alter how he is conducting business instead of trying to recreate another into fitting whatever he thinks will help his becoming. I know first handed what it cost to give up a part of yourself in order to make the best of what is."

"I have never known you to talk about your folks, or where you came from. There don't seem to be anybody who knows much about you other than that you are a good man to work for. Your people who sharecrop your land almost worship you as a god."

"I believe I'll share a secret with you today. I want you

to promise with all your heart that you won't share this information with anybody. Do you think that you will be able to do this?"

"If you trust me to that degree, I can't let you down. You have your reason for sharing a top secret with me. I will be honored to keep your secret Mr. McPherson."

"I'm sharing this with you because what I plan for the two of us to do to help the Negro people will require a lot of trust in each other. I think you are the man whom I've waited all my life to work with. My mission is to help my people to come from under the yoke of oppression before I pass on into the hereafter."

"Do I understand you to say your people? Are you talking about the Negro people? I can't see the white people needing the black people's help."

"That's the secret, J.B. You see I'm colored too. I might be a lot lighter than you, but I'm considered Colored. I have colored blood running in my veins."

J.B. could not mumble a word after hearing what the secret was. It would take a while before this sunk in and he could make sense out of the information.

"Look J.B., you look like you've been struck by lightening. You don't have to say anything right now. I'll be talking to you come tomorrow. Have yourself a good day, partner."

J.B. knew there was something unique about the McPherson family, but he would not have guessed what it was in a million years. This was shocking news, but it explained a lot. J.B. was beginning to understand this old man, whoever he was. J. drove to his church and parked the rig near the cemetery. He had to do some heavy thinking and he didn't need any interruptions.

"Why did you stop on the porch J.B.?"

"I just wanted to relax a minute. I'll be right in, mama."

J. was thinking that the old man had something else on his mind that made him reveal his long-kept secret. He was trying to prepare himself for whatever. J.B. was not hungry, but forced food down his gullet to avoid having to answer questions that his family was sure to ask. He retired to his bed earlier than his usual bedtime. He didn't go to bed to sleep.

J.B. did on Sunday afternoon what he always did on Sunday afternoon, He took Janet home from church. He had to decide whether to share his secret with her or not. He decided to honor his promise to the man. He knew there must be something else coming.

"Do you feel good, J.?

"Oh, I feel great. I have a few thoughts on my mind which I'm not allowed to talk about."

"I thought there must be some reason you haven't talked much since you picked me up for church. You and I know that's not like you. But, whatever it is you will decide when it's time for you to tell me about it."

"That might be a while. You see I made a gentleman's promise to keep this to myself. So, there you are. There are some things that us men have to keep to ourselves. You women know too much of our business already. You can't get it out of me when I'm asleep either. That's the way you women get information out of drunks. I'm not a drunk, thank you."

"Young man you do have it bad don't you? Well, you'll be all right after you get a belly full of my chicken and dumplings, plus a chunk of your favorite pie. Come on now, let's cheer up. Whatever it is will take care of itself."

"You always know how to make me feel better, don't you?"

"Yeah, I just feed you. It's hard to find unhappy men with full bellies."

J.B. could hardly wait to continue his education. The old man had mention something about doing something for his people before he crossed over into the after life. He was looking at J.B. hard when he said that. J.B.'s skin crawls every time he thought about the expression that was in the old man's eyes. There was something big coming down the stacks.

"It's looks like another one of them days, J.! We can't grumble too much though behind nearly two weeks of sun shine and plenty work to do. This might be a good time for you and me to continue our talk."

"That's exactly why I'm welcoming this storm. Boy, the puffs of winds almost blew that tractor off the road. You see I didn't bring the trailer. I came strictly to hear how you plan to help your people to live better lives."

"Yep, that's why I made a pot of good strong coffee. I heard you coming when you cranked up the rig. Yep, the wife is not feeling too good, so we have the back porch and the kitchen to ourselves. Lucy won't be here today. She never comes when the weather is bad, that is if she can help it."

"Do you want me to get the coffee, Mr McPherson?"

"No! I'll get it. You just take sugar don't you?"

"That's all. We didn't always have cream like you rich colored people had."

J.B. tried to make fun so his nerves would be quiet. He wanted to hear every word that the boss had to say.

"Now, where did we leave off at after I shared the big secret? You see we Coloreds won't ever get what we deserve until we realize what it is we have to bargain with. We have to realize the power of a good bargaining position. Have you been keeping up with what some of these trade unions are doing?"

"The paper says that they are refusing to go to work and won't let anybody else cross their lines either. They won't do the work and won't let others do it either. Do that sound fair?"

"They thinks so. They think it's as fair as it is for the man to work them to death for nothing. They do have the rights to strike. That is the law. Now, about us here in the deep south. We can do the same thing without having picket lines. There is a simpler way we can get our way down here. You see there is nobody to take our places. The Coloreds do all the work here, with the exception of the money handlers."

"Are you suggesting that we try and pull the same kind of work stoppage as them men are doing? You know what that would do to the relationships between the land owners and the workers?"

"Yep, I sure do. It would do the same identical thing that the strikes do for the workers and the owners of the minds and steel mills up north. It would create a better working condition for all. The owner often get more produced, and better quality too, when the working men feel that they are being treated fairly."

"Boy, this will require some thinking about. How would we get these folks to agree to something like that?"

"Our people will have to be educated, that's all. That's where you and a handful of young men and women will come in. It will be your jobs to tell theses people, both Blacks and Whites, how much they will have to gain by having a more equal distribution of what we have plenty of."

"How do we get something this big off the ground?"

"You leave that to me. I have a plan that can't miss with men like you leading the pack. You see I've been waiting for a man just such as yourself to come along. You see, you don't fear these people on either side. That was your greatest handicap up until now."

"Let me digest what you have already shared with me and we can go from there. I run this kind of thinking by my folks and the preachers just to get their input. I understand that this won't be an easy task by a long shot. But, it works for the coal miners, it can't hurt us none to try it either. I'll get your plans of how this can be put together later. For right now, I will chew on this idea for a while and see if I want to be in front of the mob."

"It will be yours and my jobs to see that we don't start a war between the workers and the owners. You go on and do what you have to do. Let me know when you want to get this mission under way."

"I'll see you later."

"Tomorrow, if the rains don't let up."

J.B. felt old for the first time in his life. He had never been in a position where what he did might impact the lives of a whole people. This would require some praying over. J.B. wanted to get the support of all the leader in the community that he could. He had to plan according to what his next talk with the old man brought out. He knew enough to get prepared for a rough row to hoe.

"What's on that devilish mind of your now? You have been too quiet the pass few days to be your old self."

"I'm just thinking about a few things that me and Mr. McPherson have been talking about. He told me that it was a lot that we Negroes could do to help ourselves. He also mentioned the problems that we are likely to run into. I don't know all the details of his plans, but I have a hunch of where we will have to go and what the cost might be."

"You and I know how these people are. We are so set in our ways until it will take an earthquake to change how we think. Don't you go getting your hopes too high while listening to some white man who has little to lose."

"Mama, you will be surprise if I told you all I know. But, we will have to keep some thing secret until telling it won't cause more trouble than good. It's still too wet to get back in the woods, so, I'll go and have a talk with The Pastor the first thing in the morning. I want to pick his brain and see what he thinks could be done to educate our folks."

"I wish you wouldn't get too hopeful about the good that you can do for our community. Don't forget that those who are credited with making big social changes usually don't get to enjoy the changes. I'll ask the Lord to watch over you and keep you safe and sound."

"Thanks, Mama. I'm getting the feeling that I might need all the praying for me that I can get. Good night, sleep tight and don't let the bedbugs bite."

"Don't you play with me boy."

J.B. was on the Pastor's porch before the mailman ran. He sure wanted the leader of the church on board with him when the road got rocky.

"How is you mama and the rest of your family doing, J.?"

"They are getting by pretty good, Reverend. I thank the Lord for the blessings that he bestowed on my family. How have you been Reverend?"

"God has blessed me far beyond what I deserves. Now about why you are here so early this morning. What is it that the good Lord and I can do for you?"

"You know Mr. McPherson about as well as anybody knows him. What is your opinion of the man?"

"He has the reputation of being about the most honest white man in the world. I have never heard anything bad about the man. Why do you ask?"

"You know that I have been working with him for the past few years. He and I have talked about the need for some social changes that us Negroes might make to better our lives, and even will better the lives of the White's too. He has not given me the details yet of how we might be able to do that here in our neck of the woods."

"I hear you. Go on and tell me what it is you want from me right now."

"What do you believe that the Negroes could do to make this a better place for all of us to live?"

"You know I work through God. I leave man and man's sins up to God to deal with. I'm nothing but a servant of the Lord. I will agree that changes are needed and will come when the Lord reckons that it's time. Praise the Lord."

"I just wanted you to be aware of which way the wind is blowing when the mess hits the fan. You and I know how our people are when they are forced to make chances. This will come to that, you know. I stopped believing in something for nothing a long time ago."

"Well, you know I'm here if you ever need somebody to talk to. The doors of the church will be open to you to whatever it is that you decide to do for our people."

"Thanks a bunch Reverend. I'm sure I'll be back sooner than you think. Keep them church door open for us social mavericks, we'll need all the help that we can get."

"Good hunting J.B. Tell your mama howdy for me!"

# Chapter Ten

J.B. tossed and turned all night. He would wake about every thirty minutes before he heard the first rooster crow. He was up and had the coffee going while the other members of the family were getting their last few winks. His brother was the first to come into the kitchen to see what in the name of God was eating his big brother.

"Morning big boy. Why are you up so early?"

"I just felt like getting up. Is there anything wrong with that?"

"Stop treating me like I was ten years old. I'm about as old as you are. Now, let's start over. Is there something wrong?"

"No, nothing like you might be thinking. I have a few things on my mind right now. You'll be in the middle of what's about to get going. I will tell y'all about it as soon as I get some facts. That might be as soon as today. Okay big boy?"

"Do you want me to go with you?"

"No!No! Mama has enough to worry about as it is without me dragging you on to the front line. Your job is to look after mama and your brother and sister. I know they think they are grown too, but you are the head man in the house when I'm gone."

"What are you two children whispering about?"

"Good morning mama." The two early risers spoke like they were singing a song.

"You boys know keeping secrets from your ma'ma could be bad."

"Yes ma'am. We were just talking about why J. was up so early. I heard him flopping about in his bed last night too."

"Well, we'll know what's eating him soon enough. Now, you boys make room so me and your sister can get breakfast on the table."

"Yes ma'am." they sung together.

"Good morning Mr. McPherson! How are you on this cool and dreary morning?"

"Good! I try to not have any dreary morning catch me out of bed. I look forward to what I will be able to get done during all the days. What about you? Are you ready to do some important work?"

"As ready as I can be. If we don't get this out in the fresh air, I just might go crazier than I am." "J.B. let's look at where I would be if I didn't have loyal people working for me, or should I say working with me?"

"They show wouldn't work nearly hard enough to be as productive as they are. Everybody knows that your farms outproduce most of the other shared farms."

"I will show you what can be done to make more people harder workers. It is the work that makes or breaks a business. My people supply one thing and I supply another. Neither one will work by itself. I have the land and they have the muscle power. This condition exist throughout the country. Where one group have one half of the tools, the other group have the other half. You see, neither can work without the other. There are groups that have both. Those are the independently family owned and operated businesses."

"I see where you are going with this, but what is the way

to making these people understand this and be willing to work with each other to make it happen?"

"That's what I'm about to share with you. You see one side will have to show the other side how much it has to lose by not working together in a fair way. All of us have tools that we can use to get what is due us. Now think about what I just said."

"You mean we can use our tools the same as the men up north used theirs to force the big men to share more of the wealth coming in from any business."

"That's exactly what I'm suggesting. You might look at the situation another way. Get the people to understand that one without the other is no good for either. Let's take our business for an example. What could I do without you and my other business partners in the logging business? It takes the whole crew to make our business work."

"Are you suggesting that we go on strike if we can't get better deals with these sawmills and farm owners? This would include the kitchen help too. Is this what I think you are saying?"

"Mr. J.B. I believe you might be getting the point. You see the workers holds the aces in this matter. They have the power in their muscle and know how. Do you believe any of these mill owners could run any one job at their operation? Hell no! These big-time business owners would do just like I would do without my people's help; starve nearly to death. Now that's a fact."

"This is sounding better and better, but scarier and scarier. This might upset the total way we think and behave when doing daily business. But,as you know, I'm about ready to do most anything that will make life more comfortable for all, and especially for the working people."

"I know. That's why I'm sharing this with you. You are the first Negro, other than myself, who I thought might be ready to do whatever it took to make life better for all. Now let's get down to business. You can guess what my role will be in this dangerous undertaking."

"Yeah, you will be the white man on the side of the Negroes. We will need all the white help that we can muster up."

Now let's see if you can agree with the next step in the process as I see it. You will have to get a crew of believers together to help you rally the people to get them on board with you. This might take a while. But, the way I see it, this has to be done before the other side knows what's happening."

"I've already had a talk with our minister and he has opened the doors of the church to the idea. I've been testing the idea of social change on a handful of people whom I know well. They tend to agree with the idea that something needs to be done. You know how much that tells us. Agreeing with what needs to be done versus doing what needs to be done are horses of different colors."

"Now you better get busy and hold rallies in every place you can get into. Get the people ready to stay home from working for the Whites whenever it becomes necessary. They will have to get prepared for this ahead of time. These Whites won't roll over and play dead the first few days of doing without. You all will have to get the point over that you are willing and ready to finish the job."

"There is one big advantage that the Negroes have; they can live easier off the land than the Whites can. We Blacks know how to hunt and fish for food a lot better than the Whites do. We also have relatives who owns their own land too. I can't see how we could have let this go on this long. I have always had trouble with this American way of dealing with the two races."

"Why do you think I'm letting you in on things that could cost me a great deal of misery. Your daddy was somewhat like you. You have one of the greatest opportunities to do something about the social conditions that you don't like. These opportunities go for me too. I have waited a lifetime for this. You and I would never rest in peace if we didn't exploit this chance to make a difference in the way our people live."

"I will print out something in writing to hand out to the people so they can take it home and share it with their families. Now, do you have any suggestion how I might get this done without putting somebody on the spot?"

"You just leave that job to me. You see I can get my son to write it for us, and to print as many copies as we might need. He lives far enough out of harms way to get the job done without endangering anything that he is involved in. We Coloreds don't have access to the printing presses here in our hometown. If I paid one of these folks to print what I'm gonna write it would be all over the county before the ink dried."

"We'll need fifty copies or more just to get started."

"Don't you worry none, I'll take care of that. You just get the ball to rolling among our people. Let's get off our butts and get to hustling. I'll have the pamphlets ready before you get your people ready to start the rocky road to equality."

:Good evening Mr. McPherson!"

Old J.B. drove back to his church community thinking that he might have bit off more than he could chew. He remembered his grandmother's old words "Be careful and don't bite off more than you can chew. She was not talking about tobacco or food. Yet he had the most satisfying feeling in his stomach that he hadn't had in a long time. His life had begun to take on a meaning that was bigger than one man's life could ever be alone. The mission had to be addressed by a powerful social consciousness. The boy was beginning to experience what it felt like to be all that one could be. He was feeling not only like a whole man, but feeling like a big whole man. He was on a mission and was becoming part of a great whole.

For the following two weeks the men went crazy cutting timber for the mills. J.B. was making three loads on the average per day. They were making hay while the sun shinned. That was the old saying. The hauling team worked until one or two o'clock on Saturdays.

"i saw Mr. McPherson in town today. He seemed to be getting friendlier every time we meet. He never miss telling me how proud I should be to have a son like you. You two must have a lot in common."

"More than you might ever know. I have learned more about how to run a business from that man than I could learn in a million years in school. I'm giving a talk at the church Sunday about some of the things that Mr. McPherson is willing to help us Negroes change. I ask the Preacher to give me about five minutes right after Sunday School class is over."

"I know you two must have something up y'all sleeves. I know it must be important enough for a White and a Black to agree on."

"Y'all just wait until Sunday morning, you'll see what it's all about. I want to make sure this don't get out until Sunday."

"I'll say again and again, don't bite off more than you can chew. You see what happen to others who took it upon themselves to try and change the way people live. That's a job for the Lord himself."

"That's where the preachers and the churches come in. We won't leave the Lord out. You go on to bed and don't worry about what a few social nuts are up to. Everything will be good, just you watch and see."

The paper was ready by the second Sunday after the big decision was made. J.B. was impressed with the wording of the pamphlets. The short paragraphs said all that needed to be said to a people who had all the tools they needed to become full citizens in the country that their sweat created.

"Christians! Give me your attention for a minute. Before we get our regular service under way, we have a member with a message for you. I'm asking all of you to listen to what he has to say. Mr. Smith!"

"Good morning fellow Christians. I have some very important information to hand out to you today. This information is for you to take home, discuss with your family and everybody else who will listen. I don't believe that I can say this any better than what this pamphlet says it. I will ask you to take this information to heart because the future of you and yours will be decided by what you decide to do about what's in this message. Okay? I'll hand these out and if there is any questions, save them for me until next Sunday. Thanks a lot and may the Lord bless what we are about to do."

The local gossip lines was buzzing like a beehive within two days after the revelation. It appeared that the pamphlets reflected everybody's opinions. There was no vocal disagreements to be heard. People were flagging down J.B. every chance they got to ask more questions about when and where they were gonna get the ball rolling. J.B. and crew didn't expect that kind of a explosive reaction.

"Well how is it going J.B.?"

"Unbelievable! I didn't know that we had this many unhappy people. It's looking like everybody and their dogs are dissatisfied with their lot in this here country. We better get this thing on the road fairly quickly or my neck will be in a noose. Let's get down to the next step as fast as we can."

"This is where it will get sticky. Once we cross the line there will be no turning back without doing everlasting harm. It will be all or none. Our methods won't be one that can be easily agreed to by all. You and me just might have to leave here running if the enemy thanks that would solve the problems."

"I might be run off if we don't get the ball rolling. My home has become a grand central station. Every night I have at least two or three visitors. If we don't move with this, mama will be driven nuttier than a fruit cake."

# Chapter Eleven

J.B. and Mr. McPherson set the date to shoot their biggest gun. They were about to get strung up if they didn't do what they had promised. J.B.'s neck was really close to the noose. He was not in danger of getting it from the other side, but from his own folks.

"J.B.! Are we ready to set the date for the big shut down?"

"I'm more than ready. My people think we should have called the strike a week ago. But, we hadn't gotten all the churches on board at that time. I had to go cross the county line and let them folks know what we were up to and when we planned to do what we are planning to do. They are with us too. They are ready to feed us if it comes to that."

"Isn't it a great feeling to realize how much help a people can get when they are doing the right thing? Doing something that will benefit all mankind?"

"Well, Mr. McPherson, we think next Monday will be the beginning of the big shutdown. We will announce the news through the churches, come this Sunday. How do that hit you?"

"The timing is perfect. It's perfect because this is the critical time the farmers need people in their fields trying to get the harvest out before the rains come. Yes sir, this will be the perfect time to wake these folks up."

"We will advise all our people to stay home Monday, even from their own fields. We have been working night and day for the past two weeks getting most of what is ready hauled in. The Negroes who are working for the Whites are encouraged to slow down as much as possible. This kind of working would even put more pressure on the man to see the fruits of his possible changes." Monday was upon the community before anybody had a clear idea of what it would bring. Smoke was coming from the chimneys like it was Sunday. The working class had sat down on the jobs. The mills, lumber yards, the general stores and most of the rich homes were absent of workers. The white folk didn't have a clue of how to deal with this kind of worker's behavior.

The entire community was so stunted until the news on the radio failed to recognize what was going on with the labors. The county seat businesses came to a sudden halt. It appeared that it was every man for himself. There was next to zero traffic on the roads which told how serious this must be.

J.B. followed his own advice and stayed home all day. He had advised all to remain home at least for the first day or two. They had no idea how the big powers would react to a shutdown of their ways of life. It was one thing that was super clear though; they would not like it one bit. J.B. took the mail from the mailman's hands without either saying more than a polite greeting. J.B. was expecting a little more communication than just a polite greeting.

J.B thought he might ought to drive over to the McPherson's to see what the other side was talking about. Sure enough, the old fellow was sitting on his back porch enjoying the warm breeze. He had stayed home just in case J.B. came by.

"Good afternoon my partner in crime!"

"Afternoon J.! Come on up and have a seat. I'll get you a cool glass of ice tea. I'll be right back."

J.B. relaxed and let his mind wonder. He knew that they were on a new road to somewhere, but where exactly, he didn't know.

"Here you are. I'll leave the pitcher here on the table. Now what have we to share this lovely afternoon?"

"I'm here to find out what the white folk might be doing. What have you seen that we might have to get ready for?"

"I hung around town most of yesterday afternoon and there was not much going on at all. The stores were open and remained open all afternoon. What surprised me most was that it seemed that not one white businessman saw this coming. It told me one thing and that is whatever we Negroes do will catch them by surprise. They don't seem to have any idea of who we really are."

"That is hard to believe. Do you really think that these dimwits really bought the notion that we Negroes were a bunch of happy simpletons?"

"I'm as surprised as you are. It is almost impossible to live with this much social inequality and think that all is well with the system. The next question that comes to mind is, which race is responsible for this lack of sensitivity to the social conditions of each?"

"That has been a question I've ask myself every since I have been a man. Nobody knows how to ask such a question. Our people will pass the hard questions into the hands of the Lord. They won't even try to address such questions."

"I know the sheriff's office is closed. I believe he might be on one of his fishing trips. You know how they act when they feel the high winds of trouble blowing in their direction. They don't know anything about bargaining with Blacks at all. They figure trouble is some times started by one person, or by a small minority and would soon fizzle out."

"This is what I'm asking you to do, Mr. McPherson. I think

these folk are searching for that one or two people to blame this on and take action on who they are able to pin this to."

"I'll know this when these misguided citizens get down to business. I will stop in the Elk Lodge tomorrow and see what I can learn. The Elks is where the decisions relative to problems between the Blacks and the Whites are hashed over before any action is taken."

"There is one thing for sure now, the ball has been pitched. Now let's see who will bat it back to the pitchers."

"I advise you to remain off the roads for another day or so. Okay ring leader?"

"I'll see you day after tomorrow. If anything comes up that I should know for sure, never mind. You know what to do."

"See you day after tomorrow, if not sooner."

The community businesses and other work-related goings on came to a complete stop. The Negroes were beginning to venture beyond the limits of their front yards after several days of nearly total community inactivity.

"Son, I don't like how these Whites are driving up and down the roads as if they are looking for a killer or something. I know it must be beginning to sink in that they have some big problems. I just want you to do what you have to, but just remember us."

"I'm keeping my eyes open mama."

J.B was being pointed to as the ring leader of the striking pack of a bunch of lazy people who didn't appreciate being better off than half the world. J.B. and his crew started to remain as close to each other as it was possible to be. The preachers were advising the same kind of togetherness just to be on the safe side. News began to blow in about clashes between the races but nobody had been seriously hurt. But, it was just a matter of time before some misinformed nut does something that will derail the whole mission.

"Well! What do you think J.B.?"

"It looks like we are making some progress. I believe the lack of progress is due to a lack of knowledge on both sides. We don't know how to talk to each other about money. The two races think that money means different things to the other side. I don't believe that they figure that money should buy the same goods and services for all."

"The rumor is that most of the Negroes would not have it any other way other than what they have. We have people on both sides who have been pretending that all is what their God wanted it to be. People like you and me will have to keep the pressure on for change. We will have to step up and lead our people. I would gladly get out front, but I think I'll be more good to the movement passing as a rich white man and keeping a finger on things from the insides of places like the Elks Lodge."

"Mr. McPherson, you are an educated man. Why don't you publish a small handout, maybe weekly, stating what it is that both sides could do to solve the problem. Your son could help us out a lot."

"I'm glad you came up with that idea. I can write the pamphlet, with input from you and our people here, send it to my son for printing. We can come up with the cost to cover printing and shipping. He might even get paid a small wage."

The first pamphlet was a jump starter. It opened the eyes of a new batch of workers. McPherson Jr. borrowed many steps to learning to bargaining from the unions in his city. McPherson Jr. would send materials used by the unions to his daddy to share with the local Blacks. Mr. McPherson was known to share this information with his white Elk members too.

Several weeks after the shut down, a few people started to actually negotiate better working arrangements. J.B. Knew, this undoing the old and establishing the new, would take about as long as it did to build the old if things were left to evolution instead of revolution.

"I see the cotton gin has closed for a few days in order to make some repairs. We know what that is all about. They are ginning the Whites' cotton but refusing to gin the Blacks'' cotton. They are paying less for the poor folk's cotton. I'm suggesting that us Negroes stop trying to sell the cotton. Let's store it. Let's fill every vacant room we have and wait until the pressure is put on the buyers."

The white race was beginning to get their heads together for an all out attack. What they didn't know was that the black race was also gearing up for an all out attack. The war was getting on. J.B. was finally seeing the possibilities for a Negro to become a full citizen with opportunities to stand tall and stare any man in the eyes.

"What is on your mind, Janet? You keep looking at me instead of paying attention to what the preacher is saying."

"I can't put my finger on what seems to be bothering me. I had a dream that I didn't like. I'll just keep praying and trusting in the Lord."

"That sound like the thing to do. My mama told me almost exactly the same thing last night. I told her the same thing I'm gonna tell you. But, this conversation can wait until after the service is over. What do you have to say about that?"

"That makes sense."

It was the usual uneasiness in the hearts of the people whenever there were disagreements between the Blacks and the Whites. Neither seemed to know what to say, or do with the other. The two races, and all the mixed breeds in between, live together, worked together and slept together but didn't have the least idea of who the others were.

"Me, mama and daddy was at the store the other day when we were asked the craziest questions you ever heard. Mrs. May asked daddy what it was that the colored people wanted. You know that these folks can't imagine us wanting the same thing for ourselves as they want for themselves?"

"What was your daddy's answers to Mrs. Mae's questions?"

"He told her that the Coloreds wanted the same thing for them and theirs as the Whites did. They wanted a chance to be full citizens, nothing less and nothing more."

"What did she say to that?"

"She said that they were under the impression that the Coloreds were about the happiest and the most contented people in the world. Can you imagine that? Her answers made me realize how much work we are going to have to do just to become full people to these white folk. I'm beginning to have bad dreams behind what I'm beginning to see and hear."

"I know exactly what you are talking about. I have always thought that they had no idea of how to be fair and just with us Negroes. This might have been partly our fault too. We have a bad habit of telling these folks what they are trained to want to hear from us rather than telling them the truth. This is our chance to change all this misinformation existing between the two sides."

"I don't want to spend my time with you talking about these white folk. I don't get to see you nearly enough as it is. I think I'll have the biggest fish sandwiches that old man Brooks has. Can you afford me one?"

"You can have all he has, if that will make you happy. I'm the man of your life and don't you forget it."

"That goes both ways. I'll sure be glad when this race mess settles down and we get on the road to where ever it is that we are going."

J.B.'s plans were to settle down into a way of life that made sense once the two races started making some progress. He knew what they were into would not be over in a short time. He would be happy with signs of positive progress being made.

"Morning Mr. J.B."

"Good morning Mr. Brooks!"

"How many loads do you plan to get me today?"

Mr Brooks had never addressed J.B. as Mr. Matter of fact, he barely ever spoke to him at all. He would just point to where he wanted the logs dumped at. J.B. was a bit uneasy by the change in this old redneck's greeting. It was a well known fact that the Brooks had no deep love for Negroes.

"Mr. Brooks down at the log yard is beginning to be friendly to me. I wonder what's on his mind. You haven't heard anything have you?"

"Yeah, we had a short conversation about what is going on throughout the community. He is beginning to hurt, money wise. The small pulpwood cutters and cross tie cutters were his bread and butter. He wanted my opinion of how long I thought this would last."

"What was your opinion?"

"I kind of laughed at the man to his face. I asked him did he have any idea of why this happened in the first place? I asked him to figure out the causes, or listen to the reasons these Negroes are doing what they are doing and he would have the answers."

"He then pointed out the fact that my people were still working, and more than ever. He wondered how did I managed to do that. I simply told him to check my reputation when I work with my people. I told him that I treat my people the same way I would want them to treat me if the shoe was on the other foot."

"What was his response to that?"

"He stood there looking at me as if he had never thought

about what being fare to Negroes was other than what was already. He finally muttered,

"They always seem so happy with the way things were up until somebody started to put this junk in their heads."

"This is what we will have to deal with;a total lack of seeing the issues from the Negroes' side of the fence. I get from the Elks that if a few trouble-makers could be rounded up and silenced, things would return back to the good times for both sides. I'm having a ton of letters printed to mail, and hand out at the churches etc. I want to make sure the Whites get them all over their yards. This letter will state exactly what the problems are. At least this will be a start. We know it won't change much right away."

"Well, get me my batch as soon as possible. I'll have my boys deliver them to the doors of the black folks. I won't attempt to distribute any to the Whites. I ain't that crazy. No soiree!"

"My son should have them here by the first of next week, yours that is. Ours will be mailed out from my son's home. None will be sent from here. If I was you, I would give them out at church only. I would not take the chance of walking these roads trying to delivery anything. You might not want to believe this, but we have a small number of black folks who think the same as the Whites do."

"That is a pill that's hard to swallow. I'll see you in the morning. I better get this last load to town before the yard closes."

# Chapter Twelve

The county seat, and the other county towns, were in a mess after the third week of the great black strike. The garbage had piled higher than a tall man's head, the freight was still on the trains with nobody to unload it. The worse conditions were in the country. The farm produce began to overripe in the fields, the cows were not milked, the hogs went unfed. You name it, and the lazy unskilled Whites had it. They made numerous trips cross the county line trying to hire people to work at least until their own Negroes came to their senses. There were no takers.

The extreme pressure to do whatever had to be done to solve the problem came from the white housewives. They had dirty clothes, dirty dishes and starving chickens all over the place. The eggs had not been gathered on a regular bases. These women directed their anger at the white men who they believed were not doing all that they could to find a solution to whatever had gone wrong.

The white women were ready to do just about anything to get their Negroes back in their houses and around their yards. They had gotten to the point where they had no butter and there was nowhere to buy it from. The pressure was on to at least offer some of the things that were asked for on the letters that came in the mail. The white women were the most helpless bunch of all. Half of these middle class women could barely make up their own beds.

"J.B.! I hear some terrible rumors around town. Now, when you think it is too dangerous to drive these roads, we can shut down until things get better. These white men are scared to give an inch because they believe if they gave one inch, the Blacks would be out of control."

The white men were showing their buried fears of the Negroes. They believed that they would not stand a chance if the Negroes had a level playing field. The Whites had two weapons that he trusted to use on controlling the relationships between the races-violence and fear.

Mr. McPherson thought it would be a wise move to shut his operation down. The whites were beginning to be a bit slow or becoming awfully quite when in his presence..

"Men! How is all today?"

"We have a lot to be thankful for, Mr. McPherson." The leader spoke for all'

"I want to see what you all think. It is getting a bit mean out there in town, and out here in the country too. I believe this would be a good time for us to take a vacation. I have a hunch that somebody is gonna get hurt before this thing is over. Now this don't mean that we are giving up on our mission. We are taking ourselves a short vacation, that's all. Now what do you think?"

"We've talked about the same thing. It is a weird wind blowing through the trees that we cut. We are with you, boss."

"It is done then. J.B. and I thought if it was agreeable to y'all, we would shut down until it's safe to haul down these roads again. If any of you have needs that require our help, we are as close to you as your right hand."

"We'll see you when the storm is over. We hope that won't be forever either." Mr. Moses wave goodbye.

"J.B. I'll see you tomorrow and see what we can come up with. As you know, my people's cotton and other goods for the market are stored in every space that we have. But, it will be worth all the trouble if we just make a few inches of improvements. It will be a start. We have come a ways already whether you realize it or not."

"I believe that with all that's in me. I have never told you this, now I will. I haven't gotten married because of the limited social freedoms allowed the people of color. I could not see how I would have been able to sat by and take less than what my family deserved. I know where I would be the first time I ran into certain situations where a white person show a certain kind of respect for me and mine."

"J., I already know that. That young lady of yours told me that a long time ago. I asked her when she was planning on putting the noose around your neck. Her answer was "When J.B. feel that he has enough freedom to be the kind of man he wants his wife and children to have."

"That was a true statement. There is no way a Negro could be the kind of man I have to be while married with a houseful of little ones. I don't blame any one group or any one man for the way things are. I think there is enough blame to be shared by every citizen of our country and the world. That may be the main reason nothing has been done to correct this social injustice. There was no one person who could be tared and feathered for the way it was and still is."

"That is exactly what these folks are trying to find. They are looking for one or two men that can be used as scapegoats to blame this mess on. Believe me, if they find somebody to blame it will be all over for him or her. They have already starting the search down in Red Creek community. It will be only a matter of time before it reaches here. That is if they don't find scapegoats down there."

"I'm telling my people who are making deals with their white folks to be careful what they commit to. I tell them to use the advantages that work gives them to bargain with. Both sides needs to know that whatever is agreed and accepted right now will set the stages for our futures."

"Let's keep our fingers crossed and hope that both races will be able to see the advantages of working together toward satisfying everybody's needs to nearly the same degree."

There was good news coming to the community every day. But, there was that hard headed bunch who would not let well enough do. These men, on both sides of the bargaining line, wanted more and wanted it faster. There were a number of Negroes who thought that they were due catch-up monies and properties. They felt that the Whites owed them more than just equal chances. They wanted make-up appropriations for years of being shortchanged.

"Mr. J.B.! What would you answer to the question my boss asked me Monday. He asked me what more did I want from him in addition to what he already gives me. Now how would you answer that?"

"Look John, each case is different. You see, I don't know what he is paying you at the present time. You see? If you and your boss have a good deal going already, don't rock the boat."

"I don't think he gives me a fair share of what I earn for him. No, I really don't."

"Then tell him exactly what you think and what you will do if you two can't come to terms."

"If we continue to hold back our labor what will this community come to? I don't want to sink the boat that I'm in just to get my way with the Whites."

"John, you will have to establish your own limits. You will have to live with and raise your family with whatever you and your boss come to an agreement on. Or, you can turn in your resignation and look elsewhere for a better paying job."

"Howdy J.B.! We had a full house today. Thanks to you and your ideas of social justice."

"Good afternoon Pastor. I was hoping we accomplished more than a full church house. But, the Lord works in mysterious ways. Those are your words."

J.B. wished there was some way that he could tell his people the price that progress always demanded. Filling the churches and praising the Lord was a good thing to do, but there was more to living than that. Man received according to how much he was willing to give. J.B. felt a bit disappointed in what the average Negro was willing to offer for a better life. What he was willing to offer to be a better man, a better husband, a better daddy and a better citizen of his country.

J.B. was slowly becoming the front man to ask questions of about what was the solutions to the unequal share of the goods and freedoms enjoyed by the one race of the country's population. J.B started to keep a low profile so as not to attract too much attention. He had never been gullible enough to put much trust in the average white man to do the right thing at the right time by the Negro race.

"'Morning J.B.! What's on your mind this early on this windy and cold day? It's too windy for the birds to fly."

"Nothing much on my mind today. I just feel like taking a long walk and look at the great country side. It has been a long time since I walked the three miles to town. I think it is time to get some cool fresh air and exercise."

"I'll see you when you get back. The walk will clear your head and get you away from the pressures."

J.B. decided to take the Red Creek Road into town. He could have taken the Ceder Bridge road, but there was something telling him to take his favorite route into town. The ground was frozen hard and easy to walk on. His mind was thinking of another time when another black man took a walk on Red Creek Road back thirty plus years back. J.B.'s mind was trying to picture what must have taken place long ago to another young man. He was so lost in the past until he didn't notice the pickup parked in the log road just over the hill until he heard the voice say "that's that uppity nigga."

J.B. felt something that he had never experienced before. He did not have to see who said them last words that he would ever hear. He came full circle and saw the reasons why he was attracted to Red Creek Road. His job on earth was finished.

When the news about J. B.'s shot up body reach the community shock waves nearly busted every ear drum that has sense enough to hear what this millstone meant. Doing business as usual became impossible. J.B had completed his and his father's mission.

# WHEN ALL IS SAID AND DONE

# Chapter One

Mark sat on the curb and waited for a ride out of the area of his adopted home. He was leaving a town that had been his home for over thirty years. He remembered the good and the bad times. He remembered the good friends and his worst chums. He was thinking about joining the church once he got settled in back home. His mother was heavy in the local Baptist Church.

He had decided that it was time to make a move. The past several years had been a wake-up time for the man who almost had everything. The middle-age rocket scientist was searching for a brand new highway to his heavens. He knew that there had to be an easier way to get where his dreams told him that was all his for the asking. He had his fill of dealing with broke folks. He knew that it was time to work smarter.

He jumped to his feet when he caught the sounds of a truck coming barreling down the highway. The noise got closer and closer while the hobo prepared his introduction speech. He used the old reason for being on the road thumbing.

Mark stood as tall as his six feet allowed him to as the truck began to slow. He had the good old feeling that comes with accomplishment. There was no feeling like the feeling he got when his schemes worked.

"Good morning friend! It looks like you could use a lift!?

"I sure can. You don't know how much I appreciate this, friend. I'm called Mark."

"I'm called trucker. I guess you know why that is."

Trucker was one of the kind who loved the open roads much more than he loved being tied down to one small plot of land on this whole big earth.

"How far are you going, Mark?"

"Oh lord, I'm headed to Butler Alabama. That is a far piece of ground from here."

"I know exactly where it is. I have a few relatives living near there. You might know some of them. I'm from a little snot town called Carbon Hill, Alabama. I might know you. No I don't think so. You were no bigger than a gnat when I left the south. What's your last name, Trucker?"

"My read name is James Walker. There is a bunch of Walkers living in the county."

"My last name is Williams. Williams is a common name in them parts. There is as many white Williams as there are black Williams. I believe they got the name Williams from the same source.."

"Why are you headed back to your home? Has there been a death, or something?"

"Well! I'll tell ya. My luck has been running kind of bad for these last several years You know how it is when everything you touch tend to turn to stink,"

"You bet, Mark. I have had my ups and downs. I have been doing pretty good since I've had this job. I have been driving trucks, on and off, ever since I was old enough to have a driver's licenses."

"That's why you are known by the name, Trucker. I'll bet there ain't many folks who know your real name. Is there?"

"You are right. When I kick the bucket they will have to

print the name Trucker in parenthesis, otherwise nobody will be at my home-going."

"You never did tell me how far you were going."

"Oh, that's right. I'm going to within a few miles of your town. Don't worry. I'll swing through your town."

"I wish I had the money to pay you. Maybe we will meet again down the road."

"It's no problem. The boss-man is paying me to drop you off. I love doing my kind of folks favors at my boss' expense. I'm glad to have company. You won't believe how lonely it is driving these highways with nothing in your ears but the sound of a big diesel engine."

"Who taught you how to handle a rig like this?"

"My uncle drove trucks for a white man who he had known all his life. My uncle was not the read teacher. The sons of the white owner were the boys who spent time with me. My uncle was too scared of losing his job if something went wrong. The white boys didn't have to worry about something going wrong. You see, they owned the trucks, plus, they were about the best mechanics in the county."

Trucker drove through the country and talked to who he thought was a good listening hobo. It didn't take too long of riding on a smooth road to put his hobo to sleep. Trucker sometimes wondered which usually put his hobos asleep, the ride or his ho-hum voice. He knew he had a tendency to talk too much when he had somebody trapped in the cab of his truck.

"Hey, Mark! Wake up, sleepy head. We are close to your stop."

"Ops! We just past the Raymond store. I can get out right here. You don;t know how much I appreciate the ride."

"You take good care of yourself, Mark!

"You do the same, Trucker!"

Mark took in a deep breath of the clean country are that he

had been missing so long. He thought he smelled the freshness of recent plowed soil, but he knew this was not true; it was in the fall, not spring time. His memory was beginning to play tricks on him.

"Man, just smell that fresh air. It show feels good to be home. I don't know what I was thinking to leave here in the first place. Yeah, I know what was driving me."

He remembered the day he had decided to hop a freighter and head for the pot of gold that he was sure waited for the right man to come and get. He remembered the Spring breeze and the smell of the freshly plowed fields. He had at that time no intentions of farming his home farm with his little brother and little sister as helpers. He knew there was an easier way to make a living.

Mark hesitated before knocking on the door that he had never needed to knock on many time in his life. He tapped the glass peep window so lightly until he thought the knock had not been heard. He was about to give it another tap when he heard the beautiful voice of his mother.

"Who is it?'

"It's your oldest child, mamma."

"I don't believe my eyes. Boy, git your butt in this house and let me look at you."

"I thought I'd sneak up on you. Oh, this old house show smell good."

"Just put your bag down and let me get a good look at you. You didn't even write and let me know you were coming home. How long are you here for this time?"

"That will depend on a lot of happenings. I just might be home to stay and look after my mother. You ain't getting any younger, you know."

"Neither are you, boy. I see that gray hair sticking out from under that cap. Yes Lord, it has been a spell since I laid eyes on you. I don't know whether to laugh or cry."

"Don't do neither, yet. You will be laughing your head off when you hear what I have planned for you. I came home to make you happy. Mamma, you need somebody here with you both day and night. How often is Martha by here? How often is Marvin by here? You see what I mean?"

"Go on and take your belonging to your room. You must be hungry from being on the road all this time. I see you don't have an automobile. You had one the last time you darkened that door."

"Well, Mamma, it's like this. I have run into a few bad people here recently. I don't know what the world is coming to. It looks like everybody you run into is trying to gyp you out of what belongs to you. Every job I've had here recently turned out to be run by swindlers."

"You get squared away while I fix you something to go in that belly of yours. You look like you have missed a few meals."

"Oh, come on Mamma, I don't look that bad. How is my little sister doing these days since my brother-in-law been gone?"

"She is doing much better since that brother-in-law of yours took a hike."

"That man was never right for my little sister. I tried to tell her that. It is good that my nephews and nieces are grown and have families of their own."

"I didn't think you felt that way about the man that you brought home to where your sister lived. Don't you remember introducing the man to us?"

"You don't have to keep reminding me of that. I have never forgiven myself for bring that lazy sleepyhead to my house. He sure didn't then, and still don't, believe in hard word."

"Who are you telling. If my mind serves me right, you didn't cotton to hard work either. I hope that has changed since you have turned gray-headed. I show do."

"What has the young man of yours been up to? The last time I talked to him he was trying to buy a service station, with no money,"

"That was my boy, but that has been a while since he wanted to go into his own business. He gave that idea up years ago. How long has it been since you two talked?"

"Oh, God, it has been at least eight or ten years. I think it was the time I called home to borrow a few dollars to hire myself a lawyer. Remember when I got in a little trouble with the law? I had got myself hitched to a bunch of good-for-nothing street bums."

"Yeah, you know I remember those times. You almost caused me and your daddy to lose this here piece of land and all for nothing too."

"We all tend to hook up with the wrong crowd at some times in our lives. It was just one of them things. That's why God forgives us and gives us another chance. I wouldn't have gotten locked up if I had followed my right mind. No, I had to listen to old gambling John. That was one man who could find troubles in the church on Sundays. He was something else. He finally did it. He is now serving life in the pen."

"Come on and sit down and eat you a healthy meal. I'm sure you haven't had a home-cooked meal in a while, judging from the looks of you. Tell me how is my grandson doing. Weren't you living with him for a while?"

"He is doing his thing. You know how high-and-mighty he thought he was. He and that woman he married thought I should get a job just so I could pay them high rent. Anyway, we just couldn't set horses. I told them what was on my mind and packed my few rags and moved into a shelter."

"I don't think they were asking too much of you. From what I heard you had been living with them for over two years and hadn't paid a dime to help out with household expenses."

"Mamma, that's not exactly true. I would go out and run into cheap bargains when food and other household goods came into the hood. I know of several times when I hustled up on enough stuff in the streets to last them a long time. I would often run into stuff that sold for a little of nothing. He made some cheap buys when I showed him where the stuff was at."

"Yea, yea! I know how you bring junk home that you have no use for. When you were a boy, you would raid any trash pile you saw and load up with worn-out junk to bring home hoping you could find somebody nutty enough to buy it from you. Remember son. I'm your mamma."

"There were some that we used around the house. Remember when I lucked upon that freezer that somebody thought was finished? The only thing that it needed was a new connection."

"What is your plan for the rest of your life? You ain't getting any younger, you know."

"That's what I'll be sharing with you within the next few days. I have some good plans that I know you will like. I've got more thinking to do on them before I'm ready to charge ahead. I'm gonna rest up and regain that old self of mine before I get busy with these plans that you will like. Boy, these collards are right on time."

"You are eating like you haven't had a full meal since last year. My daughter-in-law was good at keeping you fed. She was a good breadwinner. You haven't looked like much since she decided that she could do better without you."

"That's what she led you and her family to believe. She caught pure hell for a while when she jumped up and went back to her mamma's.

"Mamma, why are we talking about my long ago ex wife. You know when that was?"

# Chapter Two

"Well, I'll be a monkey's uncle. Look fellows who has been raised from the dead! Where did you come from, boy?"

"I came in last night. I thought you boys might need a hand at doing what you do best, sit on these bar stools all day. Look men, I'm only here to help you men out."

"We use to have great times. Yes indeed, I remember those good old days."

"Jake, you and Rex have put on a few pounds since I saw y'all. Somebody has been feeding y'all good."

"Mark, do you know when we saw you last?"

"It has been a good while. I believe I was home to my daddy funeral."

"That has been a few years. Your mamma didn't know if you were alive or dead most of the time. We would always ask about you, right Rex?"

"Yes we did. I wanted to know where you were because you still owes me ten dollars from that time you were here to your old man's funeral."

"Aw man! Buy me a beer before you start reminding me of a long-ago debt. Give me time to get reacquainted with my homeboys and I'll take care of them little debts later. I've got to get the feeling that I'm welcome home."

"Hey, Claude! Give this bum whatever tickles his throat. He looks like he could use a friend or two right now. Come on and tell us about what sent you home riding the back of a pig."

"That is a lot better. What have you been up to Rex? Thanks Claude."

"You might not be aware of what happened to me on that construction job I had. I had twenty years with them when I got hurt. So, I've been on disability ever since. I plan to retire next year. My time still goes on as long as I'm on disability. They will kick me off the moment I'm old enough to take an early retirement."

"What about you Jake? You sure don't look like you have been missing meals. Look at that belly you got."

"You don't need to remind me of this gut. Between my friends, relatives and the old lady I have enough folks to never let me forget this gut. You could use a few of the inches around my waistline. Good Lord, boy. Have you been eating on a regular schedules?"

"There comes times when a man is down on his luck. This was one of those times."

"We heard that you had a good-paying job and was nearly rich."

"That goes to show you that you can't believe everything you hear. I haven't been out of jail too long. You know how these bastards are. They don't want to give a black man a job if he has one little tiny mistake on his record"

"We know you ain't talking about your record. Shucks, you have a history book of screw-ups on your record. Mark, remember who you are talking to. That was one of the reasons you had to leave home in the first place."

"That was when we were boys. You two were the ones that got me into that mess. You know what you done. My

Mamma sent me to live with my uncle just to get me away from you two."

"Now we know why it took you so long to write your mamma and let her know your whereabouts. Boy, you were in the lockup. Why did they put you in jail?"

"They had a crack down on the numbers and gambling businesses and I happened to be in the wrong place at the wrong time. You know how that works. They needed a fall guy, I was that guy."

"You bet we know how that works. You have always been the fall guy, right Rex? This boy has never done anything wrong if we let him tell it. No sir, he has been a victim all his life."

"Jake and I got your butt whipped a many times while we were growing up. Right Jake?"

"Yeah, at least that's what this rascal thinks anyway. He hasn't changed a bit either. I want to know what happened to him up yonder in the city. This is the first time he has been home in a coon's age. Come on Mark. We will be all ears for the next few days just to hear your story. What happened that got you put in the pokey?"

"It was exactly like I told y'all and Mamma. I happened to be in the wrong place at the wrong time. The head man always knows when there was gonna be a raid. It's just that he forgot to tell all the people who were in the joint."

"Mark, you just didn't get put in jail, you spent years in prison. Why?"

"I had a few points on my record already. Nothing like murder or worst. What happened was that the bastard I was working for hired the sorriest lawyer in the state to defend me. The judge was in with them jokers. You men just don't have any idea how corrupt the justice system is.'

"How long have you been out of the pen, Mark?"

"I got out about five years ago. I thought that them jokers

would make an attempt to compensate me for taking the rap for the business. Instead of helping me get on my feet, they refused to give my old job back to me. Them jokers had the nerves to accuse me of stealing from the business,"

"Well! Did you dip into the till?"

"I didn't pocket any more than the rest of them cheating jokers did, and I know that for a fact. This kind of thing went on every day. Sure, I would grab lunch money, or emergency money once in a while. They all were doing the same thing. Believe me, there were some real outlaws in that business."

"Listen to this crook, Rex. What do he think he was, a preacher?"

"What he is saying Mark is that all of them were outlaws. None of them had a legal job where they could earn a living honestly. Boy, do you know how to get an honest job?"

"I tried that, believe me. These folks won't even look at your application if you have a jail record. No sir, you are out of the loop if you ever had a little trouble with the law."

"Mark, what kept you alive these years since you got your walking papers? You show didn't come home."

"I stumbled up on a cleanup job at a greasy-spoon cafe. I picked up paper and cleaned floors. You know how much those kinds of jobs pay. There was no way I was gonna work those kinds of jobs any longer than I had to. I would work just long enough to draw a paycheck at which time I would get sick and stay home."

"We know you did. Right Jake?"

"What do street business look like here at home? I heard that a man could make a killing here selling watches, rings and other inexpensive jewelry. All I would need is a stake to get started. I did some of that up in the city. There were too many of us trying to do the same thing in the same places."

"The law does the same thing here as they did up where

you got your tail in a crack at. People will be the way they are no matter where you are. Rick, Rex?"

"Jake, let him tell us how he ended up back here to aggravate the living daylights out of his mamma, and his other kin. I can't believe your mamma was over-joyed to see you standing at her door. What was her first words after she recognized her oldest child?"

"She was surprised to see me, there is no denying that. Her first words were 'what storm blew you in here?' But, she was glad to see her prodigal son."

"Yeah, we bet. Now about this business you are thinking about. I don't see why you can't get some kind of a regular job like the rest of us have. What's stopping you from getting a job that requires very little skills or work history?"

"Who is gonna hire an ex-jail bird to do anything. It's like I've told y'all. These folks don't forgive for past mistakes and give a man a second chance."

"Will you listen to this jive, Rex? This boy even thinks he can shuck and jive us. He is actually trying to run a game on us who knew him before he knew himself. This boy owes both of us money and is here asking for our money and help for him to continue doing what he is damn good at doing."

"Look my best friends, I'm more experienced now than I was in my yesterdays. I have a few good ideas that will work, I just know it. The only help that I need is a small loan to get me started. I didn't want to hit Mamma up for any parts of her pension."

"I know you don't. After all, she is putting you up and feeding your big over-sized butt."

"Jake, do we want to take some pressure off this boy's mamma and trust him once again?"

"We don't have nothing to lose but a few dollars. If he screws up this time we will deny ever knowing the rascal."

"Just this one time, Rex. I have a catalog that has all that cheap jewelry one can order from China. Then we will see if there is an honest bone in his butt."

Mark was up and running with his shady business within three weeks. He didn't do too bad for the first few weeks either. That was enough time for the cheap jewelry to start turning jet black. The boy was reaping what he sowed again. He was having to move from one area to another just to keep from getting a foot in his rump.

"Hey, Jake. When have you seen that pal of yours?"

"Who are you referring to, Mark?"

"I think you have only one pal that's running from justice all the time. You and Rex are nearly as guilty as he is. If it was not for you two the man would have gotten his rump kicked many many times. A butt kicking might have done him some good back in the day"

"I can't really call that boy a friend of mine. I don't believe that his kind can have any lasting friendships. Rex and I kind of feel sorry for the poor slob, that's all. As far as knowing his whereabouts, I don't know. What do you want with him, as if I don't know?"

"Look at this set of rings he sold me. Take a close look on the insides. Now what do you think I want with the young man?"

"You had to be looking for something cheap otherwise you would not have falling for such bull. You know the man about as well as anybody."

"I thought he had changed. You should have heard the story he told us down at the cross-roads bar. You would have thought he was on the verge of becoming a preacher. He sure made a killing down there last weekend. He had me about to start thinking that it was us who were the blame for his condition. Yes sir, that boy is some talker."

"Sonny, you and Mark are like two peas in a pod. You two are so much alike until y'all could pass for twins. I can't imagine your being sucker enough to fall for that line of poop that Mark feeds you. You were once in the same business as he is now."

"Yeah, but I soon learned how that mess could come back at you and bite you in the butt."

"That's why I'm surprised that you were taken by the same line of bull that you once peddled."

"The same line that he once peddled? The only reason he ain't doing it now is that it caught up with the boy. Sonny, just be thankful that he didn't nail you for more. You guys will never learn that there is never something for nothing in this here life. Do like we do, take a few hits and learn by experience and move on with your life. Remember, it's only a few dollars that you would have played up in numbers anyway."

"It's just that I don't like being made a fool of. He flat out lied about the values of that junk that he is selling to his friends."

"Jake, do you hear what this hustler is saying? I remember when he had to leave here running to keep John Evans from beating the mess out of him."

"Rex, have you been paying close attention to how mad these crooks get when they get caught in their own traps?"

"Hold it down men, here come the great money-maker now. Let's don't let on that we know about your luck, Sonny."

"What are you men so quiet about? It's cooling off a bit."

"How's business Mark? We hear that you are making a mint selling that nice jewelry that you orders from China."

"You know how this business is. There is some ups and downs. I'll have yours and Rex's money back in y'all's hands before the end of the week. That is if business continues like it has been going."

"Sonny has something to show you, Mark. Go ahead and show him Sonny!"

"I'm not too concerned about this, Mark. But I do want to know why this watch has turned nearly black where it meets my skin."

"Sonny, you ought to know the answer to that. I remember buying a ring from you once upon a time and it did the same thing. Remember that, Sonny?"

"Yeah I do. I also remember giving you half your money back to. Do you remember that, Mark?"

"Yep! You did that. There is something else I want you to know. Do you know what I'm about to say, Sonny?"

"I know I haven't paid you a dime, yet. I didn't complain to you, I'm just telling you what I had told Rex and Jake here just before you showed up. That's all."

"I'll tell you what I will do for you, Sonny. You can have the watch for nothing. I just ask you to shut that big blabber of your and let bygones be bygones. How do that strike you?"

"That will be fine with me. So, I don't owe you nothing and I can keep the watch too? Is that what the deal is?"

"Not entirely. What did I ask you to do?"

"You said that the watch was mine to keep for no pay."

"That's right, but what were the conditions?"

"Oh, I forgot. You want me to keep this to myself. I believed you used the term 'stop blabbering about it all over the community.'"

"Can you do that?"

"I got you. You heard him boys."

"We show did. That tells us one thing for show, "DON'T BUY HIS STUFF."

Mark was running out of satisfied customers, or customers period. He had never had a satisfied customer in his life. From the deals that he made, it's a wonder he didn't get his nose broke.

Mark had to rush off to take care of some more business. He wanted to get out of sight of his life-long pals. Rex and Jake were a good source to borrow a few dollars from once in a while, but, they were not customers.

"You jokers know where Mark is going to today?"

"He was kind of dressed up for this time of the week. He hardly ever clean himself up."

"They have a week-long revival going on over at the Holy Cross church this week. He should make out good over there. Those country hicks wouldn't know a pocket watch from a bracelet."

"Mark has done business over there before. I can't understand how he can get away with such scams without getting his behind in deep poop."

"Jake, 'y''all, remember who we are talking about. We are talking about our very own Mark."

"Yeah, I keep forgetting. Mark has a sixth sense and knows things that the average man would not know in a million years. He can get out of a tight spot just in time to watch the mess simmering from a distance."

"Rex, do you men remember when his daddy had to get the fool from them white folks who caught him stealing eggs?"

"He told his daddy the biggest fib that one could think of. He said that he was gathering the eggs for the owner and thought if he did the owner a favor he would offer him a few eggs for himself. He didn't mention the fact that he was a mile from the farm when they caught up to him."

# CHAPTER THREE

"Jake, did you get the news about Mark?"

"Not yet. I haven't seem anybody since Monday. What has he gotten himself into this time? I thought he had found a dumb white man who was religious enough to give the fool a chance."

"He had met a good man who believed half what that lying Mark told him. The old white man was a preacher too. The preacher bought the nut a darn good used truck to haul his produce to the market on. You know the preacher had to believe in God a whole lot to trust Mark."

"Even God is not fool enough to trust Mark and it doesn't matter how hard mark prays. How did he get his tail in a crack this time?"

"It seemed that the man even tried to sell his boss's produce to the man's own kin. I hear he had gotten away with it too, for a while. Remember we heard that old white man bragging about being able to buy produce cheaper than he could raise it himself?"

"So, Mark was his supplier. That boy has guts, or no sense one."

"You haven't heard the whole story. The nut tried to collect the cash ahead of time and failed to bring the goods. The idiot sold the goods twice. Can you believe him?"

"Where is the clown at now?"

"He is in jail down in Cliford City. They won't even set bail for the man. They are scared that he will disappear into no-man's land. All white folks ain't crazy."

"Let's go by his mother's house and see how she is doing. Maybe there is something that she needs that we can do."

"Sounds like a good idea to me. Let's roll."

The men wanted to know the story behind Mark's lockup. They would offer their help if they had enough information to tell them what was what. They knew that Mark was not one for doing his share of anything. His mother might have been better off when her oldest son was in the tender care of correctional officers.

"Good afternoon Ma'am. How are you this afternoon?"

"Y'all come on in. Mark is not here. I assume you boys already know that."

"Yes, Ma'am, we heard. We were wondering what happened and also wondering if you needed something done here around the house."

"No more than what I need help with even when Mark is here eating me out of a house and food. I just might need less when that boy of mine is behind bars, come to think of it."

"Where is he at as we speak?"

"He called me and told me that they refused to set his bail . He wanted me to stand by just in case. He didn't mention hiring a lawyer."

"Well, Ma'am, we will haul you a load of kindling in case you run low. We won't waste too much of your time. You know our phone numbers."

"Thanks, boys. I won't forget this as long as I live. I will make Mark's brother do the choirs around here. This way there will be a voice heard loud and clear without us saying a word. I'll see that my other boy takes care of what has to be done. This way there will be no lasting hate cooking."

"I see what you mean, Ma'am. We'll be seeing you!"

"That was a good thing they nailed old Mark with, no bail' This way his mamma won't have to worry about, or feel guilty for not coming up with any cash. We know what the boy cost his mamma and daddy back in the day. Now, he pops up and is starting to do the same thing with one exception, he is old and gray headed."

"Rex, do you believe that he will ever learn and change his ways?"

"We know others who woke up and tried to make up for what they cost their families during their young lives, but Mark?"

"Mark did have his mamma's roof fixed before he got caught with his hands in the cookie jar. I guess there is some good in everybody if only you can find which button to push."

Life went on in Mark's neighborhood as it usually did, without him. Nobody seemed to miss the boy enough to include him in their conversations other than a quick thought when they saw his mamma in church on Sundays. Then the mess hit the fire. The law showed up at Mark's mamma's house ready to do battle. There were three carloads of deputies and the sheriff. The entire community held their breaths. It looked like the boy had arrived at his destiny.

"I believe that Mark is in hiding somewhere near here. He would know better than to hold up in his mamma's place."

"My dogs were making lots of noise this morning before daylight. I thought it was a fox or something that was upsetting them darn hounds."

"Jake, I know that boy haven't lost the little sense that he had. We know he has always been ready to do most anything to avoid earning an honest living, but I don't believe he would go this farm"

"I don't know. I would not put it pass a desperate outlaw.

The man is getting to the end of the times when he can run away from life. He has been running a long time. I'll have to give him credit for doing a good job of it thus far."

"Rex, you once thought a lot of the hustler. I'll have to say though, he has had a lot of fun, and punishment. He is beginning to act like he wants to get caught if it would earn him prison time. But that's not the case this time. Them folks over where he pulled this stunt at want his hide nailed to a tree. He has to learn better soon before it's too late."

Mark had traveled by night and hid by day for several days before he came to the old old vacant house that his granddaddy built before Mark was a glitter in his daddy's eyes. He didn't dare show his face in the community for fear of somebody's tongue would start wagging. These folks had very little news to share with each other and would grab any news they could get and spread it faster than a gasoline fueled fire travels.

Mark had started probing for food and clothing at any neighbor's smokehouse or clothe line. He would sleep by day and early night and go prowling by night. He was not new to this kind of living, he knew the places where he could enter and do his work. Some of the people kept their goodies under lock and key. He knew his folks'

The problems with prowling was the good watch dogs. They could make enough racket to wake the dead. One set of barking hounds could cause dogs to start barking for unlimited miles. Mark's food supply was reduced to less than he desired.

Mark figured that with enough time the hunters would think that he had hightailed it for the north, or somewhere far away, like he once had the habit of doing. He was running out of room to live the life that he was familiar with. He thought he would wait until the right time before he could knock on his mother's front door without being under the watchful eyes of the head hunters. He certainly didn't want winter to catch him having to sneak around liked a 'coon prowling for a few snakes just to remain on the top side of the grave.

"Rex, what do you think we should do to help old Mark out?"

"Anything we can, short of getting ourselves in trouble with our own folks. We are partly responsible for him being the way he is anyway. Maybe we will have to reap parts of the trouble for the tricks he pulls on us fellow critters of his."

"Let's go see the boy tonight and see what he needs, now that we know where he must be. There is only one place where he could be hanging out at."

"I'll grab a sack of last year's jars of canned turnips and fruits. He must be nearly starved to death by this time."

The friends of Mark's went home to get their gift basket ready for a nearly dead man. There was only so much food the thief could gather from people who were as bad off as it was possible to be without ceasing to exist. Food was not usually easy to be made ready to eat. Food came in the raw right from the fields and woods and had to be made ready for human consumption. The man couldn't take a chance to build a fire that could be seen from heaven. Cooking would be the shortest road to the lockup, that is, if he was lucky.

"Let's wait until the midnight hours when most of the hounds are tucked in bed with their wives and kids. We will have to be careful or we will scare him into the swamps."

"I don't think so Rex. Don't you know the boy will be expecting us to do something. I wouldn't be surprised if he doesn't chew our butts out for not coming sooner."

"I'm sure you are right, Jake. He is no fool when it comes to knowing how to hide and when to hide. If he didn't have that skill down pat he would have been history a long time ago."

"Maybe he will retire from doing thing that keep him on the run. He is getting far too old for such a life style. Can you image you or me jumping through hoops trying to outrun some angry person who wants to cripple us for life for stealing something that is free for the asking."

The men waited until they thought the country folks were done rambling for the night before they went to where they knew old Mark had to be. They hadn't gotten halfway to the old house when they heard a voice.

"Hey, Rex! Is that you?"

The voice came from behind the bushes on the pasture side of the fence.

"Jake!"

"You can come on out from behind them bushes boy. Let us take a look at you to make show that you ain't no ghost."

"Give me that sack. You two show took your mammy-loving time getting here. I done nearly wore my teeth to stubs chewing on this raw sugar cane and eating field corn."

The hungry outlaw dug into the sack searching for something to put in his mouth right away. He didn't have time to express appreciation for the sack of goodies at the time. He didn't have time to answer the questions that his oldest friends were asking of him.

"Take it easy friend. You don't need to chock yourself. The sack is your to keep."

"How have you been doing? You don't look too bad. When was the last time you were at your mamma's?"

"Let the man get something in them there guts of his. Jake. He act like he was mad with hunger. Just take your time Mark. Let's get over here behind these trees just in case some night owl happens to come along."

The night was one of them night when there could be heard only the wind blowing through the pine trees. The owls had even gotten their fill and gone back to bed. This silence left the three friends free to try to come up with a plan that would save the maverick from self destruction.

"What's on your mind Mark? Where do you plan to hightail it to when the heat cools down."

"I have thought about going over to Lucdale and stay with an old boy who I met while we both were behind bars. I would need a ride to at least the county line. You two old rascals could set that up for me, since you two are partly responsible for the condition I find myself in."

"You hear that Jake? This boy still sees himself as being a victim of circumstances. You know he just might be right to a greater extent than we would want to admit."

"Rex! I refuse to take any credit for the life that our buddy here lives. No siree, I won't jump up and down on them hot coals down yonder for what this monkey do."

"Maybe we will be much safer ourselves if we dump this rascal off on his uncle over yonder in the bushes. When can you have your pillow case packed and ready to go?"

"I can meet you right here tomorrow evening. Is that good for you, my friends?"

"We will do just about anything to rid the county of you. I know your Mamma will be glad to see you gone and know that you are safe in the arms of your kin over across the state line."

Mark was waiting like he had been there in the brush all night. He didn't have even a pillow case full of his personal belongings. He did have a straight razor and under clothes and socks.

"It's getting a wee bit cold out there. Crawl on in here boy."

"Man! It show feels good in here. Your heater must be working like crazy."

"The two of us will help warm this thing up so you won't freeze to death. We knew you might be half froze to death."

"I'm glad I've got friends like you two. I don't know what I would do without you. You two are life savers."

"We understand, Mark. Things just seem to happen to you out of the clear air. Trouble tend to find you no matter where you go. You show can't go back north anytime soon."

"That is the truth, Rex. It ain't the law waiting for his butt either. But, like we said, his luck was running bad there for a spell. All he needs is a little time and good buddies like us. We are responsible for keeping the boy warm these cold nights."

"Y'all don't know how much I appreciate what you are doing. I will make this up to you one of these days. I wouldn't be in this mess if some jealous bastard hadn't gotten into something that was none of his business. Them old white folks got ten times more than they need. All I was doing was helping out the folks who needed help. I think it might have been one of the ones I helped who let the cat out of the bag."

"Mark, you don't have to prove anything to us. We know how sympathetic you are. Don't we Jake?"

"Yep, we show do. He has a heart as big as the state of Mississippi, if you ask us."

"And just as poor. It would be hard for this boy to live among totally civilized city folks."

# CHAPTER FOUR

Mark moved right in with his relative with out a hitch. He had become a professional at homesteading in the homes of relatives. He had gotten pretty good at sleeping in the fields and abandoned houses too. He was sure his luck would change once he was given a fair chance. Yes, he could feel it in his bones.

Mark's uncle had his hands in the hands of God. He was the pastor of a church. Mark could almost smell the good luck flowing into the highways leading to his tomorrows. He followed his old graying uncle nearly everywhere he went, except to bed and the outhouse.

"I want to introduce my nephew to y'all today. This is my sister's oldest child. His name is Mark. That's all I can tell you because we have not lived around each other much in our entire lives. But, I feel that God has his reasons for getting us together at this time in our lives......"

That was the open door that Mark had been waiting for all his life. He could smell success in the air and all he had to do was find a vehicle on which he could ride to his heaven in. These folks were heaven sent. His gold mine was right under his nose all the time.

"It's good to have you in church with us, Mark. If you are

anything like your uncle, we will all benefit by having you among us. Praise the Lord."

"It is a blessing to become a part of your congregation. I believe it is the will of God that we are together at this time in our lives."

"Praise the Lord. The Lord knows what he is doing, all we have to do is to trust him. Praise the Lord."

Mark went around for a few week floating on cloud nine. There was one member of the church who was into selling household goods. He had the area sowed up to. Everybody within twenty miles was in the man's ledger. Mark hired on with him because the man had too many customers to serve. But, Mark wanted his own kingdom to rule. He got his wish one day when he least expected.

"Hey, Mark! Have you ever thought about going into real estate?"

"Yes, Mitch. Once in a while, but I never got into it. I hear you will have to go to school, etc so on."

"That's true but, that won't take forever, you know."

"Yeah, but, I have a jail record. Do you think I could still qualify to be an agent?"

"I'm pretty sure we can work around that record of yours. You see that was a long time ago. It's worth a try. What do you say?"

"I have nothing to lose. Where do I start on this road at?"

"Give me a few days to get the paper work set up. I'll get back to you next week. How do that sound?"

"This sounds better and better the more I think about it."

"I'll see you Monday or Tuesday."

"See you Monday, Mitch!"

Mark could hardly wait to share the news with Rex and Jake. He was waiting at the store where they always met to grab their day-starter. They were at the age when a small energy booster helped to crank them up for the day.

"Hey, you men. Listen up for a minute before we go inside. I want to know what you two think about my chances of becoming a real estate agent?"

"Mark, are you joking? What company would be desperate enough to trust you?"

"Shut up Jake, let the man tell us what has made him fall completely off the deep end. Go ahead Mark."

"I met a guy who thinks I will make a good real estate agent. You know the fellow I've been helping sell the pot and pans for the past few months. Mitch, y'all met him last month."

"Yea, we know who you are talking about. Tell us how did you two arrive at your being good material for a super salesman?"

"I don't really know why he thinks that I would make a good salesman. But, it is good to know that there are people who think I'm good for something. Now what do my best friends think of those apples?"

"Mitch must have bumped his head, or something to come up with that opinion of you."

"Wait a minute Rex. Let's take a look at what a real estate salesman does for a living. What will be the man's main job? Will he be in a position to screw the daylights out of the customers?"

"You might have a point. Go on Mark, what did you two come up with?"

"Mitch seems to believe that my jail times won't be a problem. He thinks that it has been so long ago until it will not show on my record. He knows somebody who will sponsor me. This real estate company will have the responsibility for whatever I do."

"When are you gonna get this dream going?"

"I'll know the first of next week."

Mark could hardly wait until Monday to know if he had a shot at becoming an honest man. He had a hard time even visualizing himself being an honest man. This would be as strange to him as it was to his best friends. He thought about how much he should tell, if asked, about his past life. He even lost his appetite for a short time. There was something bothersome about having to live up to a level of honest behavior required in a real estate business. He didn't really know how to be a man that could be trusted. He had always felt that he had let himself down the few times he didn't get all that was for as little giving on his part as possible.

The real estate school was easy as taking candy from a baby. Mark could relate to putting on an act of honesty when honesty was serving his cause. The selling of real estate was a way of making money without working and being honest all at one and the same time. This was hard for the man to believe.

"How is your schooling going, Mark?"

"You two won't believe how easy it is. I'm at the top of my class. My instructor says that he has had only a few students who was as quick to catch on as I am. I have always tried to tell my customers what they wanted to hear. This schooling trains me to do just that without my having to give in count of the outcome. The final results will be between the customer and the finance companies. Once I collect my commission, I'm free to go."

"I've never met a real estate agent in my life and knew it. What is the Job? What training do he needs?"

"The only things he needs to watch out for and learn is how to fill out the paper works and where to send it to. There are a few who wants to buy way above their heads, which the system will not go along with. The good part of being an agent is you are out there mixing with the people and having a good time. There is no back-breaking hard work involved."

`"What do you think about what all this boy is telling us, Rex?"

"I will have to wait and see more of what he is doing and how successful he is before I make up my mind. Mark can do the unbelievable at times, then turn around and screw the whole thing up. How many times have you and me heard this kind of tale before coming from him. He is always on the edge of becoming richer than rich and all in an easy way."

'It might be like the gambler said, 'if a man plays the numbers long and often enough, he is bound to get lucky once in a while. Maybe this friend here of our has found his pot of gold."

"I hope so, then maybe he will stop begging us for what we have busted our butts for. Right Mark?"

"You guys go on and don't wish me luck when I need a little encouragement from my buddies."

"He has a point, Rex. Let's pray for him to be super successful and if the Lord answers our prayers, maybe this boy will pay us all the money he has borrowed and forgot to pay."

"Are you listening Mark?"

"You guys go on and have your doubts about me. You will be made to eat them smart words one of these day after my horse comes a galloping in. Now, lets get down to brass tacks men. I can feel this thing is exactly what I have been waiting for all my life. Now, I need you two friends of mine to believe in me. Okay?"

"We know there is several others who will be more glad than we will be if you hit that home run that you feel so strongly about hitting."

"I'm telling you men that this real Estate is for me. I don't know why I hadn't thought about becoming a salesman before. You guys just keep your fingers crossed and pray for me."

"Jake, I wouldn't be surprised if this boy didn't become a preacher sooner or later. He show has the gift to gab which is one of the skills needed for such jobs."

Mark had his real estate card in his wallet and his license on the wall of his broker's office with time to spare. He graduated at the top of his class.

Mark felt pretty blessed for being given a chance like he had. He always had a sliver of fear that his sponsor might learn his life history. He thought maybe his record was not considered to be a problem because he would not be handling cash. There was one thing he needed badly. He needed some transportation. He had to talk his boss into signing for him to rent a car His sponsor had seen him driving his mamma's car and thought it belonged to him.

"I saw you going in your office carrying a briefcase, Mark. You looked all business-like too. Did your boss buy you a briefcase for your graduating present?"

"How did you guess that, Rex? That was exactly what he did. He told me that he expected to earn a lot of money because of his giving me that briefcase."

"Mark, you can thank your boss for saving Rex and me the cost of that briefcase. We thought we might have to get you one from the salvation army store. But, thank the man for us."

"Now, the only thing that will hold me back is transportation. A car is a must. I'm thinking of asking the old man to give me a hand, but I want to show him what I can do before I spring the car on him. I'll have to use Mamma's until then. She wants to see what I can do too."

"We know she do. Don't we Rex?"

"Your mamma has more to gain from your good works than anybody. She wants to get your sorry butt off her dependent list.

"I don't know what you two deadbeats are talking about. You know Mamma is getting up there in age and is needing more and more help with the old place. My sister and little brother have their own places to pay attention to."

"Looking at it from your point of view, I can see where you two would be better off with each other than without each other. Maybe that was the reason why you never amounted to much. What do you think Jake?"

"This boy is making me believe in a power greater than man. His mamma might have been blessed when she had what we saw as a worthless hunk of meat. Do y'all think we all are born for a specific purpose?"

"No, Rex, I don't and I won't let this rascal off the hook that easy, come to think of it. This big headed joker is doing what he has always been good at. Jake,we have always wanted to believe that the creator didn't make mistakes when he made some of us, even though it appeared he came close. He couldn't have come closer than when he decided to blow breath into this boys nose."

"Well, boys, I have to get on with my work. I don't have time to be sitting around jabbering with the likes of you two. I'll see you good friends of mine tonight after work. Did you two hear those last words? After work? I might have to work overtime, if you two know what that is."

"Good luck."

Mark had never been so fired up over working before. Rex and Jake thought he might be falling over the edge even further than he had already.

"I certainly hope Mark all the luck in the world. He sure could use it. He sure seems to have a mission to shoot for. You know, Jake, we might have missed our calling. We might have been better off going into the selling business."

"No I don't think so. Them kinds of opportunities were not around for people of color back when we started work. We had to make do with what was."

"You know how long ago it has been since you and me put on our working gloves? Shucks, we are nearing retirement now and this Mark is just now going to work. I would like to have heard what line of do do he fed his real estate broker."

"Rex, he might not have fed the man anything. We know this friend of ours has the gift to sell just about anything if they didn't know him. Just imagine meeting him for the first time and listening to his line of bull. What would you think?"

"I see what could be a talent that he has that will be beneficial to him for the job that he has. The boy was dressed for the occasion too. He almost looked honest."

"Mark's age, and his street wisdom might be exactly what the doctor ordered. Let's start to encourage him to get on the last train going his way."

"I'm with ya."

# Chapter Five

"Okay, you bums, come on and let me treat you to the best meal and drinks that you bums ever had. I'm looking for somebody to help me celebrate my big success. You two were the only buddies I had. Don't hold back now. Go for it."

"We heard about the big deal you pulled. We didn't have any idea that the old Greek's son was gonna sell his store. We thought he would take over like his daddy had done."

"I'm telling you boys how it is these days. These white folks are hightailing it for the country. They are selling out like the world is coming to an end. Their world that is. I'm gonna help them with their running from the new times. Haven't you men noticed how these folks are sticking "for sell signs" in their front yards and on the light poles all over our neighborhoods?"

"You know we don't have an eye for such. Rex here is nearly sleep all the time. We are getting on up there."

"That's the point that I have to shout out at you men. Maybe it is not too late for some of us to reach for higher rungs on the ladder to success. Our time might still come within our lifetimes. You guys thought I was a nut all these years when I didn't want to spend my life serving the white folks. You see what is happening in our towns and cities here lately,don't you?"

"We realize one thing that is for sure. You have the experience to ride this horse on to wherever you decide is your destiny."

"I'm trying to get something else over to you smart old men. This might be your chance to become a part of this big change. Age is a benefit in this business, instead of a handicap. I have run into something that we could tap into, and that is fixing up these homes that the white folks are dumping. You know who is coming in here and making a mint fixing up these properties?"

"We see that. How do you think we can benefit from this business you are thinking about?"

"You men won't have to do much of any of the backbreaking work. You can hire it done. Do you old farts realize how many Blacks have the skills to do the work? They don't have the license, and so forth, but they do have the skills. Who do you think has been building the homes and businesses all these years?"

"Come to think about it, you have a point there. The upper class never did the work, did they? We have been the builders of this country, but we never were given credit for it. Come on and tell us more. What have you seen in your travel that makes you think that us two old worn-out friends of yours could become somebody like you did?"

"I have a plan that I copied from a few men who were in real estate classes with me. These men were mostly white, the same as the agents, but they were studying the business of doing the kind of business that every neighborhood has to have. The homes need electricity, plumbing, roofs, and you name it, the houses have to have it sooner or later. Who do we call now to do our work? Most of the time? We call nobody. We have the skills right here among us."

"Do you really believe that it ain't too late for men as old as Jake and me? We are part of an over-the-hill gang."

"I'll say again, you will provide the brain and supervision and let the young do the work."

"What are you grinning about, Rex?"

"The more I listen to this hot-shot, the more I believe he might have a point. You know we don't have too much to lose at our age. I show would be proud to leave something back here to be remembered by."

Mark continued to break sales records like nobody could believe. The man loved the business so much until he was willing to live in his office just in case somebody needed his services. His office was the only office open for business seven days a week. There were days when the fanatic would spend the night in his office sleeping on an old couch he had bought at the Salvation Army store.

"Hey Boss-man! How is the hammer hanging this beautiful morning?"

"Don't tell me that you three goons came by here because y'all were interesting in how I'm doing. No, let's get to the real reasons you bucks are here before I have had my breakfast."

"You hit the nail on the head, buddy. We came by to ask you to join us for breakfast. We are on our way to a big helping of grits, eggs, and bacon for breakfast. How would you like to join your best friends and let them fill that empty pouch of a belly for you?"

"Okay, what is it that you old worn out Negroes want from me?"

"You have a nice big office here and all by yourself too. Go ahead and tell this boy what we have come up with, Jake."

"We thought that you needed some company down here and would welcome partners to share your office space and expense with. Now, let me finish before you speak. This place has to be kept clean, plus you need somebody to answer the phone when you are on a mission."

"What have I got to put up with to get this kind of tender help?"

"We have decided to try out the idea you told us about. We want to start out slow with a house cleaning service. We would be ready to clean up homes before they are listed for sale, we would be in a position to hire the needed repairs done that we could not do ourselves. How do this sound so far?"

"Go on."

"Answer this question, Mr. Big Shot, Where do you go to get done what you need done before you can hope to make a sale?"

"I hear what you are saying, so what do you two think will be a solution for us and make sense. You boys already know if it is no benefit to me directly, I'm overboard."

"What do you think about this office sharing idea?"

"It sounds good to me. I'm getting tired of sitting here alone, half asleep waiting for the phone to ring. At least I;ll have somebody to talk to. When can you boys start to move in? I'm on board for now."

"Let us see what office furniture do we need. You can help us with that. You have been in business for a while."

"Let's see now. Both of you want your own desk and chairs for customers. Now that would require us cleaning out the room where I store stuff that I've been getting out of these homes. My customers throw away some good stuff at times."

"When can we start to clean her out and where can we get the chairs and desks from?"

"It's like I said, go to the Salvation Army second hand store. They have some good things for nearly nothing."

"You are still using your mamma's car, ain't ya?"

"Yep, somebody has to drive it once in a while."

These future millionaires went to work with dreams of becoming the colored role models for their whole race. They would show their people how it is done in the modern times here in these United States. These men were up and running in less than a month. They could hardly believe how easy it was to get the thing up and running. Mark had customers waiting before they got set and hired a crew to do the manual work.

"Rex, what could we have done if we had gotten into this business when we were twenty years younger"?

"There is no doubt by now we would have been too rich to be colored."

"It is still hard to believe that our partner, Mark, had this kind of brains in that nappy head of his. This boy comes up with new ideas every day. He is thinking about starting a paper that would serve as a handbill to let our people know when we have good deals."

"You know what Rex? He hasn't been too far off course yet with his radical ideas and I'm ready to go along with whatever the sorry butt comes up with."

"Did you get in contact with Roy, yet?"

"I show did. I went by his watering hole yesterday. He and his tramps were doing what they usually do when they ain't on a job."

"Is he ready with his bunch to go to work big-time? He will have to understand that we are all business and will not put up with sloppy work."

"You know Rex, we have been wrong about what we thought about our people when it came to business. Gosh, I would have never thought that we two would be this deep into organizing our own organization to take us to the top. I can see us now not only becoming the richest colored folks, but becoming the richest folks in the community, baring none."

"Roy said that they had bought his uncle's old truck and they are getting it in good working order. You know that pickup that was in his uncle's barn all these years. His uncle fell and busted his leg years ago and has been sitting on his rear end ever since."

"Roy is a good man who we can trust to make our contacts with the junk dealers. It is always a wake-up call when I open my eyes and mind to what is really out here for the taking. Our no-good life-long chum has changed the way we see ourselves. It's a good thing."

The gang was busy as honey bees all summer making good money from their brand new way of making use of their time. Mark had done a good thing for him and his friend, and by the same doings, had become a positive role model for the Coloreds in general.

The J. R. Maintenance Troupes was fast becoming a monopoly in an area that covered the entire county. These boys had found their pot of pure gold. They hadn't changed what the lower class members had been doing since time begin, but they had started to get paid for it.

"Rex, you have a birthday coming up pretty soon. What do y'all plan to do on your big sixty-fifth birthday?"

"You know we stop celebrating birthdays the same time when you and yours did. A birthday is nothing but a reminder of a time that we would rather not think about."

"This is the point. We should celebrate every minute we have left because we know what time it is getting to be. Why don't you let us take you out for a plate of your favorite bowl of beans and rice? You can have all the corn bread that you can eat too. How do that sound to your guts?"

"I'm ready. All you had to mention was a bowel of bean soup. We are far too old to be chopping down on a big birthday cake. With your cholesterol out of control, cake is out of the question. You might not even have a sip of our happy juice either."

"I'll agree with part of your saying but, let's don't go crazy now. How can a man celebrate another birthday without something in his guts that makes him feel lucky to be having a birthday? Now what do you buddies of mine have in them knotty heads of y'all'?"

"You just be ready tomorrow afternoon about three o'clock. We'll do the rest."

"See y'all tomorrow, Jake!"

The big-timers didn't have too much time for pleasures like hanging out at bars and cafes during the working hours. They were too busy making money and providing services for their community. Their office had become a place where the entire community had to stop and catch up on what was the newsworthiness of what was going on in the entire world.

"How does it feel to be over the hill, Jake?"

"Speak for yourself, Rex. We are all done passed the expected limits for a bunch of low-class .porch monkeys. I'm beginning to envy those who crossed the great river at a young age. It's no fun limping around getting in these young folks' way."

"I know who you are thinking about. Earl was the first of our generation to say goodbye. He was younger than all of us, but he was doomed to a short life when he was diagnosed with that blood disorder. I still believe that I saw relief on his face the last time I looked into them big brown eyes of his. We were by his side when he took his final breath."

# Chapter Six

"Morning, Rex! Get up off your butt and let's go. Mark and I don't have all day to waste fooling around with your puny butt."

"Have a seat, Jake. You and Mark don't have any place to go or be except right where you are. You two old rascals have already been to all the places that you will ever go. So pour up yourselves a coffee and shut up."

"Tell him, Rex. You two use to jump on me for being in a hurry going nowhere. Look where I'm at after all these years of breaking sales records. I had to leave here, go to the big city, become a ghetto big-shot, spend half my young life behind bars, you name it, I did it. Now, look where I am. I have been there and done it'

"We didn't think that you were ever going to make it to your twenty-fifth birthday. But, we were wrong. You are here suffering the pains of old age the same as the rest of us. You have proven beyond a shadow of a doubt that the good die young. If the bad died young, you would have never seen your first birthday."

"Au, come on you nuts, give me some good credit for something. If I had crossed the great river when I was young, where would you two old geezers be today?"

"Jake, the boy do have a point even if we don't want to admit it. I'm beginning to believe that it was us who was out of tune with having a great life and a beautiful future. Yes, it took a social reject to open up the possibilities for people of color to be themselves. I appreciate the man like I appreciate no other man."

"Thank you Rex for that compliment. I once wished I could be like the two of you. You men had jobs, respect and the girls. Y'all had what money could buy and that was what made men, men. But, I had a problem with what we had to act like to get to these men-making things."

"We know how you acted that kept you in trouble with our social rules. No sir, you were not the kind of fellow that I wanted to be. You were not made of good husband, daddy, employee or friend material."

"I knew that too. Those were my main reasons for leaving home and heading for the city slums. We were sent to prison for doing the same kind of businesses as were legal for the white people to do. We had to operate outside the law, his laws. Therefore, when we became too successful and penetrated his circle of business we were charged with committing crimes."

"You know Mark, we could not see what was really the truth in a million years. Most of the people thought that was the way it was and there was very little that one could do about it and remain on the streets."

"I spent a lot of time with men who thought like me. The majority of the men that I was locked up with was of the same mind that I was. These people were not bad people. No siree, not by a long shot. They would have been considered heroes if they had been White. We had plenty of time to share ideas, read books and just plain think. The more we shared, read and thought the more we were convinced that we were doing the right thing and had no notions of changing our minds.

"That was why most of you jail birds would end up right back in jail. Rex, Roy and I use to bet on how long it would be before you were in trouble again after they kicked you out of the slammer. You never let us down while you were young."

"I realize that my getting them years in prison might have saved my life. It was easy for an overly ambitious policeman to use people like me to get promoted. You men know how that works. Shoot a bad Black to death and become a white hero."

"That was one bet we lost. We were betting that you would not live to middle age. How wrong we were and we are glad that we were. It is men like you, Mark, that make it possible for us to be men like us. You've gotten us to where we are today."

"What have you got to add Roy?"

"I heard my daddy say a many times that Mark would not live to see his eighteenth birthday. He was right if Mark had been doing these things twenty years sooner. That's what was spread throughout the community. You were the role model that the mothers and daddies used for training their boys not to be like."

"Ain't we glad that you were the kind of tainted man that would one day show us the way? Here we sit with all that a man could want and use. We are by far the richest four men in this here town, baring none, who would have ever thought this could be in our lifetimes?"

These few men were paving the way for others of their kind to follow to their social independence. They were the lights for others of their kind and ambitions to follow. The social climate was changing all over the Americas. Black men and women were getting elected to powerful political positions where the differences were being made. It was the beginning of the time when it was an advantage to be people of color.

The old men were beginning to walk like old men. They

were satisfied to remain in their office in a climate-controlled atmosphere. They preferred to do the remembering and talking about what once was, and let the young do the work.

"Hey Mr. Mask, You forgot your bag!"

"Thank ya sir!"

Mark stood there looking into the eyes of a young white man who had just addressed him as Mr. He was nearly in shock and had to get his mind up and working before he could grab his forgotten bag. He was spellbind. Instead of grabbing the bag and moving on, he stood there looking like an overgrown old nut. This was further proof that both sides of the racial equation will have their work cut out for themselves. This new way of being a good citizen was kind of like wearing a new pair of shoes. The people had to break themselves in to these new relationships.'

Mark had new sensations galloping through his brains like a runaway mule. He had to walk off to a private spot to think about what it would be to be treated as a total human being by a member of the pretended superior side of the track.

"I have something to share with you old knuckle heads. I'm being addressed as Mr. more and more these days. My problem is that I'm having a hard time being comfortable with this new thing. Have you men been getting the same gut reactions to the new?"

"You bet we have. Rex and I just finished discussing this new identity we have. We have a job on our hands. We have got to learn how to see ourselves in a new light."

"We will have to make adjustments in how we deal with each other, when all is said and done,"

# THIS IS MY COUNTRY

# Chapter One

John sat near the radio so he could hear the news over the noise made by his younger brother and his nephews. They were just being their usual selves after filling their bellies with a giant meal of beans, hock-joints and cornbread.

The news were blasting through the airwaves about Japan bombing Pearl Harbor. John and his people had never paid too much attention to news about things that they believed didn't matter to them. But, this news was different somewhat. He had heard the white folks mumbling about them darn Japs. John was at the age to be drafted into the arms forces if he was a white boy. It was obvious what the white young men were doing. They were lining up at the draft board to enlist in the services. The more news came about the American lives lost in Pearl Harbor, the longer the enlisting lines got. There was next to none people of color lining up to enlist.

"Walter! What is your thinking on this war mess?"

"The only thoughts I have is copied from what I heard Granddaddy say the other day."

"What did he say that made you believe that you don't need your own opinions?

"You know the old man was in the last war, don't you?"

"What has the last war to do with this war? This is a

different war from the other one. They didn't bomb our own people as close to home as Pearl Harbor is. Pearl Harbor is just a skip and a hop from us here."

"My grandpa said that he would rather go to prison than go to the army and help these white folks to continue to treat Blacks the way they do. He thinks that we were worse off by our serving our country in the capacity that we did. The arms services made fools of us in the eyes of the whole world. Up until that time the world was not upon how the Blacks lived here in our homeland."

"Yes, that was then. Do you know how long ago that was? These folks may be ready for a change now. We have to remember that times moves on. This is a new day for all of us."

"Tell me something. Why are you so fired up over this white-mans war?"

"If we served in this war maybe we will make the Whites see how much our country needs us. I mean really needs us. We might have a chance in this war that we didn't have in the last big one. Do you see how well we get along with our fellow white neighbors? We will do just about anything for each other."

"You are right, John. We can depend on our white brothers and sisters to help us live as second class citizens. If you don't believe this, try to go to their side of the movie house. You will then see how fast they will put you in, what they call, your place."

"Now you are getting the point. I want to make sure that I don't sign up to give my life for a second-class citizenship in the country that I gave my life for. Why don't we ask Tommy what is it that he is enlisting to fight for. Let's see what his answer is."

John and Luke were always trying to figure out exactly where they stood as citizens of their great country. The renegades had nothing better to do than sat around questioning who, what and why they were.

"Hi Tommy. What are you two up to this evening?"

"Luke and I were wondering what you thought of this new war and what the big fuss was all about. Could you give us your side of the picture?"

"I'll be glad to share my thoughts with you boys. I think like my daddy. He says that these little red men are trying to destroy our democratic way of life. We have the rights to choose our leaders, etc. We can decide what is good for us as a group. These other countries don't enjoy democracy to the same degree that we do. Even you boys can understand that."

"Thanks for your thoughts, Tommy. We have been knowing each other all our lives and we value what you think about this great way of life we have here. Tell us one more thing, how do you believe that me and Luke would fit in if we joined the great defense?"

"You boys have a stake in this beautiful country too. Look at what you have. You boys are better off than the people are in most countries that don't have a free and democratic country. Don't y'all agree?"

"Yes we do. We realize that this country belongs to us as much as it belongs to you, if not more. You see, we were here long before your people came. That's what your granddaddy said."

"Me and my cousin are going down and join up the first chance we get. What about you two? There will be plenty of ways that y'all can serve. The army will still need cooks, housekeepers and etc. Yes sir, we will all have a job in this great fight to defend our democratic way of life."

"Thanks Tommy. We appreciate your sharing your opinions with us. We'll be seeing ya!"

"We'll be looking to see some of you boys signing up. We could go together but y'all have a separate day, place and time to enlist. But, anyway, get in there and help us protect this wonderful way of life we have fought so long and hard for."

"Luke, did you follow his thinking on the subject of war, democracy and what all of it had to do with us?"

"Yeah, but, I can't believe that he is sold on all he was telling us. He told us what he wanted us to believe. He would have to be a fool to put himself in our shoes and do what he is suggesting we do. What did you hear him say?"

"Yes you are right. He is not big enough a fool to apply to himself and his cousin the bull he asked us to believe. He thinks that we Blacks are foolish enough to go for what he told us. No, he would not buy into that crap that he fed us in a million years. But, he was right part of the way and that is, this is our country as much, if not more, than it is his."

"The man could believe what he said applied to us under only one mindset, he had to think that we are content and happy to be who we are. We appreciate our white brothers,"

"Daddy, I have an important question to ask you. Get ready now, I want your true opinion."

"Go on, ask the question."

"Me and Luke have been thinking about joining up with the army. We think this is a good way to prove that we Coloreds are worthy of first-class citizenship. Think before you give me your answer." "We thought that you and that boy might be thinking about using the army to pay y'all way to see the world. Don't expect too much appreciation to come from your countrymen. You are aware of what your great uncle had to go through when he was fighting in ww1."

"We think times have changed since his time. We are of the mind that with the new generations we will be given more respect and freedoms if we show our countrymen what we can do, and are willing to do, for our country."

"That sounds good, but don't expect too much change in these people of ours. I think you two eggheads are wanting to go into the arms services for more than the reason you just gave me. You boys are using the army as a way of getting from under the house-rules of y'all homes."

"Even old Tommy told us that we could become more deserving citizens by showing this country that we are ready and able to come to her defense. We didn't buy into all what he said. He didn't have sense enough to realize that we knew he was telling us that serving in defense of our country was a good way for us to prove something that he didn't have to prove. We knew he was not capable of seeing us deserving the same as he did."

"I see you boys have been taking this thing about what you can accomplish by defending democracy which you don't totally have, yet. You boys proving that you are ready and willing to do what is required to be truly Americans will put the pressures for equal sharing of the goods here in the hands of out brothers."

"We will go down to the local board come this Wednesday. Tommy and his cousin are going down to the board Monday. It's a shame that the Coloreds and the Whites can't report on the same day. We hope to change that for the next war."

"You boys think there will be another war after this one?"

"We learned in history classes that there has always been wars. This tells us that we better become warriors who are ready and willing to fight for our own. We haven't shown that side of ourselves to the citizens of the world. Other people don't believe, or never have read about, our people fighting for what we feel is necessary for us to be fully deserving people.

# CHAPTER TWO

The two, American to-be first-class citizens, were in line at the local board long before the doors opened for business. They were somewhat surprised to see a line building up as the minutes ticked away. They could feel the dreads of the unknown moving through the young men standing waiting to see what their future could become. None of the waiting expressed any opinions about what he hoped to be the results of his being in line early on Wednesday morning.

"What are you thinking about this line, Luke?"

"I see we are not the only ones who thinks by letting our folks know that we are ready and able to serve our country and defend her way of life."

"Excuse me Mr., did I hear you right? You are down here to volunteer for the army?"

"You heard right. That proves that there is nothing wrong with your hearing. You stand a good chance of passing the physical with flying colors."

"I think you have it wrong. I'm here to flunk the physical. I don't want any part of the man's fight. I don't see that I have much to gain by getting my behind shot off for something that I can't have."

"Just maybe we will have something to be proud of if we

show that we deserve it. I don't know for sure, but the ball will be in the white man's court. They have to be the rotten apples in the barrel if they don't recognize our proving that we are truly citizens of this country that we call America."

"I wouldn't mind fighting for what I already have, but for something that belongs to somebody else? Not on your life;"

"You have a point there. We don't know how the man feels about having to share with black heroes in uniform. If we prove ourselves beyond a doubt that we deserve better, then maybe they will change their minds about what they allow us to be and do here in our country."

John and Luke became members of Uncle Sam's army. They had their orders and could hardly wait until they got the chance to kicks some butts. John and Luck could not believe that the majority of their kind was not eager to join up and prove that the Coloreds were better citizens than many other ethnic groups.

"Luke, don't you think this army would be further ahead if they would at least give us the same quality of barracks as they give to the others?"

"It seems that would be a good thing. But, you see that we don't even have colored officers. That old boy who got rejected might have been right. I certainly hope not though."

"Those boys were putting us in a worst position by their playing crazy so they could be rejected and sent back to picking cotton. Their actions were proving what the others think we are."

John and Luke had to grit their teeth at times because of the officers' rotten attitudes toward the men who were only asking for an opportunity to show the world what kind of men they were.

"Do you think we might have been wrong John?"

"Wrong about what?"

"You know what I'm talking about, boy. Don't you try to pull that dumb act on me?"

"The Whites will change their minds once they see us in action. They haven't seem our people in action. You and I know there ain't a white man nowhere in Mississippi who can beat a Negro fighting. Could Tommy and his cousins take down either one of us? Hell no.

"I do hope you are hitting the nail smack on the head."

"You just wait until we step off the bus when we return home with our clean army uniforms on. Folk's eyes gonna pop out of their heads. I would show like to see the faces of those boys who played crazy to get back behind their mules."

"We will gain something, if it is nothing but to get to see the world at tax payers expense. Plus we get room and something to eat and wear, all at tax payers expense. That's something to be thankful for."

"You left out the main thing."

"What did I leave out/"

"We are from behind the plow and out from under the cotton sack. That was a big one for me. Luck, you and the whole community knew how much I hated working in the fields and woods."

"Yeah, those white folks show were not running to hire you on. You had a snotty attitude to. There were times when I thought about ducking you when I would see you in town."

The colored recruits were given the bottom-of-the-barrel white officers to get the Colored ready for combat. These jokers were either drinking on the job or sick from a hangover. It was rumored that these officers were unfit to train the Whites. Therefore, they would be sent to the colored boot camps as punishment and to get them out of the sights of the green white recruits.

"All right you black birds, let's see you double-time it around these barracks twelve times. I'll be sitting right here where I can see every one of you darkies. If I see any one of you falling out of formation, that person will have to deal with me one on one. He, or they will have to keep up with me and I will be fresh and ready to run. Do you boys hear me? Let's hit the trail!"

The officers would sit on the hood of an army truck so he could observe every man's steps. They would have something to talk about at supper time if they had to punish a few Blacks for passing out before the drill was called to a halt.

"Boy, this was a rough day. These officers are crazy. Mike and Jerry had to be carried to the medics."

The white medics didn't come out in the heat of the day to check on a Black unless he was near death.

"That crazy sergeant must have come from somewhere where Blacks are hated. Half the platoon was dying from thirst before that bastard called the drill to an end. I hid behind some of the others. Gosh, I didn't think I would make it for a while."

"I was right behind you, Luke. I had planned to hang on to your shirt tail if I felt myself falling."

"This might be worth it when we get back to our hometown. I want to walk through the colored quarters with my head held high. I want to see what Pearl thinks of me then. Yes sir, I want to have a chance to ignore that uppity gal just once."

The boot camp stay lasted for ten week. This was four weeks longer than the other boot camps lasted. They said that this was because the colored recruits needed more training than the white boys. But, the graduation day finally was upon the proud colored men in uniform.

The proud professionals were eager to get on the bus for their homes, they didn't know how heroes were supposed to behave, but they were practicing every day before they were given their riding orders.

"Make sure that your extra uniform is ready for church Sunday. I'm gonna have mama press mine before church Sunday morning."

# Chapter Three

Finally the bus driver let the black soldiers board. These boy still had to wait their term to get on board even though they were going to the back. The Whites were loaded first. This way they were sure to have enough seating. If there was a shortage of seats, the Blacks could stand.

"John! It would be nice of the bus driver if he could see his way to treat all us soldiers like we are going to the same war."

"Don't be too hard on the man. What do you think he would have to put up with if he did what you said he should? That boy might have to leave the country. He sure would not be driving this bus after his boss found out about it. Just take it easy, our time will come. Let's just sit back and enjoy how we will be treated by our folks the coming days before we are off to the war."

"I want to make these butt-holes sorry they ever thought that we were less deserving than they are. Yes sir, I'm gonna have big fun watching them and their women change their minds about how we should be treated."

"You have the same wish I have Luke. I want to make these joker eat their own racist attitudes. We will show them how wrong they have been all these years. This what we are planning shouldn't be too difficult because we are better men than most of them. I can't wait to get at them enemies of ours."

John and Luke didn't realize that America had the number of fighting age men that they were seeing. It looked like every man in America was in uniform. This gave the boys unshakable faith in their country's power to beat the socks off any of those backward countries across the big ponds.

Boot camp was not as hard on the farm boys as it was on the city bunch. Working in the fields, log woods and sawmills made strong men out of boys. This was especially true of the Blacks. The Whites, the Blacks thought, didn't stand a chance of winning any war without the help of their black brothers.

The proud black soldiers could not believe their ears when a few of their white brothers and sisters had something to say.

"Howdy John. Tell me something, John. Why do you boys insist on wearing those army outfits every day? Those garments are for y'all to wear when you are doing army duties."

"Mrs. Bea, we see your Billy wearing his navy uniform all the time. Why don't he change cloths when he is home?"

"Bill's wearing his uniform ain't the same as you boys wearing y'alls. You see, Billy is a full American who is proud to be who he is. He is showing everybody how proud he is to serve his country. That's the difference, boy."

"We can't see why we can't do the same thing as Billy can. We are glad to get a chance to show off our thankfulness for being good American citizens too."

"I've never heard such ridiculous nonsense in all my fifty years. You boys claiming to be citizens equal to that of a white boy? You folks can;t even vote."

John and Luck didn't let what the old white lady have to say dampen their pride in wearing the uniforms of their country. The voices of the Whites didn't bother the proud trained colored soldiers as much as the opinions of some of their own kind did.

"What are you boys grumbling about, Luke? Somebody done stepped on your pride?"

"Mr. Slater, you wouldn't believe what Mrs. Bea told us today. She thinks it is a shame for us to wear our army uniforms when we are not on the base. How can she come up with that kind of thinking?"

"Easy son. Even I think that you boys just might be disappointed in how your fellow country people view what you boys are doing. You see, everybody knows that what you boys are telling yourselves that are the reasons for your being in those uniforms in the first place ain't true"

"That's the point, Daddy. It might not make good sense today, but look how it will look after we win the war for this country. Then, them bastards will have to eat every negative word they ever said about us colored soldiers."

"I'm not trying to discourage you boys, I just don't want you fellows to be so disappointed in your folks until you give up on becoming good citizens. I can remember when we had colored men going into WW1 with those same notions. I know that was a different time and people. Y'all just don't expect from others something that they can't, or won't, give."

"This is the part that I don't understand. They don't have to give us anything. The benefits that we have for our citizens are our already. We ain't begging for handouts. We will get what we earn and pay for. Now is that asking for too much?"

"You heard what Mrs. Bea told you about how she saw you men in your shinny and fitting uniforms. You might have been reminding her of something that she ain't ready to think about."

"We won't need her kind of approval after we show the whole world what we are made out of. We met some Blacks who felt the same way as some of the Whites. They used every trick in the book to get out of being inducted. We will have a chance to show them a thing or two."

The all Americans could hardly wait until they showed the world their true grit. The boys had the girls showing a different attitude toward the decked out young men. The men stood out at church as much, if not more than they did in town.

The end of their leaves came much too soon. The men were given their orders to ship out, they were being sent to parts of the world that none of them ever heard of. It seemed that most were told to report to the west coast to be sent to some distant places in the South Pacific. Up until the final days the men thought they were going to Europe or somewhere that they had read about in their history books.

"I'm sure glad that you and I will be stationed together, Luke. We will miss home and our folks for a while. At least we will have each others' shoulders to cry on."

The boys were seen off by half the people they knew. There were a few Whites standing at the station watching the sad bunch wave good bye to all that they knew, and head into an unknown future. It was one thing that the boys agreed on and that was they would all be heroes once the guns were silenced. They would return home bigger heroes than what they were before. They would prove their love for their country. The future heroes were on a mission.

"Luke, I wonder if there is a reason why we don't have shells for these nice M-1 rifles. Do you think that the white boys got empty rifles too?"

"Maybe they did and maybe they didn't. The officers might figure we might go crazy and turn on our own people. I wouldn't be surprised if some Blacks would get upset over the way some of these Whites treat them."

"It is hard to hold your peace when you are insulted at every contact you make with the upper class. You see how we were packed on the buses and trains while you never saw one White standing because of a lack of seats."

"Let's face the facts, Luke. Look where we are corralled in the hole of this ship. We have pretty good accommodations which is true, but what would happen if this ship was attacked?"

"There would be a bad time for us poor Coloreds. There is no way we could escape behind the Whites who are close to everything. I don't believe we will receive any better treatment when we get to where ever we are going."

"Luke, just keep in mind why we are so willing to stick out our necks for our country. This is the kind of bull that we are trying to change. If we do the job right, these white boys will hiding under our beds at night."

"I still can't forget what the folks back home told us. The old folks who recall the end of WW1 and the trouble the Coloreds had the moment they stepped off the trains at their homes. It was made clear to the returning heroes that nothing had changed for them here at their homes. The truth of the picture was that the returning black heroes were made fun of."

"John, I wonder why these people are the way they are. If they are afraid of not having enough to share equally, they are dead wrong. Our country has more than enough of everything to satisfy the cravings of all."

"You are forgetting one main factor to what goes with all that having enough of everything. Remember how we have to get at what we have buried beneath the soils and growing above the ground?

"Oh, it takes a lot of work, yes. But it is there for the taking."

"Think about what you just said. It takes lots of hard labor to mine the treasures offered in our country. If one is willing to work hard, the world is at his fingertips. Just think about that one thing which make the big dreams come true."

"I'm getting it. These sorry bastards are allergic to working in the hot sun and in the woods. That's what they don't want to share with us."

"You are getting the picture. They will give us all the work, but will limit your share of the harvest from the work that you do. That's the only thing that the man will gladly give all of to us. He is not greedy when it comes to sharing the labor."

The food on the ship was prepared by Blacks, with the exception of the officers. The eager beavers were seeing their jobs getting bigger and bigger. They would soon change all this kind of relating. They believed that nobody could be so selfish and lazy to be blind to what he would gain by sharing everything that a democracy had to offer with all its citizens.

"Roy, what do you believe will change by us showing these brothers of ours who they are dealing with here?"

"Well, John, I'm on this ship because this was one way out of the sugar cane business. You men think that cotton is a tough crop to grow, you should try your hands at cultivating sugar cane. Most of the Coloreds flunked the physicals for the army. We were lined up three deep to join up."

"Why did such a high number flunk the physical? Was there something wrong with Blacks in your neck of the woods?"

"No more than anywhere else. It was those big cane growers who controlled the draft. The only Blacks who could get into this man's army were guys like me."

"What kind of man are you?"

I'm what is considered a lazy no-good black man. The draft board would have found me fit as long as I could breathe without a breathing machine."

"You know, some of that kind of crap was going on at our home. The only difference was our men were begging to be exempted from going. Some who had a powerful White to put in the word, he got disqualified. You were the other way around. Isn't this a messed up system?"

"I hear you two making plans to change the way the cards are stacked against us by showing these folks that we can measure up to the best. I got my doubts about your heroic deeds changing anything for your betterment."

The more these men shared their dreams with other like themselves, and a few of the Whites, the more they began to feel that their job of making change in their duties was getting bigger and bigger. The ship sailed on into the western horizons with no land coming into sight.

"I wonder how far have we traveled?"

"Luke, we are not even half way yet. We are headed for the Hawaiians Islands, or something like that. I wonder what kind of people live there and will we be fighting them. This war is getting more confusing as we go."

"It's one thing for sure. Luke. You won't be able to kill many of whoever with a rifle and nothing to go in it. Ha. Ha."

"Ammunition for our weapons won't be a problem once the first shot is fired. You men just wait and see. They will need us to help reduce their losses. You know how much our brothers in arms love their lives and their ways of living them lives."

The white sergeant heard the conversation between the colored boys. He had kept his mouth shut until he thought enough was enough. These men deserved to know what their jobs would be, he thought.

"I couldn't help from hearing you boys talking about the empty rifles you were issued. You might have a better understanding of what is if you know what exactly your jobs will be. You folks won't need ammunition for them there guns you boys are so proud to have. Your jobs will be housekeeping, cooking, washing clothes, digging crappers, and so forth. You show won't have time to be shooting at the enemy."

"How in hell are we to defend democracy with a pick and shovel in our grips? Can you tell us that?"

"Can y'all look at it this way. These assignments that will

be given to y'all are nearly as important as the actual fighting. We couldn't be free to fight the enemies if we had to do what you men are drafted to do."

"We want to get in the thick of the fighting the same as you men do. How do we prove ourselves sweeping floors?"

Luke! He ain't the one to jump on about how we are to be assigned our duties. There have to be many opportunities for us to jump in the middle of the fray. The sergeant doesn't know everything that's gonna happen. This is his first time in this corner of the world just like it is for us."

"I sure hope you are right. We sure didn't go through what we went through to wash dishes. Can you see us digging holes for johns while ducking bullets?"

"Don't you worry Luke, I'll write home and tell the people how you got your butt blasted off while you were bent over digging a hole for the white soldiers to relieve themselves in. You will be recognized as the great fighting man that you are."

The wanted-to-be heroes were getting a bit worried about what their future in the arms services would turn into. If the sergeant knew what he was talking about, the colored men will be the laughing stock of the world. The men had to figure out a way to be the men that they knew they could be.

"Just you men wait and see before going jumping to conclusions based on what our dumb sergeant says. We know he is our sergeant because he was too dumb and low-class to be a sergeant in the white outfits."

"You are right. What does that idiot know?"

"I'm wondering if there might be a sliver of truth in what the white idiot said. I am also wondering who will be doing them women jobs if we don't? Somebody will have to do the dirty women work."

"Not really. The men can do their own personal work until the bullets start to fly and then washing dishes and so on will be the last thing on a soldier's mind. We will all be needed if we expect to win this war."

"John, and the rest of you, what would you tell your children and grandchildren about your army time if it was spent peeling potatoes and shelling peas?"

"Men! Men! We will do whatever it takes to fulfill the mission that we promised ourselves. We ain't on this boat because the white folks need us to do their women's work. We are here because we are fulfilling a duty to our country. Do that clear things up a bit?"

The sea got a bit rough when they encountered a tropical storm. Half the men got so seasick until they were darn near ready to jump overboard and end the suffering. Most of these boys had never been sick a day in their lives. They sure started praying for better weather so they will be able to perform once they hit the war zone.

"These seasick pills don't seem to be doing much good. I don't remember ever feeling this bad in my whole life, not even when I had the mumps and chickenpox."

"Maybe we can beat the enemy by giving them what ails us. I bet they don't get seasick. They have to be used to this wild ocean by now,"

Sickbay had standing room only. The Coloreds were usually the soldiers who had to stand and wait for the longest before being waited on. This practice only made the colored soldiers more determine to measure up and bring about change. This won't be the case on the return trip home.

"Boy, it's getting harder to wait until we get our chance to prove to these idiots exactly who they are messing with. What do you men say?"

"John! You and Luke didn't make good sense when we were in boot camp, but I'm beginning to see what you men had on your minds. I can see your points now. We have never been given the opportunity to be on the front line when it came to defending what these folks call democracy. We were not given the chance to fight much in the Civil War. That war was about our freedom. Our history books skip over the good part that we played even then."

"You went to college too, didn't you?"

"Yes I sure did, but it did me more harm than good. That is one of my reasons for joining up."

"You thought that the modern army would give you a chance to be appreciated?"

"It would give me a job in addition to a chance to use what I've learned. Sometimes I wonder, though."

"You just hang out with us. There will be a new attitude toward the Coloreds when we show these idiots what we can do. We aren't fighting for them anyway. We are proud to be Americans too."

The more these boys felt discriminated against the stronger their desires for change grew. They were getting to the point when they would turn on the Whites without much provoking.

"I wonder what was that old boy doing in line with us anyway. His people have been served already and here he is back here with his ears cocked in on what we are talking about."

"Do you think he was put in our line to spy on us?"

"No, I've seen that rascal eating with the Colored before. He might have been brought up by Blacks and feels more comfortable hanging around us."

"John, you two might be missing something. Have y'all ever paid close attention to the way he talks? Does he sound like an average White?"

"I noticed that right off when I first heard him speak. I think it's because of what part of the state he comes from."

"There is something peculiar about that boy. I'm gonna ask him a few questions about where he came from the first chance I get."

The flotilla finally arrived without anybody jumping overboard. The boats were all in one piece. The Whites unloaded first as usual. Blacks had to spend an extra few hours in the bottom of the boats. The extra time gave the Coloreds time to get to see the Islands from the ships decks. They had never seen lands that pretty in their short lives.

"Luke, have you ever seen a land looking that peaceful?"

"Nowhere near. Maybe that's what the big fight is all about and not about democracy at all. I know the war is about something more than what they tell us. You and I know these people don't believe in freedom for all anymore than an ape do."

"That's about what our people have been telling us for years. But, we gonna make a change in that attitude if we have to beat it into our own brother citizens."

"Okay men. They have given us the signal to start for the gangplank. Let's see where we will be stored. I don't want to think about what we'll be assigned to do."

"At least we are here where the actions will take place. At least that's what our country thinks anyway. I can't imagine how anybody could be mad here in a paradise as pretty as this"

# Chapter Four

"Well now, these quarters don't look too bad. They show make what we had back home look like prison cells. Come on boys, I think we are on our way."

"What do you think now, Sargent?".

"I want all of ya to fall out for inspection at four o'clock sharp. Do y'all hear me?"

"We got it, Sergeant!"

The men saw a glimmer of hope shining from the horizon. Maybe they were feeling the effects of being out of the bottom of the ship. They would be able to look out of the window for the first time since boarding the troop ship.

"These natives remind me of the Indians in the movies. They don't look exactly like our Indians, but come close."

"What kind of folks are they, John?"

"Let's ask the know-it-all Sargent of yours."

"Their ladies show look better than most of the women back home. Maybe it's their fruits and vegetables diets they eat. Whatever is causing it, it makes them pretty."

"Let's don't forget what our purpose for being here is. These women's opinions of us might be carbon copies of the opinions of our white women back home. We don't have a clue about how they see us."

"You are right John. We are not over here in this man's war looking for women. Where are their men at?"

"I thought I saw a few unloading one of the freighters when our boat was docking. I show hope that is their jobs and not ours."

"These men have no reason to be fighting for our country, so they will need us to fight, not to handle freight. No siree, we are soldiers, not dock workers."

"We will know soon enough. I want to get at them there Japs. You know what they told us about how much the Japs hated Americans. We will show them little slant-eyed men a thing or two. You heard what the Captain said when we were getting ready to get on the ship. He said that them buggers were natural born killers of anybody from our side of the big waters."

"Quite y'all. Here comes Sargent. Hey Sargent! We want to ask you a question about the men and women over here on this island."

"What is your question?"

"What kind of people are these?"

"They are called Orientals. They are sometimes called Asiatic folks. Don't ask me any more because I'm like you boys. I had never heard of these folks until a few months ago."

The men got squared away and fell0ut for inspection and to be given assignments. This would be their wake-up time. The Whites had been given their orders and it was time for the brave and eager dark-skin boys to learn what their major tasks will be for the duration."

"Line them darkies up in lines of nine each. Let's get moving!"

The sergeants started yelling orders like the house was on fire.

"You, you and you, this went on for what seemed like an

eternity. The men were thankful that they were not back in Mississippi where the sun was hotter than hell itself and with no breeze. At least there was a nice cool breeze blowing here on the island.

After nearly and hour standing at attention in the sun, they were divided into work groups of nine each and assigned to a white sergeant or corporal. The men were beginning to have a few questions they wanted answers to. John and Luck didn't want to get the troops any more disappointed than what they were already. So, the picked colored leaders kept their mouths shut. They had no idea of what was to come next.

"John, you heard where we are destined to. We are assigned to dock 43, whatever that is. What do you make of this stinking mess, John?"

"Luke, I'm as confused as you men are. I have no idea what we will be doing on the dock. Maybe we will be security guards or something. I certainly hope the Islanders will be doing the loading and unloading the ships."

The men were beginning to get the feeling that comes when there is an ugly surprise coming their way. The men could sense the hot and cool waters used to wash dishes and clothes for the ruling class. They began to dream up ways to make it hard for their white officers who might be in charge of whatever they would be assigned to do.

"You boys fall out over here along this wall. I want to get one thing clear to you men and that is what exactly your jobs will be. You will be ready to fall out at four in the morning and work until the job is done, or until told to quit. Do I make myself clear? If you have any questions, now is the time to ask them. Now, you boys will be responsible for all cargo arriving at this pier. You will have days when there won't be any work at the pier when it will be my obligation to assign you other work. That will be my decision. A ship of supplies is due in here tonight. So, you men are dismissed until work time in the morning. Good day gentlemen."

"Can you hotshot soldiers believe that we came halfway around the world to unload grits off a boat?"

"John, you are the leader of the men from your neck of America, but you were way behind on the real happening for the black soldier boys. I have heard you and your bunch making plans to become great deserving heroes. It will never happen. The best you can do is to do as little work as you possibly can and feel good about that."

"Your name is Rob isn't it?"

"You got it. We are from the East edge of Alabama. I don't know who told you, boys, that you all would be soldiers like the Whites."

"I don't believe that we had to do all the training that they put us through in order to become dock-workers. We could have done mule's work with the know-how that we had without all that boot-camp training."

"You boys have a lot to learn. One of the facts that you will have to live with is that nothing will change how these folks think your job is. You and your men will have to accept what is and leave the big jobs to God."

"John, Rob is beginning to sound like the preacher who was our rector back on the base."

"You are right Luke. I will be your minister while we are here in the south pacific. If you have any problems of a psychological or social kind, I'll be on call twenty-four hours per day."

"Tell me something Reverend, what do you hope to gain from your sacrifices?"

"I will leave the rewarding in God's hands. I will try to bring comfort to his servants and leave the rest up to the Lord."

"Reverend, what part do you believe the Lord plays in these conflict between the powerful nations?"

"The Lord has the final say in all of what men do. I refuse to try and speak for God. I just try my best to pass his word on to his creations. I hear that some of these countries involved in this war don't even believe in the one God. Now, you tell me how is one suppose to deal with a people who refuse to believe in the one God?"

"Thanks, Reverend for your thoughts. You gave us something to think about which we didn't have before talking with you."

"Any time, young men. That's the reason I'm here."

"I guess the reverend got you boys on the right track, John. Now that you know to leave the heavy thinking up to God and the man, y'all can focus your minds on following the orders given you. The Reverend just made your jobs a piece of cake."

"Aw shut yo mouth. That man set the stage for more questions to think about than we had before he came on board. Now I really have some tough questions, but I will give him time to think about his answers to us today."

"How did you swallow what he said?"

"I was trying to believe in something higher than man and the games that man plays with each other, but now I don't believe in much of anything. Luke! What are we supposed to believe is the reason why we are here?"

"We are back at square one. I still believe we have to come up with our own reasons for being here or make the best of a bad situation. I can't really blame this human mess on a god or a devil. That's like pointing the finger at the other guy while exempting us from all blame."

"Hold up John, here comes our orders."

The sergeant was coming in high gear. He had the kind of expression on his face like a man has who is pure business.

"All right boys, let's get to stepping. Get the lead out and get to your positions on the ship. We don't have forever to get this boat ready for another job."

"The sergeants competed with one another to see which one could get the most work out of their crew. This high production was the white boys way back to a position with the white soldiers. It was no crime to drive the colored boys to the breaking point and when one did fall out, it was not because he had been overworked. It would be due to his being a lazy bastard.

"Luke! What will you tell your folks was your great heroic contribution you gave to win this great war? Huh? Tell us how your washing down the mess hall gave this country the winning edge in this war?"

"I'm gonna tell the same lies that you gonna tell. This might not be telling pure lies because my washing down the mess halls freed up other soldiers to fight the war. We will be right in the thick of it just like all the others."

"Right, you tell them how we won the war without firing our guns one time. We fed them bastards to death. We can tell our homeboys that they were not good citizens when they deliberately faked insanity to avoid the war. No sir, we won the battles without firing a shot."

"Come on John, what have we to brag about to make us proud to be American soldiers? There has to be some noble lies we can tell about the part that was given to us Blacks to play."

"You are right, Luke. Now let's look at who we are and what sacrifices we are called on to make and what the rewards are waiting for us at the war's end. We will win, you know. Who is the hero of an action, the ones who give less and receive most, or the ones who give most and receives less?"

"That depends on who is telling the story and who is listening."

"That's is so true. You see we will tell our own story. Our people will know what the deal is anyway. They will be able to spot a lie a mile off. So, we need a noble truth to tell. I think we have all we need to be the greatest heroes of the whole war."

"I think I know what you are about to say, but say it anyway. Our men need to hear it more now than ever."

"Our original mission has not changed one iota. Matter of fact, it has gotten more to our liking than it would have been if we were given a part in the killing. We have to remember whose country we are fighting, or, cleaning and cooking for. Men, this is our country that we are protecting from the world. Sure we will have to protect it from some of our own people too. You and I know that will always be the case."

The good old colored boys increased their commitments to assuming the full responsibilities for what they considered theirs. They were of the mind that the United States of America was more their country than it was anybody's else.

# Chapter Five

The war in the Pacific was taking its toll on the American troops. The little slant-eyed and so-called monsters were good jungle fighters. The American white boys were not conditioned to the kind of heat, humidity and hard work that the enemy was. They began to depend on the colored soldiers for more than driving trucks and forklifts.

"Sergeants, assemble the black boys in the yard in front of their mess hall. We have to make some changes to what their duties will be from here on. Let's jump to it, now!

The sergeants rounded up their men who were all nearby because they were not given many okays to leave the base. When they were given passes, they were escorted by the few black military policies that were on duty for the single purpose of keeping an eye on the black boys. They had no legal power over the Whites.

"Instead of this getting better, it's getting worse. We are now given the responsibility of patrolling the jungle to protect these sorry white boys. Can you men believe this?"

"We sure can, Mule. So can you. You men expect these folks to change? Not in a million years. You haven't been paying attention to what we have been doing. Our jobs have always been to do the work while the other folks enjoy the results. Don't you men ever get the point. Tell them, Luke."

"John is right. We are doing nothing over here that we were not doing back home. We will be given the same credit that we were given back home too."

"Thanks, Luke. Men, listen to what we are trying to get across to you. We are not fighting so white people can give us nothing. Let's leave them out of our business as much as they leave us out of theirs. We are not here fighting for their country, we are over here in the hot jungles fighting strangers to protect our country. Do you get our point?" "How are we to take America from the white folks and the others who think that it is theirs?"

"Roy, we don't have to take anything. It is ours from the jump. Let's keep our mind focused. The members of the other ethnic groups will be working for us from here on."

The colored soldiers were sent into the jungle even before the white soldiers were. The army knew which was the strongest and could handle the killer heat and humidity. The soldiers had to have something to believe that he was fighting for in order for him to do his best. Each group believed that they were fighting for themselves. If they didn't think that they were protecting something valuable to their lives they would be sorry soldiers. A negative state of mind could not win the war.

"Sergeant! Get your boys together quick. Lieutenant Morris is pinned down and need assistance. You take your colored men and circle the Japs and come in from behind them."

"Captain, I have a crew of fifteen men. They are not really trained for hand-to-hand combat."

"They can serve as decoys and create some more targets for the Japs to shoot at. Get moving!"

"Yes sir!"

"Fall out you men! Grab a box of shells and follow me. Let's get the lead out!"

"This is what you men have been hoping for, Luke. Here is y'alls' chances to become real soldiers."

"This has the smell of do, do, John. I heard the orders, decoys? You know what that sounds like."

"It sounds like our chance to show America what we are made of, this is the chance that we have been waiting for, so let's don't blow it."

The brigade of eager beavers moved into the edge of the swamp determined to come out great heroes. They had the orders to become true soldiers of the finest country in the world.

"Run as close to the ground as you can, men. This way you won't be an easy target."

The sergeant had been with the men so long until he felt more like one of them than he did of his white brothers. The first main reason he wanted his men to fight as professionals was his life was in their hands.

The soldiers proved to be more than a decoy. They were the best fighting bunch the whites had ever seen in action. The white witnesses found what they were seeing hard to believe. The men didn't miss a shot. The White soldiers could not believe what they were witnessing. They could not take their eyes of the Japanese unarmed soldier marching into the open fields with arms over their heads.'

"What the hell! I don't believe what I think I see. Are we insane, or what?"

The captain could do nothing but turn around and go back to his desk and make out the report. The only believable report that would be accepted by the big boys was to make heroes of the white soldiers. If he reported what he thought he had seen he would be thrown in the brig for turning in a false report. He might even be discharged for being shell-shocked.

The Blacks could be heard celebrating late into the night. They celebrated without their white brothers in arms. Their white partners acted as if they would rather the Japs had won the fight. These men had accomplished something that the real soldiers could not do. They were on their way to a life that only heroes enjoyed.

"Listen, you men! Can I have your attention for a few minutes? I want all of us to hear this news at the same time. I got a letter from home today. You can see that I haven't broken the seal yet."

"Come on you men and listen to what they are saying about us back at home. Go on with your reading Roy."

'Okay, here goes."

Roy took his time opening the letter. He wanted the men to be on edge to hear what a great job they were doing in the jungles.

"Howdy Roy! We are doing well here at home. Your daddy has been promoted on his job. He took the place of his foreman who is cleaning them jungles out over where you are. We are beginning to wonder where you and your platoon have gotten to. The papers here at home are filled with news about our white heroes and how they are taking more Japs prisoners than they know what to do with. We are concerned about you. The papers haven't printed much about where you boys are, or what y'all are doing."

Roy didn't finish reading the letter. He gently folded the letter, put it in his shirt pocket and slowly walked back to his bunk and lay down to think.

What the letter said hit the troops where it hurt. Nobody had words that would come close to explaining what the letter didn't say.

"John! What do you make of Roy's news from home? If the papers that his folks are reading is an example of what they all are writing about us, we are the forgotten heroes. Of course, that can't be the case. I would like to know what paper they are reading."

"Let's assume that the paper is the norm for gathering news about what the soldiers of color are doing, we have our work cut out for years in the future. We can't stop what we are doing just because a few rednecks can't accept our being the heroes of the South Pacific. What do we do from here on? Start ducking our responsibilities? Will that make us feel better? I don't think so. We will be falling into the holes that the newspapers are digging for us. We will be conducting the funerals for our own heroic deeds."

"Which enemy should we be pointing our guns at? Them crazy bastards?"

"Roy! Roy! This just means that we will have to tell our own story. We can write letters to our people and encourage them to publish the truth as it applies to us. Let's get to writing men."

The army started to censor all outgoing mail. The army did not want high classified information getting into the wrong hands. The outgoing mail was either edited or thrown into the waste baskets. This was especially true for the letters being written by a bunch of angry black soldiers.

"Remember what we have been talking about, men! We figured this might be the case, at least with us. We are fighting on two fronts. Sometimes I don't know which front is doing us the most harm. This war thing is the short timer. We will have to go back home where the real fight will be and that one will last for generations."

"How can our country expect the colored soldiers to give his all for a country that won't recognize the gift?"

"Nothing has changed, Roy. We know the job before us is a big one. This war thing is nothing but a platform from which to launch our social missile from. The more we are denied, the more fuel for our battle. We have to have solid rational reasons to do what we will be faced with. These folks are too dumb to realize that what they are doing is nothing but defeating their own purposes."

"What John is trying to tell us is that without incontestable proof of the social injustices our case won't be heard by the right people. Our fellow countrymen are giving us exactly what we need to make our case. We will get support from all sides."

"Do we get it? This is working in our favor. They are giving us everything that we will need to bash their hard heads in with."

The local news back home didn't even get in print who and what the body-bags were filled with when the body-bags went directly to the black funeral homes. There was beginning to be some news relating to black casualties of the great war. This news was mostly coming from the limited black-owned and run black presses. These news media had no direct line to the front from which to gather accurate news about the underrepresented black soldiers' sacrifices. The more the poor dishwashers were denied, the harder they worked. They were being driven more from frustration and anger than anything else.

As the casualties of the white soldiers fill the hospitals the colored hospital workers became indispensable. The black medics got to see even more of the insides of the American one-sided news telling. They had to read some of the mail from home to these wounded white heroes. The newspapers back home were filled with their heroic news. There were no limits to the celebrating when a body-bag arrived at the bus station containing the body of a white heron. No sire, the streets were decorated with flags and banners of all kinds. The fire department and the police paraded down every main street of the dead hero's hometown.

From the obvious attention paid to the fighting yanks, the world would never believe that Blacks were even in uniform.

There was no room in the American psychic for the recognition of any other ethnic heroes except Caucasian men. Even the American Indians were not given heroic status except under specialized conditions.

The Indians could claim some kind of ancient kinship and worm their way on the inside to work as spies. The Japs often made the mistake of believing that the war between the Whites and the red men was still raging like it should have been. The Japs made the mistake of thinking that the Indians were fighting for democracy. They were not fighting for democracy, but for their country. The Blacks were on the same team with their Indian cousins. They too were in the war for reasons other than the right to vote in the local elections.

The war in the South Pacific was taking its toll of American's lives when it was decided to drop the atomic bomb on the Japanese civilian villages. As far as the Japanese Empire was concerned, the war was over. Germany had thrown in the hat a few months earlier.

"With Germany out of the action, we could have beat Japan without having to drop the bomb on those innocent people."

"It seems like we could have. They didn't stand the chance of a snowball in hell of winning. I wonder why we didn't drop the bomb on Germany?"

"I think we all know the answer to that question without having to think about it at all.'

# Chapter Six

The trains and buses were loaded with discharged ex-soldier boys on their way home to enjoy the freedoms that they had paid a dear price to protect. One could see lines of ex-soldiers still wearing their uniforms proudly. Even the Blacks were more than proud to be ex-soldiers for their country.

The Blacks were to soon learn that their fight on the home-front was not over and was nowhere near the negotiation table. It appeared to most of the ruling class that there might not be a class problem at all.

"Did you see what that hillbilly did? He actually pushed me out of line."

"Look, John, we might as well get started on our second war right here and now. Are you gonna let that bastard, who was not fit for the army, push you around?"

"Not on yours and my lives. Watch my back and see that nobody else gets in on this butt kicking."

"You can bet on it. Go get the rascal and give him some licks for the rest of us."

John went after the man with more hatred than he showed while fighting the Japs in the South Pacific. He had a clear idea what this fight was all about. He had no doubts whatsoever.

"Hey, mister! Did you mean to push me out of line?"

"You Nig…"

The poor redneck didn't get to finish his answer before darkness blacked out his vision. John didn't know he could strike a white man with such a hate-filled blow. With one lick the man was out cold.

"Okay, John. You have done enough. Let's get back where we belong."

The men didn't have to worry about others joining the downed White. It seemed that he was not well thought of by the Whites either.

"John, you had to come back home and beat the daylights out of your own homeboy before you could become a hero. Can you believe this?"

"We knew the Japanese were not our enemies. They might have been the enemies of the Whites in the islands, but they were no threat to us here on the mainland. We knew where our biggest fight would come from. Believe me, this mess has not gotten started yet."

The tongues were wagging all over the country before John got the feeling back in his right hand. He was feeling to see if he had done himself more harm than he had done the poor army reject. He didn't feel any broken bones.

"Your hand feels okay, John?"

"I think so. I'll soak it in some alcohol when I get home. Even if it is fractured it was worth it. I hope I broke the runt's jaw."

"With what you have started you'll have plenty of chances to break your fist and more before we are finished with these 4fs. We always knew this kind of thing could be, but this boy was trying to tell you what he thought about us black boys coming home thinking of ourselves as being fighting heroes."

"He was right about us thinking that we are entitled to a little respect. We are gonna get some respect if we have to take it. I'm just getting started. How about you? You got as much satisfaction out of the boy's busted lip as I did."

These citizens were still confused about what was due who. They had no idea of how much, or how little, they were expected to recognize the part that their American Blacks played in the defense of their freedom.

John and Luke thought they had better ease on back to their part of the county while the going was good. There were those who would do harm to Blacks for anything a Black did to a White no matter who the White turned out to be, or what the White had done to the Black. By the colored men vacating the area, it made it easier for the decent Whites to ignore the racial violation.

"John! Do you think it's safe for us, or other Blacks to hang out at night for the next few days?"

"It has never been too safe for us to hang out on these roads at night. This is especially true if one is alone. You know how these bored cousins are of ours. The problems with the way we live are that it doesn't give us enough good to do for our neighbors."

"The old boy acted like it was your fault that he couldn't pass the army's mental test. Everybody knows that not only him, but his whole family suffers from some kind of psychic handicaps."

"Don't we all have a few problems with our heads. I sometimes think that this is a world-wide problem. I even thought the Japs were one upon us when it came to having good sense. You saw what a hard time we had as police. These men of ours had to be watched all the time. When they weren't chasing the local girls, they were drunk as skunks."

"I don't think we would have won the war if Germany had stuck in there and we didn't have the atomic bomb. I haven't forgotten the part we played either."

"Don't ever forget the part we played. We had to babysit our great men just for them to have full bellies and clean underwear to put on. But, I will never get tired of saying that we were not fighting for our white cousins' sake. We can't forget that fact for one minute."

"You did a good job reminding us of that when you knocked that poor devil out cold."

"That's the last time we should do something like that. That kind of problem-solving only makes it worse. That kind of anger will not help our country to become more than it is now and that ain't good enough for us."

"How do you think we will be able to avoid them kinds of run-ins and them kinds of people?"

"I don't have all the answers yet. But, I believe we can start by going up to that redneck and telling him how sorry we are that I hit him. I want the whole town to know that we offered to make amends for his busted mouth."

"Luke! What have you given John to smoke before y'all got here?"

"I'm as shocked as you are by what I just heard come out of his mouth. Check him and see if he has a fever with them illusions he is suffering with."

"You men stop and think about what I said. By us being the good guys, but taking no mess, we gain the upper hand. We will be in a position to recruit an army of good white Christians to support us. They will see what our overall game is."

"This is something I've got to see for myself. I want to be there and not only see the white boy's reaction, but I also want to see how the people watching will react. Yes, sir, I want to be there when the man asks John to let him punch the daylights out of him."

"John. When do you think would be a good time to do

this crazy thing you are planning to do. Is this to be done on Saturday when everybody and their mothers will be spectators?"

"Yeah, I know this will be a unique act. It will have to be done when there ain't many people watching and with a sad apologetic look on our faces. I just might offer the man a hamburger from the same place where this happened at. How do that sound y'all? Especially to you Luke, since you will be with me."

"Wait a minute you two. Are you saying that you and Luke will be the only witnesses to this great event?"

"You got the point Whiskey. This will have to be done really carefully. We will have reduce as many opportunities to get emotional as possible. This goes for both sides. It will look more real for our side if we go unprepared for any kind of physical challenges."

"You must love your country more than you love yourself, or you are nuttier than a fruitcake."

"Don't you know what heroes are made of? We did a few life-threatening things in the South Pacific that were more life-threatening than this will be. We claimed it was for our country. Have you men forgot the body bags coming back with the men who had given their all for a worthy cause?"

"I guess you have a point, John. It makes more sense now that you make it the same thing look like the same fight that we were fighting for on the islands and in the jungles."

"You bet it is. In the South Pacific, we were in more danger from the fever carried by the mosquitoes than we are by what I'm about to do."

The normal citizen tends o have a tough time getting their minds around certain realities. The decisions that they have to make on their own carried a different moral and social weight than the decisions made voluntarily. John and his close knitted-bunch had to plan their missions to be seen as benefiting the total people. They had to avoid at all cost of making the people think the mission was to give one side an advantage over the other side. They had to convince a high number of citizens that the total population had more to gain by supporting John's leads than they had to lose.

"Come on Luke. Let's go and find our man with the busted lip. It must have healed by now. I know where he hangs out at during the weekdays."

"Are you sure you are doing the right thing, boy?"

"We'll know pretty soon. We will gain something no matter how it turns out. Can you hear in your mind what the grapevine would say it they did us some bodily harm after we went to their hangout to make amends?"

"It sure wouldn't make them look like they didn't want trouble. If they did you some harm they would have to explain your non-violent approach. They have done this before, but those were different times. This change in how the public perceives relationships between the races shins an evil light on what they once could get away with."

"The man hangs out at the service station on Dixie Highway. You've seen him there pumping gas for the owner. He is just a worker doing colored men work. That should tell us that he was not worth troubling ourselves with."

"Yeah, I get it. We can't let our contacts with the likes of his kind destroy what we are trying to do. He does not count much anyway. He is lower than the average colored in the eyes of his own kind."

"The man gave him that job of pumping gas because he was part of the family. I don't know what kin he is, but I hear that he is close kin to the owner, old man Britton."

The two social engineers headed for the service station on the border between the white side and the colored side of town.

"I see the dumb rascal. What in the dickens is he doing?"

"It looks like the man is trying to wash a pickup. He has his own way of doing it, that's all. He takes the water to the truck instead it being the other way around. Ops! Here comes his uncle."

"You boys are off your usual beat, ain't you?"

""Mr. Britton, we stopped by to apologize for my punching your nephew a few days ago. I know you heard about it."

"You want to do what?"

"I want to apologize to Roy for me getting out of line and losing control and hitting him."

"Well, if this don't beat all I've ever heard or seen. You stay here until I get the boy."

"Howdy Roy! You know me, don't ya?"

"Yea, yea. I know who you are. What are you here to start this time?"

"No trouble Mr. Britton. I just want to apologize for what I did the other day. I had no business acting like a fool and hitting Roy."

"You stay right there until I get the boy. Roy! Come out here right now. There is somebody here to see you!"

"Howdy Roy! I think I owe you an apology for hitting you the other day. I'm sorry I had to act like a crazy man all for nothing."

"What do you want from me now?"

"I just want you to forgive me, that's all. Will ya?"

Roy looked back at his uncle before giving his okay."

"I guess it's alright. I forgive you as long as that kind of thing won't happen again."

"You got it. So, can we shake on it?"

The two white men were never so confused in their lives, not over who stood where when it came to race. The rules were not written in stone but were written in the hearts of the citizens.

The two Black thought they had pushed their luck far enough for one day. They headed back for their end of the road.

"Here them two brave cranks come. They still have their heads on their shoulders."

"We were expecting to see you two hanging in a tree by now. How did it work out?"

"Y'all should have been there. The two white men didn't have much to say. They were tongue-tied. They were still standing in the drive looking in our direction until we were out of their sights."

"That's a shame, John. You two up there crawling on your knees asking for forgiveness for a wrong done to you. You have forgotten who's sacrifices made it possible for them two to be here in their rocking chairs, reading the news about their soldier boys while you and Luck were getting your butts shot off. Are we crazy, or what?"

"We have talked about this a thousand times. Me and Luke were not fighting for them. We were fighting for y'all and this country. They had their own men in uniform."

"Yeah, we know what you were fighting for, but it still remains true that while you two were ducking bullets, they were here snug in their beds..."

"That was good for us fighting men. At least we didn't have to babysit them and fight them all at one and the same time. We had our hands full looking after those we had."

"Well, you won't have to worry about the two from here on. You really clipped their wings. It will be hard for them to show their faces at their church for a while."

"I believe you men are slowly getting the point. You see we need them folks about as bad as they need us. This country will be strong as long as it is strong inside."

The black soldiers learned a valuable lesson in the jungles

of the South Pacific. They learned that their shoulders were the foundation on which their country set. Their proof of their own importance was provided by the boat loads every day. It came from their fellow countrymen.

The Blacks ex-soldiers found another chance to grow and become bigger than life. They were having problems getting the benefit monies in the government programs designed to help the fighting men catch up with the boys who failed to pass the physical for enlisting in our country's war of defense.

"What do you make of the GI Bill turning down an unlimited number of the boys when they apply for help?"

"I don't make too much of what they are doing. I do think that we could have predicted what it would be like. You know there are no free rides. I really believe that it is right down our alley being that way. Do you think we need those few dollars and an open path into our business? If we use the government's help, we are asking for them to make the rules relative to how the money is to be used. We don't want that. Do we?"

"I guess not. They would be riding down on us at every chance they got. I can hear them now, 'you men will have to plow up some of your sugar cane,'"

"Luke, are you going to the party tonight? You and Lou don't miss too many chances to whirl around the dance floor. There is nobody who can come close to competing with you two on the dance floor.".

"I didn't learn to dance until I met Lou. You remember that. You and I were too busy trying to get drafted to think about dancing."

"You are right on that one. You had a difficult time walking, much less dancing."

The young men were calming down to the point of thinking about getting into some kind of business to support themselves. They wanted to become men in every way possible that would make their folks proud, especially their sweethearts.

"Listen, you nuts. I hear that Charlie Wayne is sick and is not expected to make it. He has closed up the store because there is nobody to run it. Do you think he would consider selling the business to us?"

"Where did you get this information from, J.C,?"

"My mother works for the man's brother. She has big ears and tunes in on everything."

"Let's get together and talk about such a big jump. I can see us now becoming richer than the McCanns. Yes indeed, that would be something."

"You know who would give us the most trouble, don't you?"

"I sure do. That would be the legal connections. The license, the buying from the whole-sellers, the loss of white customers and maybe trouble from some of our own. This will be just another engagement with our cousins. But, let's do it."

"I thought you men would say that. I will have the wife put the question to the old man while he is still in his right mind."

"It won't hurt none to ask the man what did he plan to do with his business. That store has been operated by the McCanns since this country was occupied by the red men."

The business ball had to start rolling from somewhere. This looked like an ideal starting point. John and gang knew that a society had to have a good business foundation to be strong enough to stand up against the social, political and economic storms that are a part of all societies.

"John, the old man wants to see us as soon as possible. According to Lucile, he thought that us Blacks were never interesting in running a business."

"That just goes to show you how much we know about each other. We thought our fellow didn't encourage our business interest because they didn't want us to compete with them. Now, this man says he thought that we were okay with what we had. Most of that kind of thinking was our fault. We didn't show them that we were interested in becoming our own simply because we figured they would try to hinder us. Tell the man to set a date and time and we will be there."

The date was set after the men did a little digging up information about businesses. Rob had a younger brother who had majored in business administration in college. The young man had to teach a bunch of men, way older than he was, the fine arts of running a business. They had to learn what a beer license cost, and so on. But they were ready to start the wheels turning before the week was out.

"When will the master store owner be feeling up to having company?"

"He said he could be ready at the drop of a hat. He just had to have his lawyer there and that wouldn't take but an hour or two. He is waiting for you men to set the date."

"Tell him that this coming Friday will be fine with us."

"I will pass this on the first thing in the morning. I'll wait until I have fed him his breakfast before I tell him. He always has a better attitude on a full stomach."

"You know your people. Please give him his favorite meal Friday. We'll see you and him Friday afternoon."

The man appeared more than willing to make a deal. This old boy had always been known for his being fair to everybody he did business with. There was not one family within miles of his place that didn't owe the man at the present time.

John and Luke left the meeting as the new owners of a little country store. They knew that people no longer did their weekly grocery shopping at country stores, but they did enough local beer buying and what-nots to keep the men in business. They would have a gas pump to save the locals from having to drive miles to buy two gallons of gas.

"Well, what do we have here, Luke?"

"I think we are on the right road. We will be serving our children their pops, ice cream and other goodies that children find it hard to live without."

""We know we won't get rich from this business. The white owners didn't get rich either. It brought in enough cash for them folks to sit in the shade when the sun became unfriendly to bare heads"

"Don't forget we have a meeting to plan how we are gonna get our people to register to vote. I get a feeling that this won't be an easy task. But, it has to be done. We know most all our citizens don't vote and this includes the white folks too."

"Our colored people ain't the big hold-back that some of us want to believe, you know. I'll admit that we do our share of dragging our feet when there is work to be done. Maybe if we become more socially responsible, others of our citizen would follow suit."

# CHAPTER SEVEN

"Sampson, where were you going in such a hurry yesterday afternoon? I started to follow you to see if you needed help or what. You passed the store like something was chasing you."

"I got a call from the Sheriff's office that my son was there and I better get out there right away."

Go on!"

"It was not as bad as he was trying to make it out to be. You know how Sam is. He tends to think that he is as good as anybody else and deserves the same treatments as everybody else."

"Well? What's wrong with that, Sampson?" "The boy was in the bank to draw out a couple of dollars when old man McCray's daughter-in-law got in line to do the same thing. The clerk peeped around Sam and asked her what could he do for her."

"Yeah, I can guess what happened next."

"If it had been a man in line behind Sam there would not have been a word said. But this was a rich man's daughter."

"What did Sam say to cause the Sheriff to be called?"

"The boy never said a word. He stepped closer to the open window and blocked it. When Sam was told to step aside, he refused to move."

"I know the clerk could never let him get away with that. The truth is, the clerk would have done the same if Sam had been a young white man."

"Especially if the woman was a McCray

"The Sheriff thought it was funny. He just wanted to make sure that Sam was okay. The law and the McCrays never set horses anyway. Remember when they had the run-in back when we were doing our national duties?"

'I show do. That almost turned out to be a real fight. They still didn't tell what it was all about."

These kinds of small encounters hardly ever developed into anything more than an exchange of insults. The rules for proper social behaviors for getting along with each other were taught and practiced from the cradle to the grave. When there was a conflict, the stable citizens usually could settle down the eruption without much harm being done.

"Luke, you know the mess Sampson"s boy got into was brought on because of them northern people arousing up our young folks. We know that something will have to be done, now that the whole world has its eyes on us. But you and I know that any kind of violence will just make matters worse."

"I know I'm not gonna be part of anything that will do harm to our neighborhood and country. I dodged too many bullets to save our home, so why should I help destroy what we killed other men for?"

"You mean, we did some inhuman things to other human beings to keep what we have here. These jokers who are acting up were not over yonder with us."

"I get the point. We will do whatever is required here at home to preserve what we have. Now let's get to what that is that we are gonna have to do to make the United States a better place than it is. We do have some loose ends to tie up."

"How are we coming along with this voting thing?"

"Not good enough. I don't think that we are doing what is needed to get our citizens off their buttocks. We will get all our people together and try to fire them up to address this voting thing. If we don't take actions to address this voting issue, the busybodies from who-know-where will."

"I'm ready to go from door to door delivering the time, place and whatever we decide."

"Let's get together at the watering hole Friday night. This way we won't be at a private home or club. Let's meet at the roadhouse. They have been serving mixed racial customers since it was not a cool thing to do and be accepted."

"John, you get the topic down pat and I will do the rest. I'll get the men together and primed."

"Get busy boy! What are you standing here waiting for? There comes your first victim"

The peace-loving men got a representative size crowd together for the big social and legal project. These citizens had never gotten together to address the voting issues. This was the perfect time and place.

"Alright, ladies and gentlemen! Let's get this started before we get into the fun stuff. I see some of you licking your lips before you found a seat."

"We are waiting!"

"Okay, Bill. I'll get right to the point. All of us know that it will be a short time before we have the boys from up states setting up places to register us to vote. I don't believe that any of us want them meddling in our affairs here in our community. So, we are here to take care of this voting issue without the help of strangers."

"What do you suggest that we get our shoulders to so that we can prevent the outsiders from taking over and doing more harm than good.

"We haven't had racial troubles in our part of the great

state of Mississippi since Rover was a pup. We certainly don't need any trouble now. What do you think should be our first move Sheriff?"

"We should start at the beginning. What is it that the Northerners are doing all across the state? Getting the citizens registered to vote. This will apply to the Whites too. Half of our Whites ain't registered either."

"Mr. Mayor, what do you think about what our sheriff just stated?"

"I'll agree that will have to be the starting place. After which comes the hard part, getting the citizens educated and registered."

"If you, Mayor Gilbert, can get the tools together and call a special registering day, we'll do the rest. Believe me, we will hold a meeting in our schools, churches and the local gambling joints. We'll get the job done and you can bet on that."

The community of mixed racial members and kinfolks were not about to let outsiders come into their homeland and drive wages between them. No, if there were changes to be done in order to keep up wi6h the times, they would make them from the inside out. These homeboys and homegirls were not about to turn their lifestyles over to strangers for them to fix, according to what they thought was required, they would decide what was their legal rights and the legal wrongs that are created by the daily living of their own kinfolks and neighbors.

The local citizens were progressing with no ill-doing or feeling when the surprise happen. They knew how likely this was to be and they were sort of prepared to take action.

"Luke! Get the gang together fast. You hear what is going on down at the bus station. We might have trouble on our hands if we don't put a stop to this bull."

"We will meet you and Roy down there."

The facts were that a colored boy, from who knows where

had gotten into a scuffle with a local white boy. The tussle was not racially motivated, but boy and girl motivated. The black outsider started the trouble by getting fresh with a white local girl. Her brother stepped in to protect his sister from what he understood to be an insult to his sister.

"Hay there little white girl! Have you ever been made love to by a hot and ready northern black boy? You don't know what you are missing."

"Look whoever you are, she is my sister. I think you owe her an apology, right now!"

"I don't care who you are. All I want to do was to get between them..."

That's was the Black's mistake.

# Chapter Eight

John and crew arrived at the trouble spot just in time to intercept the news bunch. The news people were the bad guys. They were eager to print the news that would sell the highest number of papers. The sheriff was also in on the confusion by the time the newsboys got their cameras focused,

"Everybody move back to give us room to settle this mess down. I'm sure there has been a big misunderstanding. I said to move back!"

"Sheriff! What started this skirmish? Was it something that happens quite often in Your town?"

"No, this kind of things is only because of you people coming in here provoking up trouble where there has been none. The best thing that you folks can do for my town is to crawl back on the bus and hightail it to where you are needed and wanted."

"Sheriff, we are just doing our jobs, the same as you are. We are not here to cause trouble at all"

"Trouble might not be your intent but it is a direct result from your being here. Trouble usually follow the news teams. You boys know that better than we do. So, I want you folks to stand back and let us bring a close to this misunderstanding."

"Who are you, Mister? What do you know about your

racial problems here in your town? Do the law pester you black folks more than is necessary to keep law and order?"

"My name is John. Just for your information to print in your newspaper, we don't have any racial problems here. You people brought the trouble that you see here with you."

"What's your name, Sir?"

"They call me Luke. I agree with John here one hundred percent. We don't want or need you folks here among us causing trouble. We fought in the war for what we have here today and we are willing to fight here at home to maintain peace and harmony among our people. We are not about to let you and your bunch of outsider come in here and cause trouble."

"You two sound like you are the spokesmen for the ethnic groups here in this town."

"You could say that. Look around you! Do you see trouble between us? Both white and black men fought heroically in the wars for one reason only and you men should know what that was."

"I was in the army too. I have scars to prove it."

"Then you ought to know know what the war was about. Do you?"

"I think I have a good idea what we were killing and dying for. Yes, I do."

"Now, suppose you tell me what that was you men were fighting for?"

"Everybody knows what the war was about. We were defending our democracy and our country. It does not take a smart man to see that."

"What do you think we Blacks were fighting for?"

"What? What were you fighting for, you are asking me?'

"Is that such a hard question to answer? You see, I don't really think that you have a clue of what the black man's game was In the United States' army was. I will tell you. If I tell you will you print what I tell you? I want to see it in your paper and that will do more to promote peace here where we live and were fighting for in the war."

"I can tell you what I was fighting for. I can't talk for all the fighting men. I thought I was protecting a way of life that we love in this country. I did not find the freedoms and ease of living in other countries that I had the bad luck to visit. I have had just about anything a man could ask for from his country's resources."

"You sound like the common reason that Whites will tell you he was killing and being killed for. Your answer comes close to stating the reasons I were sweating in the South Pacific jungles. I was not defending what we Blacks had, but what we Black were gonna get. You see, we never had what you claimed that was yours to defend. I can't speak for all my people either, but I can speak for a few of us. I got to know the men who I was stationed with. I knew none who was satisfied with their social privileges they had back home. This was the home they were talking about. Do you follow me so far?"

"Yes, I'd think I do. Go on. This is turning out to be the story of the month. Let me turn up this recorder. I hope you don't mind."

"By all means. You will have to understand the difference between loving one's country and loving the social conditions of one's country. These two don't have to be the same. I, or we, didn't like the racism practiced in yours' and my country, but we love this country as much as you do. You appreciated the easy way of life that racism afforded you. We didn't have that to motivate us to fight. We had less than you to fight for, therefore, we were heroes of a different kind than you and your kind."

"Go on. I'm recording this to print later. I will let you read it, and approve it before I send it to my publisher."

"If we Black were to use violence to make the changes that we are attempting to make, we would do more harm than good. Violence between the races and on our front steps would benefit none of us in a positive way. You will have to understand the new mindset of the Blacks. There will be big changes. These changes will be riding in on the wings of peace and brotherly love. If you Whites can't understand how this equality idea will make a better country for all, then you guys aren't as smart as we have been giving you credit for being. This I can tell you right now. There will be changes for the better with or without you people's help. We are determined to get the job done and if your folks are too dumb to see the benefits that we all will reap, we don't need your kind of help"

"Could you hold up for a minute? Let me change tapes here. I don't want to miss any of you people's messages."

John had been waiting for an opportunity such as was taking place. This was his chance to speak for his kind. He and his close associates, both Black and White, had worked at learning the proper wording to say what he was attempting to say.

"Okay, John, you can continue."

"I want you, citizens, to jump in if I should get off track. We need all the support we can get to make this brotherhood idea work. I'm telling our fellow citizens, and the world, what will be. We are going to be all that we can be by freeing all our citizens so they can be the American citizens that they want to be for them and theirs. We all will be free to live our personal idea of who and what we are without hindering our next-door neighbor. America is big enough and has enough to fulfill all our honest dreams. That is the America that I fought the war for. Has anybody else got anything to add to what has been said?"

"I don't believe so, John."

"Thanks, Luke. So, print what has been said and add this note. We will do whatever it takes to be a country that will be worth fighting for no matter who you are. Now come on all, let's say this together that this is my country. All together now, "'THIS IS MY COUNTRY!!'"

OTHER BOOKS BY THE AUTHOR: